Secret
Sacrifice

PETRALIA J. L. FISK

PAGE PUBLISHING, INC.
New York, NY

First originally published by Page Publishing, Inc. 2019

ISBN 978-1-68289-723-2 (Paperback)
ISBN 978-1-68289-724-9 (Digital)

Printed in the United States of America

Contents

Chapter 1

Meet the Matthews Sisters

Standing before my grandma Marsh, I couldn't help but fall helpless at her mercy. Her sweet, round face always had a soothing effect on me, so I welcomed her insightful words without hesitation. Her voice was soft and poetic. "Life as you know it is in for a complete turnaround." Her bright-green eyes sparkled as they demanded my attention, pulling me in to share her knowledge.

She wrapped her fingers around my hand; I was always amazed at how soft her skin was. My thumb rubbed the lines of life that covered her hand with well-earned creases. I focused on each word that she spoke, repeating them in my mind as I had heard the life-after-graduation speech many times. Yet something about my grandmother's voice never made the speech sound repetitious. My nerves for the day's event stayed tranquil as I listened closely to her comforting words of wisdom.

"You are young and have many paths before you. No matter which you choose, remember there are never any dead ends. You will no doubt encounter many bumps and may have to turn around and backtrack down a path or two. But you must never forget, you may stop and ask for direction at any time . . . My door is always open to you, and I am never too far away." She held my eyes with hers briefly before closing her speech with a wink.

"I won't forget." I smiled and gently squeezed her fragile hand.

"I remember that same speech from the day *I* moved from home." My mother entered the room; her eyes were the same brilliant color of green. I too was blessed with the amazing glittery-green sparkle, something I was thankful to my mother for. I was also thankful that I missed out on her fire-red hair. Mine, no doubt, had the red tone but was more auburn than a fire-engine color. The freckles, however, did find their way to my cheeks, and I hated them. Aside from the bright color of my mom's hair, I looked a lot like her; from the fair skin to the slender yet curvy figure.

I wrapped my arms around my grandma, warming with delight as she returned the gesture. I rested my head on her shoulder with my eyes fixed on the view outside. My heart skipped a beat as my eyes shifted to the movement on the other side of the large bay window; the black image was that of my dad's vehicle. Watching the shiny black Tahoe ease up the driveway, I gave her a quick kiss on her pink rouge-painted cheek. "Thanks, Grams, but I've gotta go talk to Dad." I released my grip and quickly darted around the couch and out the front door to greet him.

I'd been waiting for the perfect opportunity to speak to him in private. But now that the house was crowded with relatives due to graduation, I figured it was now or never. I bit the bullet and rushed down the flower-lined sidewalk leading to his parking spot in front of the garage. I brushed my fingers through my long auburn spirals to keep them out of my face as the breeze played with the strands.

When I arrived at the end of the walkway, he was stepping out of the driver's seat of the vehicle with briefcase in hand; his knuckles shone white with his tight grip. He was wearing a dark-blue suit with a white button-up shirt; today his neck was ornamented with a gold-and-white tie that he had already loosened for a more comfortable ride home. This was his usual lawyer attire; Michael Matthews was a well-known name in these parts, and he had great pride in his good reputation. His tall figure was a great intimidator in the courtroom, and I often felt the fear in his large shadow myself.

"Hey, Daddy. I would like to talk to you real quick, if you got a second." I placed my hands in the back pockets of my jeans and rocked gently on the heels of my white sneakers—much like I had when I was a young child.

"What's up, Clare-bear?" He walked around the front of the rig, keeping his pace, as if to push me to spit out what was on my mind.

I looked down at my black tank top until my chin touched my chest. Exhaling, I found the courage to hurry with my rehearsed speech. "I've been looking into some photography classes," I said as he walked past me and continued toward the house. "I've got an interview with the *Tribune* on Wednesday for an internship. I'm really excited and would like your opinion . . . and some help with the classes . . . I'll pay you back." I walked in his shadow up the path to the house.

He stopped on the front step, and looked down at me. "Photography? I thought that was just a hobby?" With his broad shoulders and stern look, he raised his eyebrows. His blue eyes widened as if they were waiting for my response. I kept smiling to hide the knot that had formed in my throat. I rushed up the steps and stood between him and the door and continued my proposal. "Mrs. Roland thinks I have real talent." My voice rose as my excitement to have his attention became apparent. "You always said we should enjoy whatever we do." I kept eye contact, even though I was shaking frantically inside.

I waited patiently for his usual scratch of the head that would indicate he was actually taking my words into consideration. Standing in silence in front of the blue door leading into our two-story white house, my lungs were as still as my body as I found it hard to breathe in the suspense. He lifted his arm; his fingers rubbed swiftly at his short graying brown hair. My body calmed as the corners of my mouth raised, and I was able to breathe again.

"True." He nodded. "Why don't you go ahead and get up to the school? I'll talk to your mother and we can discuss this later. Okay?" He reached around me and turned the knob on the door.

"That's fair, very fair," I nodded with a grin that elated my entire body. I threw my arms around him for a quick squeeze of gratitude and ran inside.

I continued to sprint up the stairs to my room, where I grabbed the two matching blue graduation gowns hanging on the back of the door. I threw them over my arm and cautiously maneuvered through the small amounts of tan carpeting that were exposed on my side of the room. I carefully made my way through the organized chaos that led me to the white wicker dresser. I hastily pushed the messy pile of clothes blocking access to the top drawer onto the floor, adding to the heap that already occupied that corner of the room.

Upon opening the drawer, I proceeded to dig through the clutter of mismatched socks and wrinkled undergarments. Under the pile of wadded clothing, I found the pamphlets for the classes I was eager to take. Enthusiasm accompanied the mixture of emotions that had already settled in my muscles as I ogled the booklets—anytime Dad said he'd talk it over with Mom, we stood a good chance of getting our way. Envisioning the conversation with Dad, my stomach fluttered with additional excitement.

My knees were weakening as the nervous flips my body was encountering had begun invading my entire being. The combination of events was proving to be a bit much as the reality of graduating grew closer. I shook the stress from my mind and disguised my tension with a smile and flew from my room—the quicker we could get this over, the better.

Tucking the robes under one arm and gripping the pamphlet tightly in my right hand, I slid down the cherry wood banister. Reaching the end of the ride, I jumped to my feet on the bottom step. As I planted my feet in a perfect landing, my sister appeared from the family room and snatched one of the gowns from my grip. "Thanks, Clara!" Tara grinned as she threw the gown over her shoulder.

"No problem. So are you ready?" I said, looking at my mirror image of a sister.

"Of course, I've spent my life working toward this very day. You, on the other hand, should be grateful to *me* that you are even getting a diploma."

I faked a slight laugh. "Funny!" My nose crinkled in a sneer. She was right, though—if it weren't for her, I would probably still be struggling with my freshman year science class. Having a twin defi-

8

nitely had its advantages. We had learned at a young age that there were few people who could tell us apart. For that reason, we did our makeup and styled our long wavy hair the same way every day.

The schools were always persistent on keeping us apart in classes in order to help our self-growth. This worked out great for us. Throughout high school, I had two different gym classes every day—not Tara's strong suit but probably the reason I did well in sports. She ended up with my science class—probably the reason she turned out to be a borderline genius.

Though our looks were the same, we were complete opposites. Tara was well organized and did everything by a schedule or routine. Her grades were perfect, and she always did well in everything she tried. I, on the other hand, had a life. I didn't like to study and kept my grades average, which was fine with me. Tara was destined for great things, and everybody knew it; in fact, they expected it. I was simply her tool to follow in her shadow and be recognized as needed. Nobody expected much from me, and I liked it that way.

I patted her on the shoulder as I walked past her, ending the conversation to join Dad in the kitchen. He was discussing the driving arrangements with the grandparents when I slipped him the pamphlets. My movements were suddenly timid, my skin clammy and my nerves reduced to a juvenile state. I found it impossible to make eye contact—Dad still had a way of making me feel like I was a preschooler.

I delivered the information and quickly grabbed my keys from the counter to remove myself from the situation. Deep down I knew I was being silly, feeling uncomfortable about asking for help to achieve my dream, but on the surface, I was terrified that they would find my request to be less of what they wanted from me. I had been playing my rebuttal speech over in my head as I feared their rejection.

Holding the keys up, I gave them a slight jingle. "Well, gotta roll." My eyes were still unable to connect to my dad's.

"We'll see you up there, sweetie, drive carefully," Mom added as she finished up the few dishes left in the sink.

"Yes, Mom, I always do." I rolled my eyes as she conveyed her usual words of precaution.

I raised my hand and gave a quick wave as I left the kitchen. Tara was waiting in the dining room, still hanging onto her gown that was draped over her shoulder. "Clara, I forgot to tell you . . . Todd called earlier and said he'd meet you up at the gym." My unsettled stomach was instantly replaced with excitement. The mere mention of his name always gave me goosebumps and made me smile uncontrollably.

"Awesome. You ready?" I honestly couldn't help but glow with passion when ever his image settled inside my mind. We'd been dating for over a year, and he had become so much more than just someone I could give the label as my boyfriend. He was my best friend—the one person I could tell all my dreams, hopes, and secrets to without the fear of his reaction.

My family had taken longer to warm up to his charming ways. My parents were sure that his politeness was too good to be true. Then there was the slight concern about his age that seemed to enter every other conversation that went on within our walls when we first started to date. I was barely seventeen then, and he was twenty-four, but they soon found they were unable to resist his charismatic presence and saw him as part of the family.

"See you up there!" Tara yelled toward the kitchen then headed for the front door. "Come on, we don't want to be late." She waved me along. I rolled my eyes at her enthusiasm then quickly followed. She reached the front door first and spun to face me. "All right, Clara, give me the keys." She held out her hand and waited for me to fill her request. "Not gonna happen." I pushed her aside and darted out the door. My graduation gown flapped gracefully behind me in the breeze as I rushed across the lawn for our purple Saturn parked on the curb in front of the house.

"Come on, Clara, you know it's my turn to drive." Her cries of reason only pushed me faster as she ran close behind. I paused to catch my breath once I reached the car. "I'm driving there . . . you can drive back." Opening the door, I threw my gown into the back, then quickly jumped into the driver seat. "Fine. I don't feel like arguing," Tara frowned as she got in the passenger side.

With a grin from ear to ear, I ran my fingers through my hair and fixed my bangs in the rearview mirror as Tara fastened her seatbelt. "I'm sure you really meant to say you don't feel like *losing* an argument. But whatever, same dif, right?" I winked.

"Yeah right . . . just drive." She struggled to keep the smile from winning the battle against her forced frown.

Eager to see Todd, I started the car and began our drive toward the gym. We lived within a mile of the school in a snobby urban neighborhood. My mom, Cece, quit her job when we moved here over five years ago. She used to tell us that she stayed home to assure that she would be there for us when we needed her. Her reason sounded sincere, but I always felt it was in order to comply by the rules of our uptight community.

I carefully maneuvered through the bends of the newly paved roads while tuning the radio to a station to something a bit more upbeat. "Can't you just drive? .It's not a safe driving practice to be fiddling with the radio. Just tell me what station you want, and I can put it there for you." Tara tried pushing my hand away.

"I won't know what station until I hear it." I smirked with pleasure, knowing how much it irritated her.

In a feeble attempt to ignore me, Tara waved at various neighbors who were taking advantage of the nice day by mowing their lawn. The men folk were all mowing in the same direction on riding mowers. The women were pulling weeds in attempt to keep up the necessary appearance of the Marque Manor rule books. Looking around, I gave a slight chuckle, as it almost looked like we were driving through some surreal movie set.

I pulled our card out from the visor as I approached the wrought-iron gates that provided the only access to our snob prison. The entire neighborhood was fenced in by an eight-foot brick wall. Even though beautiful landscaping with large blossoming trees helped to hide the faded red-and-gray design of the wall and the edges of the fence were softened by the greenery, it still made me feel like we were caged animals.

"Bet you won't miss this when you leave for Harvard . . . you lucky dog." I swiped the card to open the gate.

"Actually . . . I think I will miss the security around here. We're lucky to live in such a nice place. You need to learn to appreciate things more. Dad works hard to give us this nice life, and all you do is complain." The irritation showed in the crease that lay heavily between her eyebrows.

As the fancy prison gates opened, I placed the card back in the visor. "You're right . . . In fact, I'll be sure to send him a thank-you card . . . maybe I'll even send you one for having enlightened me." I laughed silently to myself as I pulled out onto the road, inhaling the sweet taste of freedom as we headed toward the school.

It took only a few minutes to reach the parking lot. I gasped at the sight as we arrived; the lot was already crowded with vehicles and anxious bodies. I hurried into one of the few spots left and parked the car. It only took a moment for my eyes to locate Todd sitting on his well-polished motorcycle—the chill that ran up my back tickled my neck and made my shoulders melt. Its chrome flickered fiercely in the sunlight and provided a natural spotlight around him. If I didn't know any better, I would have sworn the earth stopped momentarily for the world to admire the amazing piece of art before them. He removed his helmet and shook his short blond hair.

I swallowed in some air as a reminder to breathe. Collecting myself, I climbed out of the car. Tara was already slipping her royal-blue gown on over her street clothes while I continued to admire Todd walking across the parking lot. He moved like a vision. His vivid blue eyes flickered like sapphires as he smiled, exposing his sterling white teeth. The summer weather had colored his skin an intriguing golden-brown color that complimented his well-sculpted arms.

Todd was a karate instructor and his body was incredibly fit because of it. I found myself starring at him in awe every time he approached me. "Hey, sweet, you ready to do this?" Todd said in his deep sexy voice that warmed my insides instantly.

"I am now, rebel." I wrapped my arms around his solid form and dissolved into his embrace. Tara grabbed her belly with her hands and wrinkled her face in disgust. "Please stop . . . your cute pet names are making me sick."

I pulled myself away from my security long enough to slip my gown on over my clothes, finding a brief moment to stick my tongue out at my sister; who simply shook her head. Once I placed my arm back around my escort, Todd threw his other arm around Tara. He pulled her close in a playful hug.

I exhaled in anticipation. "I'm ready." The words escaped as the excitement of finally being able to say good-bye to this eyesore of a school took control of my body. I pulled myself closer to him as we walked across the parking lot to the entrance of the gym. With a kiss on his cheek, I left him to find a seat inside as we proceeded to the other end of the building, to the band room.

My mind barely noted the steps I took along the sidewalk. I felt like I was floating over the top of the concrete path, unable to feel anything beneath my feet. My body and mind were nearly numb as my focus became a haze while I admired the multitude of people that appeared to have spilled out onto the courtyard. There were countless faces that I had never seen before and probably never would again. There were people I had tagged as parents straightening the gowns of students. Students that I had grown up with but never knew well enough to know their family. A couple of familiar faces ran past us with looks of panic to get to their fixed position in the lineup.

My mentality was brought back to attention as I nearly collided with Chase, who ran toward us from around the corner. His hands landed on my shoulders as we halted in place. He was wearing his cap and gown, which still wasn't enough to take the attention off the piercings that decorated almost every one of his visible features. "Clara, don't miss my party tonight. Hey, bring your sister this time. The more, the merrier." Chase's dark-chocolate eyes sized Tara from the ground up; his eyebrows rose with approval once his eyes met hers. Before I could answer, he was running off to invite another circle of friends.

"He's right, you *should* come." I slapped her arm with the back of my hand. Tara responded with a simple shake of the head. "I'll take that as 'you'll think about it'. This conversation is by no means over," I simpered.

We reached the back entrance of the building where Mrs. Roland was holding the door open. She was one of the nicest adults I knew and the best teacher I'd ever had. Her short and slender build gave her the potential to be attractive, but her shy demeanor and lack of fashion sense passed her off as cute at best. Every time I saw her hair pulled back in a messy bun while wearing a loose-fitting dress that covered her from neck to ankle, I had to struggle to not attack her with a complete makeover.

"Clara, will you be attending the classes we talked about?" She pushed her glasses back up onto the bridge of her nose. I raised my hand and crossed my fingers. "I'm hoping to. I'm waiting for an answer from my parents." I shrugged my shoulders as I stepped inside. "Tara. Congratulations on your acceptance into such a fine college." She rested her hand on my sister's arm. "Thank you, Mrs. Roland." Tara's face lit up with pride.

I felt no need to rush as we continued through the door and walked down the hall. I half-expected someone to pinch me and wake me from this familiar dream. We turned before reaching the gym entrance and entered the stuffy room of nearly seventy blue gowns. Weaving through the crowd, we found our positions in the lineup.

"Hey Clara, Tara," Cindy, our friend since grade school, said with a nod.

"Cin, are you gonna be at the party tonight?" I took my position next to her in the row of girls.

"Wouldn't miss it. Rumor has it that Chase's parents are leaving for the beach right after the ceremony. They have left the house to Chase for the whole weekend. This is going to be a party simply for the books for sure." Cindy lowered her voice to share her findings.

"My parents would never do that . . . never." I shook my head.

"Mine either . . . in fact, if they knew the Nelsons were gonna be gone all weekend, my parents wouldn't let me out of the house for sure." Cindy leaned in as her voice remained hushed.

"I hear that." I nodded in agreement.

"So, T. M., will you be going to the party?" Cindy leaned forward to make eye contact with Tara.

"I don't think so." Tara shook her head.

"You really should come this time, sis. You can hang out with Todd and me. Seriously, it's not like you can use studying as an excuse this time. It's the last party, and it's going to be the best one yet."

Tara continued to shake her head as I spoke, not even humoring me as I nearly begged for her to join the fun.

"Come on, you leave for college in a few months. This could be a great farewell and the last opportunity to show everyone the 'fun' Tara." I showed her my sad puppy eyes, hoping to get more of a response than the hopeless shake of the head.

"It's not going to work, I'm not going." Tara crossed her arms as she looked away to end the conversation.

Oh, that's too bad." A familiar voice summoned our attention from behind. We all turned around to face the deep and charming voice of the school's football captain, Bradley Moretti. He was standing with his left arm hanging casually down at his side and the other hand hanging onto it, as if it could fall off his powerfully built body at any moment. I rolled my eyes as I noted his weight shifted onto his left foot in his usual I'm-too-cool-for-my-own-skin stance.

Most girls shrieked at the mere sight of him. I, on the other hand, couldn't care less. I would never argue the fact that he was attractive; after all, I am human. He kept his jet-black hair shaved on the sides and the top styled with short messy spikes. His brown eyes contained a sparkle that seemed to pull you into them, nearly taking you captive. When he smiled, he got a cute little dimple in his right cheek.

He was Italian, and his olive-toned skin added to the many factors that made him stand out in a crowd. Bradley was almost irresistible. I say *almost* because it all changed the moment he opened his mouth and the conceited covered words spilled out and oozed ugly all over the place.

Cindy and my sister were among the groupies that swore they hated him. Yet they clammed up and their knees turned to mush every time he walked by. "Tara, I'd really like to see you at the party." Bradley took her by the hand and then looked back to me. "It'd be nice to see the friendly Matthews girl at the party for a change." He looked back to my sister, who was helplessly lost in his gaze.

"Still bitter after all this time." My eyebrows lifted along with my shoulders as the words escaped before I could control the natural defense that his presence brought out in me.

He dropped Tara's hand. In nearly a pout, he stared angrily at me with crossed arms. "You don't know what you're missing out on . . . but luckily for you, it's not too late. You could still drop that wannabe jock you're dating and come experience bliss with the real thing. I'd be willing to give you another chance." He stood with open arms, as if waiting for me to jump at his proposal and throw myself at him.

"Always wanting what you can't have." I remained calm and shook my head slightly.

He stepped toward me, his face a ruler's length from mine. "The offer won't stay on the table forever . . . I suggest you give it some thought."

Dismayed by his determination, I stared him intensely in the eyes; firm to hold my ground and refusing to back up from his shadow of intimidation, I raised my voice, losing my calm. "Well, Bradley, I've given your kind offer some thought, and I'm sorry to inform you, but it's not gonna happen . . . ever !" My foot stomped as I delivered my message loud and clear.

"Well, let *me* inform *you* of something." He took a step forward, causing me to lean back in a quest for some breathing space. "Bradley gets what Bradley wants." His stare pierced into me like hot daggers; sending chills of creepiness down my spine. His hand made its way to my face; he rubbed my cheek with his fingertips. My body heat rose in anger; I knocked his hand away and stumbled backward to get away. Collecting my composure, I stood tall and lost control of my volume. "Not this time, Bradley!"

Before he could start in with his defense, Principal Stevens walked in. She asked the boys to get on over to the other entrance to get ready for the march to our seats at the foot of the stage. Bradley walked away to follow the instructions, blowing me a kiss as he joined his friends. "I wonder what makes him think he's so special anyway?" I watched him laugh with his jock buddies as they exited the room.

"You're the only one in this school telling him he's not. Why didn't you go to the homecoming dance with him last year anyway?" Cindy said, still trying to get a glimpse of him as he left the room.

"I was already going with Todd . . . Bradley only asked me because I was already spoken for. He's persistent, though, I'll give him that. I'm just not interested, and I wish he'd give it up." I looked around the room to make sure I hadn't caused too much of a scene. Fortunately everyone was too busy focusing on Mrs. Stevens to show any interest in my crazy life or my little outburst.

"I wish he'd focus that kind of attention in my direction." Cindy's eyebrows danced as she fluffed her short blond hair.

"Cin, you can do so much better than that." I placed my hand on her shoulder, begging for her to listen and hoping she would never get involved with him. My gut screamed that he was trouble, and my heart told me it was certain.

"Are we looking at the same guy? Cause I ain't never seen anything better than that amazing piece of art. Okay, your Todd's a close runner-up, but he's off the market, so that leaves Brad. Really, what more can I say?" Cindy chuckled.

"Looks aren't everything." I shook my head slowly.

"That's easy for you to say, you've got one that has looks, brains, and money. Hey, T. M., don't you think it would be better to have a guy with a body like Bradley's?" Cindy looked to Tara for approval.

"If I ever get a boyfriend, I would hope that he'd be both of the intellectual and attractive nature. Yes, I would be lying if I didn't say that Bradley does have some features that would look mighty nice standing next to me . . . he just needs to keep his mouth shut, that's all." Tara answered with a silly laugh.

"I'm sure going to miss you when you leave for Harvard." Cindy slipped past me and grabbed Tara with tears in her eyes.

"I'll be home for the holidays." Tara nearly cried as they held each other close.

"Yeah, not the same, T. M., and you know it." Cindy pulled away from her hold and wiped away the moisture on her cheeks.

"All right girls! It's showtime!" Principal Stevens announced as she opened the doors. Her words hit my stomach like an aluminum baseball bat as the day's emotions and reality collided inside me.

Chapter 2

It's Showtime!

One by one the line-up was let loose out the door to meet up with our walking partners. As classmates walked out the door, it all started to sink in. My grandmother's words became vivid. She was right—life as we knew it was definitely about to change. Friends I had made might soon become long-lost buddies as they move away to college, with a good possibility to never be seen again.

The room grew silent, and all I could hear was the beating of my own heart, which was pounding painfully inside my chest. I slowly inched toward the door, bringing my turn to leap closer and closer. Excited to be out of here yet scared to be let loose out into the real world as an adult. I felt I was preparing to jump from an airplane. As I stepped out into the hall, I prayed my parachute wouldn't falter.

My surroundings felt unfamiliar, even though I had traveled between those walls numerous times before. My eyes scanned the dingy white walls begging for a fresh coat of paint and the blue-and-white checkered floor that only a week prior had been an eyesore that I couldn't wait to bid my farewells to. As I marched my final trip down the hall that should have been echoing the musical sounds that would generally flow from the band room, they filled my ears with the emotional tunes of the graduation march.

Every sense told me this was not a normal day, and although I had craved for this moment and knew things were changing, I struggled inside to grasp onto something that was recognizable to anchor my feet to the ground. My legs forced the motions of carrying my lifeless body down the hall to the opening to the gym as my eyes stayed focused on the image before me. Dressed in her graduation gown, my twin mimicked the vision I'd had of this day. As she marched down the hall ahead of me, her vision flowed in a dreamy haze, causing me to question the reality of it all.

Tara reached the doorway first. My visions of the sweet dream skidded to a halt as Tara began her journey of confidence and pride down the edge of the gym's floor. This was happening; the picture before me became clear. The corners of my mouth lifted, and I exhaled. My shoulders dropped as I collected myself and found the strength and excitement I'd imagined I'd hold for this day. Able to see clearly, I looked through the sea of half-occupied chairs that waited for our arrival. Tara's escort was marching at the same pace as she was. At first, I thought nothing of the face on the other side, but as I realized it was *my* escort Kyle Nelson instead of her assigned partner, Bradley, my heart fell. My nerves were electrified with unsettling energy. My cheeks flashed red as sweat beaded on the back of my neck.

Once Tara reached the end of the row of chairs and began her march toward her partner, I stepped out and started my final walk on the hard wood floor. Hesitant, I slowly shifted my eyes to the other side of the gym. First, I filtered the classmates already standing next to their assigned seats in the middle of the room. Confused as to how the routine had gotten fouled up, I focused on my partner on the other side of the chairs. My fear was confirmed as I laid my eyes on Bradley walking in sync with my step on the opposite side of the gym.

What could he be up to? I considered my options. My first thought was to stop and run back to change places with Lucille, who was now standing in the doorway. I glanced up at the families that filled the bleachers on either side of the gym and knew I couldn't run and cause a scene. I continued my march and bit my lip; after all, what could he possibly do in front of all these people?

As I reached the end of the chairs I turned to face Bradley. He smiled conceitedly as we moved closer to one another. I kept a straight face and played as if I hadn't even noticed he had changed places with Kyle. We reached the aisle down the middle of the chairs and walked side by side between them; I tensed as I waited for him to say something.

"Impressed? I paid Kyle twenty bucks to switch with me," he whispered. His face was close enough that I could feel the heat from his breath on my cheek, sending chills of disgust down my spine. I clenched my fist, remaining silent. I said nothing; in fact, I was speechless. I honestly had no words to respond to his childish game. Ignoring whatever attempt he was trying to make, I forced my attention to the vacant seat next to Tara.

"I know I've been kinda pushy this last year. I just wanted to apologize." His voice was soft, almost sincere. I slowly shifted my focus in his direction with my eyebrows raised but still remained silent as we continued the march. "I'm serious, Clara, you're so beautiful and high-spirited, I always thought we'd be perfect together. I just don't handle crushed dreams very well. The thought of you actually hating me, well . . . I'm sorry, that's all."

We reached our row of seats and parted to stand next to our assigned chairs. My thoughts raced to uncover his true motive to his sudden burst of ruefulness. My eyes fell to the floor in concentration as the rest of our class made their march to join us.

"What did he want?" Tara said in a hushed voice as she placed her hand on my arm. I lifted my gaze from the ground and looked curiously in her direction. "My gut tells me he's up to something." I could feel his stare burning into the side of my neck. Challenging the strength of my willpower, I refrained from looking in his direction as the rest of the class filtered in.

I vaguely recall the faces of the last couple to march down the aisle to find their seats, but the thunderous noise of the moving chairs that echoed off the tall walls around us might stay embedded in my mind forever. It was at that moment that I felt my own personal applause at my accomplishment. It was at that moment that I looked up at the audience and found the smiles of approval of my parents. That was my memorable moment of self-worth and pride; it beamed through me as I sat down to relish this milestone.

Once the room grew silent, Mr. Cruz; our senior advisor, took his place at the podium next to Principal Stevens. He cleared his throat, bringing all eyes to him. "I would like to now turn my position over to Tara Matthews, the valedictorian for the class of 2006." I watched her approach the podium with a stance of pride, and I forgot about the words spoken by Bradley. I watched in admiration as she delivered her speech with the utmost confidence. Her hands were steady, and her eyes focused as each word she spoke rolled off the tip of her tongue with ease.

She honestly belonged up there. I looked into the crowd lining the walls of the gym. They were hanging onto her every word. I couldn't have been more proud of her. The person she had become made me proud. An uncontrollable smirk arose as I gazed at the image behind the podium. The thought of her being my mirror image seemed almost comical. I could not deny the fact that we shared the same look. Our outer appearance was identical, but the people we'd become were complete opposites.

I was inspired by her strength when it came to her smarts and having the ability to address a crowd; that was something I never could do. Now socializing one-on-one with new people was one of my strong suits, not something she found easy to do. Like I said, complete opposites.

Memories of our first day of kindergarten rushed into my thoughts. The vision of us wearing matching purple jumpers with our pink short-sleeved shirts filled my mind. I remembered walking in the classroom hand in hand, with a look of fear on our faces as we studied all the strangers that would be our classmates. Neither of us cried as we held onto each other's hand tightly, relying upon each other for support. We were a package deal, and we tackled every obstacle together. As we approached each new year and each new phase of adolescence, we remained each other's backbone and supported the other through all the obstacles that arose—some more enduring than others, but we made it. We made it, we actually made it through high school.

Realizing this would be the end of our schooldays together, my eyes overfilled. A tear escaped over the ledge and trickled down my cheek. I hadn't noticed I was crying until I felt the wet tickle rolling down my face. I quickly wiped my face dry and shook myself from the trance. Finally getting a hold of myself, I watched Tara introduce Mrs. Stevens, giving up her position on the stage.

My mind quickly reverted back to the scheming of the infamous Bradley as Tara stopped next to him. He was leaning forward in his chair; his lips were moving, but they were too far away from me to hear what he was saying. The glowing shade of pink that had settled in her cheeks was still noticeable, as she slowly maneuvered through the legs leading to her seat on the other side of me. "What did *he* want?" I looked in the opposite direction and aimed my focus straight at the evil smile painted on his conniving face.

"He said he liked my speech." Tara sat and looked back at him with a smile.

"Be careful, I'm sure he has an ulterior motive." I looked back at her and kept my voice soft.

"Why? Was my speech *that* bad?" Her face lightened as the confidence escaped her with my poor choice of wording.

"Your speech was perfect. I just don't trust that guy, and his 'Mr. Good Guy' act gives me the creeps." My whole body shivered.

"Are you sure that deep down you don't secretly like Bradley?" I could feel my eyes tense as they glared in her direction. I gritted my teeth to keep from yelling in outrage.

"Sorry . . . I was just kidding. But I honestly feel you're reading into his actions too much. I think he's a normal guy who likes to impress his friends. I bet one on one he's a totally different person." Tara's eyes escaped mine to look back to him.

"Yeah, and at night when we're all sleeping, the sun glows purple and does the cha-cha with the moon . . . I'm not buying your theory. I have always been a good judge of character. Trust me, I've seen a look in his eyes when I've turned him down. Really, I can't describe it, but the look on his face has honestly given me the chills. I think he could be trouble."

"You're impossible." Tara shook her head and focused her attention on the graduates being called up to the stage to collect their diplomas. I didn't know how to respond. The fact was that after today, he wouldn't be an issue anymore anyway. Deep down I knew I shouldn't be worrying myself with his petty actions, but I couldn't ignore the unsettling knot lingering in my gut. Something told me he was up to something; in fact, the message was screaming loudly inside my head, and it was telling me this was not over and things were not going to end on a positive note.

Trying to shake the unnerving feeling, I placed my hand on top of hers. Her eyes met mine and told me she could read that I felt a part of her rationalizations could hold some truth. Like every other girl in the school, there was a time I had liked Bradley. My feelings changed when I met Todd. Bradley's persistence had, however, become an irritation, but now I wondered if it could also be playing a different kind of emotion, one of danger—a threat to my self-control, my weaknesses.

I broke the eye contact and pulled my hand back. I moved my attention to all the smiling faces returning to their seats with papers of success in hand.

"Tara Rose Matthews." Mr. Cruz stared out into the crowd. Tara gripped my hand tightly as she maneuvered around my legs. She released it as she continued past me to accept her diploma. Watching her walk gracefully down the aisle of gym flooring, I held my breath, waiting for my name to be called next.

"Clara Rae-Ann Matthews." I stood up as Tara reached our row of chairs.

I worked my way past the three other girls and grabbed my sister; I pulled her close and whispered, "I can't believe this day is really here." I tightened my grip briefly before literally running up the path to Principal Stevens. I could hear the applause of my family and friends as my feet carried me quickly over the shiny tan trail. The cheers of encouragement and excitement of graduation fed my energy.

I reached the steps to the stage with such enthusiasm that I stumbled my footing on the bottom step. I lost my balance and fell forward. It happened so fast I barely had time to extend my arms out to grab the edge of the stage at the top of the stairs. My left knee had banged off the middle step with such force it instantly sent shots of intense pain through my thigh. My teeth took hold of my bottom lip as I fought back the yells of pain. My knee was surely bruised, but the damage done to my ego hurt much worse. I got back onto my feet and raised up two thumbs.

I smiled, but my glowing red face showed my embarrassment. I felt like such an ass. I wanted to hide behind the podium and stay there until everyone had left. Knowing that wasn't an option, I accepted my rolled-up piece of paper. Holding my diploma with a death grip of pride and humiliation, I stared at its small structure; I cringed with disappointment as I noted that it was much too small to hide behind.

Principal Stevens extended her hand for a proper shake, but after all the visits I had paid to her office, I decided a hug was more appropriate. I wrapped my arms around her and clutched her tightly. I then spun to face the crowd and raised my arm high up into the air to show off my hard-earned reward.

* * *

After the graduation ceremony, everyone gathered back at the house. Luckily, Chase's party wasn't to start for a couple hours, which left plenty of time for me to be sociable before having to run off to the real fun. The parents had a barbecue set up in the backyard. They were still placing out chairs and food when I joined the circle of grandparents under the shade of the large maple in the corner of the yard.

"Hey, sweet." I felt Todd's warm arms wrap around me from behind. "Nice save on the stumble." He chuckled.

I felt the heat return to my face. I spun my body to face him. "Did you really have to bring that up?" I said softly while gritting my teeth. He answered with a simple wink and a grin. I nudged him briskly in the abdomen with my elbow, which only caused him to laugh. My circle of compassionate family instantly joined in the laughter with Todd. Ordinarily I'd be a victim of his contagious sound of amusement, but being the butt of the joke appeared to be my antidote to his appeal. I stood silently as the cackling continued. They eventually retired the sound and regained their composure.

To make matters worse, my Grandpa Marsh decided to add salt to the wound. "That was probably the best part of the whole ceremony. I bet the whole town will be talking about that one for years to come." He lifted his glass to take a sip of his iced tea as the group started with the laughter again.

"So you don't think they'll remember my speech?" Tara interrupted as she joined us under the shade.

"Now that was an amazing speech. You should be very proud. No doubt, the ceremony was a success due to the wonderful Matthews sisters . . . an obvious trait you inherited from your *mother's* side of the family," Grandpa Marsh said with a smile. He threw his arm around Tara and pulled her close.

"Harvard is very lucky to have you Tara," Grandmother Matthews jumped in. "We are all very proud of you. Your smarts are no doubt a gift from your *father's* side."

I looked to Tara to share a silent laugh. This was the norm for any Matthews family affair. Grandmother Matthews—or rather, Belle; she hated being called Grandma. She was a proper woman with exquisite taste and a healthy bank account. Grandfather Matthews was a great lawyer and an even better investor. They had more money than they knew what to do with, and Belle wasn't ashamed to let the world know she was better than everyone else.

Grandfather Matthews was a man of few words and stood quietly amongst the group as usual. He blended in with the rest of us in his faded blue jeans and a plain black T-shirt. By looking at him and his long shabby gray hair that framed his round, rosy face, you'd never guess he had money. "I can't believe you didn't get that mop of yours cut before coming down here." Belle rolled her eyes at Grandfather Matthews as she looked at him in disappointment. Grandfather said nothing, even though all eyes were now looking in his direction as her harsh tone piqued everyone's attention.

"I would hope that if there will be a wedding in the future for one of these girls that you'll be able to dip into that wallet of yours, for a new outfit at least." We all noted her disappointment as the words escaped like daggers in her nagging voice. He again said nothing. The simple smile on his face told us he could hear her scolding words but was either used to it or couldn't care less about her complaints. Either way, we found it rather humorous as her words went in one ear and out the other, without so much as a flinch from him.

In an obvious attempt to break some of the tension between the Matthewses, Grandfather Marsh, with his arm still wrapped around, Tara asked, "How does it feel to finally be getting out of high school? You looking forward to being on your own when you leave for college?"

Tara nodded. "I'm a little nervous, but the change will be kind of nice. I hope."

"Of course it will!" Belle snapped. "You're a Matthews, and we're not only smart and beautiful but we're also fearless and independent. You'll do fine on your own . . . you'll see. You've a lot like your father, which means you've got Matthews blood running in your veins, and with that comes only the greatest of things."

"I think that means you're invincible." Grandfather Marsh smirked as he gave Tara an extra squeeze.

"That's *exactly* what that means," Belle replied with her chest and nose pointed to the sky. As her eyes drifted in my direction, I waited for my dose of criticism that usually followed Tara's praise of Matthews' perfection. "Clara, stand straight." Belle demonstrated her request by pulling her shoulders back. "You're slouching. You wouldn't have any height at all if it weren't for your father. You should stand tall and be proud, or in no time you'll look just like your mother." I knew she meant it as an insult, but I was proud to hear those words; I'd have liked nothing more than to be just like my mother.

Family gatherings were always entertaining, to say the least. The tension between the two different worlds my parents came from filled the air; the combination of the two would intertwine like hazardous fumes. The outcome would almost always end in some kind of explosion. Unfortunately, it was usually in the form of tears, shed by my mom after everyone had left and Belle had criticized her about everything she did.

"Time to eat," Mom said, waving a handful of royal-blue napkins high above her short stature to get everyone's attention. My mom was slender, short, and quite possibly the most elegant person I had ever met. She was soft-spoken and kindhearted. She kept her natural curls that flowed down to her waist, up in a ponytail with her bangs combed perfectly straight in front and always a spiral curl that hung on either side to frame her fair-skinned face. Mom never wore a lot of makeup, but she didn't need to; she naturally glowed whenever she smiled.

The family filled in the chairs that were placed around the table that was decorated with a blue cloth and an array of delicately prepared side dishes. Mom had gone all out, filling her best crystal bowls with fancy dips made of the finest ingredients in an eager attempt to impress Belle. "Wow! Everything looks wonderful, dear," Grandma Marsh looked to my mom, who was carrying out the cake.

"Thanks, I hope everyone's hungry. I've made plenty, so dig in."

Dad carried over a plate of hamburger patties he had pulled from the grill and placed them in the center of the table next to the garnishes. Todd reached for the fixings first, setting things into motion; arms from all directions instantly joined the fight for food. I delayed the preparation of my own plate as I watched everyone else.

Smiles were abundant as everyone's plate became covered with samples of all the varieties of the spread on the table. The guys wasted no time in stuffing their faces; in fact, Dad had a hamburger in one hand and a handful of chips in the other. I continued to scroll over everyone, pleased that everyone seemed to be content—for the moment anyway. I shook my head slightly and shared a private snicker with Tara as we spotted Grandma Belle eating her hamburger with a knife and fork.

That moment sizzled itself in my mind like a memory of prominence—the connection between my sister and I that could never been broken, the image of my family brought together to celebrate a day of great importance for my sister and me. The weather was perfect; the sun was shining with a subtle breeze that helped the temperature to be neither too hot nor too cold. This would be a day I would remember forever.

The background noise of singing birds only added to the memory video that was recording and saving itself in my brain. The busy bird feeder in the far corner of the yard provided the orchestra of chirps while the flowers beneath them released the faint smell of lavender. I inhaled the subtlety; the aroma of the lavender had to compete with the scent of the food. My belly grumbled as the smell of the food begged to be noticed and eventually triumphed in the fragrance battle. I felt at ease as I sat back and watched everyone talking and enjoying the meal. I tingled with delights as I noted *life was good*.

Belle glanced at me for a brief moment before shifting her attention to my sister. "So, Tara dear, do you have everything set up for school? Will you be staying in your own apartment, or nesting in the dorm?" Belle wiped the corners of her mouth gently with her napkin. I was amused by her proper ways and had to fight the urge to grab my own napkin—in an attempt to imitate her 'look how much better I am than you' gestures.

"I have a job already set up as a mail girl. It's at a law firm not too far from the dorm where I will be living."

Tara reached for another roll—missing the look of horror that swept in the color of crimson across Belle's face. "Working! You should be worrying about your studies, not a job . . . I thought your scholarships and grants were supposed to cover your living expenses!" Belle's attention shifted to my mom as if she was the main cause of Belle's disapproval.

"They will cover a lot of them, but I wanted to be working among the profession I was studying. You know, make sure it's really what I want to do." Tara sat tall and spoke in a confident voice to deliver her rebuttal. She was a natural; Belle didn't stand a chance.

"I see . . point taken." Belle took a breath then smiled, half a smile showing she was somewhat impressed.

Dad was one of the few who had noticed Tara's abundance of attention that left me on the sidelines. As my personal protector, he had a way of reminding people of my existence if things seemed to be navigating toward my sister like a magnet. As the smile swept across his face, I knew he about to shine some light in my direction. "You know Clara has some exciting news," Dad said, slicing himself a piece of cake. I felt my cheeks warm as everyone adjusted their eyes to focus on me. "Clara will be attending some photography classes and already has an interview for an internship at the *Tribune* next week. It looks to me that we should be very proud of both my girls." He looked in my direction and gave me a wink.

I jumped up and ran into his arms. "Thanks, Daddy, this means so much to me."

While I was still in his arms, Belle started with her criticism. "Now taking pictures is more of a hobby than a job . . . don't you think?"

Before I could respond, my grandpa Marsh jumped to my defense. "I happen to know some great photographers who make a fine living and who have had some amazing traveling opportunities. Sometimes life isn't about who will make the most money in their profession but, rather, who enjoys and does well on the path they have chosen."

Belle simply shrugged her shoulders and looked in the other direction. Excited about the opportunity of working for the paper, I grasped my dad tightly to thank him once again. Feeling more confident about the new role I was expected to play after high school, I stole a piece of cake and returned to my seat with a smile. I could feel my body was beaming with an overload of excitement. I wanted to jump up and down screaming with joy, but now that I was out of high school and no longer a child, I controlled myself.

Chapter 3

A Life-Changing Party!

I scraped the last of the cake from my plate and savored its moist, chocolaty taste. I wiped the frosting from my lips with a bright-blue napkin. My focus drifted to Todd. He looked at his watch and showed me the time. Getting his subtle hint, I nodded then turned toward Mom, who was sitting at the end of the table.

"Well, it's been fun, but I've got to go in and change for the next party." I stood, pushing my plate aside.

Before I could step away from the table, I heard a heavy sigh. "It's kinda rude to leave your guest at your own party, don't you think., dear?" Belle's eyebrows raised; her stare stabbed into me.

I opened my mouth to respond, but Dad was already excusing me for the evening.

"Go ahead, honey, and have fun . . . I'm sure your grandmother didn't come all this way just to see you. You'll see her again tomorrow when we go out to breakfast." Dad watched his mother cringe at the use of the word *grandmother*. I enjoyed her apparent pain a little too much as I joined his side and gave him a kiss on the cheek, a thank-you for coming to my rescue yet again.

With a new burst of energy to hit the party scene, I rushed into the house to find something to wear. I sprinted through my door-way, instantly zoning in on each scatter of clothing that was thrown carelessly into various nooks on my side of the room. My fingers found comfort in my hair as they grasped at my auburn roots as I became overwhelmed at the scene. Shaking my head at the choices before me, I opened my closet and thumbed through the collection of hanging dresses.

"So . . . what does one wear to a party like this anyway?"

I whipped around in disbelief, drawing my attention to Tara standing at the door.

"Does this mean you'll be going?" My body leaned toward the doorway, anxious for her to verify her remark was genuine and not a joke.

"I've been doing some thinking, and I figured it couldn't hurt to see what all the fuss was about."

She entered the room, sending chills of excitement through me.

"This is gonna be great!" I looked back to my closet and grabbed a navy-and-white floral-print summer dress from the floor and threw it at her. "Wear this!"

Tara caught the dress with one hand before it could hit her in the face. Her eyes widened as she pinched the thin spaghetti straps and held the dress out in front of her. I watched her reaction of disapproval as she examined the low neckline.

"Trust me . . . you are gonna look great." I nodded with a wink, counteracting her slowly shaking head.

"I think I'll find something that will cover more skin." She threw it onto the bed.

"Wear your navy-blue hoodie with the short sleeves." I tapped my bicep to indicate the shortness of the sleeves. Her eyebrows raised to show her doubt in my suggestion. "Just try it on, then you can judge."

With a sigh of irritation, she went to her side of the room and walked straight to the hoodie I referred to. I envied that, the organization she had, the neat and tidiness of her side of the room. I often considered trying to be more like that, but I just didn't have the time for that petty detailing.

As she closed to door to change into her outfit, I finally spotted the perfect choice for me. I pulled off my low-rider jeans and slipped into my faded denim miniskirt with the ragged hem. Remembering the red halter I had bought recently, I ran to my dresser. Once my fingers snagged onto the strap of the halter, I flung it onto my bed and stripped off my T-shirt.

The red shirt was long enough to cover half of my skirt and fit snug. The draped-style front showed off the cleavage of my C-cup chest. I tied the strap behind my neck and then pulled my sandals with a subtle heel out from under my bed. As I stepped into the worn-out pair of shoes, Tara shook her head. "When are you going to retire those old things?" Her laughter was a stab at my fashion sense, but I didn't care.

"I've finally got them broken in. These are the most comfortable pair of shoes I own. I will never throw them out . . . ever." I picked my oval chain belt off the floor and swung it around my waist and fastened it at the hip so the smaller links dangled down my left hip.

We both met at the full-length mirror near the door. "You look great!" we said in unison.

"Should I leave my hair down?" Tara pulled it back to see if she liked it better up. I grabbed two small clips from the vanity table and pulled back one side of her auburn curls and placed the clips side by side.

"There, it's perfect." I stood next to her and admired our reflections.

"I look like you." Tara stepped in toward the mirror to get a closer look.

"You're just now noticing?" My eyebrows dropped with concern.

"No. I mean my style or, rather, your style . . . everyone will think I'm you. Good thing you have that bruise on your knee to help people tell us apart." She smiled as she pointed out my colorful leg. I punched her in the arm before she could finish with her wisecrack remark.

"Ouch!" She rubbed her arm and stepped back with a giggle. I fluffed my hair and touched up my makeup to keep my freckles hidden. After applying the lip gloss for the final touch, I followed Tara out the door.

Standing before the French doors in the kitchen, I pulled my sister closer to my side. Tara opened the doors, and we stepped out onto the patio together. Todd's eyes automatically gravitated to us; the smile on his face showed his approval. I almost forgot we weren't alone. Our eyes locked as he drifted over the grass, slowly eliminating the space between us. Taking his place next to me, he took my hand into his. His breath tickled my ear as he leaned in with hushed words that shivered my insides. "You look amazing." My voice was frozen by the flattery; my only response was given in the form of a coy smile followed by a subtle shrug.

I looked out at the family. All eyes were staring directly at Tara and her new look. "I'm sure gonna be the envy of every guy at the party when I walk in with the hot Matthews sisters on my arms," Todd broke the silence.

Tara leaned toward Todd with a whispered tone. "So do I look all right? I'm kinda nervous, this being my first party and all." She looked down at her bare knees.

"You look awesome, and I'm sure you'll have a great time," Todd said with a smile, reassuring everything I had already told her.

I tried not to laugh as I noticed Belle's expression; she looked as if she had sucked a lemon. Her face was all tensed up as she glared at us in disgust. I almost felt guilty for the humor I found in her reaction. When I was younger, I craved the approval of Belle. She was, after all, my elder, my grandmother, and as a child, I was raised to show respect. Of course, now that I was older and had wasted endless counts of energy on her, I knew finding her approval was a lost cause.

My new challenge in life was much more rewarding now I liked to see what different reactions I could get from her. The look of disgust was not a new one, but it was one of my favorites. With feelings of satisfaction by her current reaction, I couldn't help but run to her with open arms. "We'll see you in the morning at breakfast." I gave her a loving embrace as she gently patted my back with one hand, as if afraid to touch me. "I love you, Belle." I gave her a peck on the cheek. Feeling her cringe in my arms, I was elated. I imagined she was revolted by my touch and the filth I may be transferring onto her, as if I had cooties.

Looking over to Grandma Marsh, I could see her natural glow as she smiled. I released my grip on Belle and ran to her expression of invitation. I fell carelessly into her arms. As she held me close, blanketing me with comfort, I clenched on tightly, knowing that I was welcome in her embrace at any time. My heart fluttered with enchantment as if I were a small child again, and I loved it. "You have fun, sweetie. You look so hip it makes me remember the days when I was young and skinny." She grabbed me by the waist and pushed me out in front of her to take another look. "I love you, Grandma." I beamed naturally at her genuine praise.

"Love you too, dear. Call me with the details on your interview . . . I want to know every detail." Grandma Marsh shook her finger, turning her request into a demand. "I will." I nodded.

Tara had already said her good-byes to Belle and was tapping my shoulder. I stepped aside and let her say her good-byes to our best friend of a grandma. Grandma Marsh was easy to talk to and could always be trusted with a secret. Growing up, she played the role of our armored knight who would come to our defense, and for that we were grateful.

"All right, Dad, we'll be in by midnight." I walked past him to take Todd by the arm.

"That sounds fine, have fun . . . but not too much fun!" he said as we ran around to the front of the house. Todd pushed his bike up to the side of the garage then ran back down to the car and jumped in the backseat with me. Tara sat patiently in the driver's seat.

The party was only five minutes away, five short minutes I spent clutched onto Todd's arm like a child with a new teddy bear. Chase's house was located on a dead-end road with no close neighbors. The sky was starting to turn a brilliant purple color as his home came into view. It almost looked like a painting of a country cabin. The two-story rustic home had a large fenced-in yard with borders of brilliantly colored flowers and a backdrop of large oaks.

Excitement rolled through me as I noted the crowd of cars that already filled the large driveway. The mix of familiar cars rang truth to the rumors; this *was* going to be one hell of a party. Tara hesitated, then eased the car behind the lineup that was collecting along the gravel drive in front of the house. She shut off the engine, but kept her grip on the steering wheel as she continued to sit quietly. I stared at the multitude of bright windows that decorated the cabin. The large number of people inside could be seen dancing and laughing. A muted version of the music playing inside filled the car as she looked blankly toward the source of the toe-tapping beats.

"You ready?" I leaned forward, peeking my face between the front seats to get her attention. "I think so . . . is there alcohol in there?" she said, never peeling her eyes away from the cabin. "More than likely, but you don't have to drink. There are generally cans of pop somewhere. And if it gets too crazy for you, just say the word and we'll all leave *together*." I reached my arm over the seat and rested my hand on her shoulder.

She leaned her warm cheek against my bright-red manicured nails. We waited in silence until she gained her courage and lifted her head. The door handle clicked as she opened it. "I'm ready to do this."

After climbing out of the driver's seat, Tara adjusted her dress in an attempt to cover more of her legs. Todd paused briefly to assure Tara was not going to jump back into the car. When it was apparent that she was going through with it, he pushed the seat forward and slid out the driver's door; I followed his lead. He sandwiched himself between Tara and me, and our trio approached the front door as a team.

The music grew louder as we walked closer to the house. My foot barely found support on the bottom step of the front porch when the door flew open, and out ran Cin and Tracy. "T. M., I'm so happy you made it, come on!" Cin grabbed Tara by the hand and pulled her inside. Todd closed the door as I watched our friends drag my sister through the crowd. Her giggles assured her approval, and without worries, Todd and I gravitated to the dance floor.

I scanned the crowd of faces and felt relieved that Bradley didn't seem to be anywhere around. The normal circle of jocks was blocking the stairway in front of the entrance door. This was where Bradley would normally be spotted, but tonight he wasn't among them. I waved back to a couple of girls from school that were migrating toward the eye candy in letterman jackets. As I rolled my eyes at the popularity of the stereotype, Todd pulled me close to him. "I'll go find us some refreshments." He yelled over the music then leaned in and gave me a kiss on the cheek.

I grabbed his sleeve before he could vanish into the sea of dancers. "Make mine the non-courageous kind. House full of family, you know." I shrugged my shoulders to my request for a change from my usual party beverage.

"Gotcha!" He slipped through a small gap within the crowd of party people.

As he disappeared, I caught a glimpse of a streaker near the door. Surprisingly enough it was Annie. No doubt she had plenty to show; if I hadn't known her since the third grade, I would have sworn they were fake. However, I was there when she had bought her first bra in the fifth grade and was the friend she would cry to when the girls would make fun of the freak with the big breasts.

We had grown apart in high school when she had discovered how much the guys loved her freaky characteristics. She still had on her short black-and-red plaid skirt, but her top was bare. Annie spotted me standing in the middle of the floor and ran past the wide-eyed group of guys sipping on their cans of suds. "Clara! Thish is a great pary. You look sho beauful." Annie slurred her intoxicated words as she bounced her way to me.

"Annie, it appears that you may have misplaced your shirt." I looked through the crowd to see if I could spot Todd, trying not to stare at her massive double Ds. She looked down then quickly covered with her hands what she could of her naked breasts. "Sho I 'av . . . oh, ew know tha' Bradley . . . he muss have done tha' when we were in da closet." The mention of his name made my skin crawl. He *was* here, and he was already up to no good. "It sho goo to see ew, Clara, I mish ush, you know. Us." Her face dropped into a pout.

I listened to her muttered words, barely making any sense out of them. I smiled uncomfortably as everyone began looking in our direction. "Whoa! Hello, Annie," Todd said, staring at her hands that were still hanging onto her voluptuous mounds of flesh. His eyes bugged out for a brief moment as he held onto a cup of punch in each hand.

"Helwo yoshelf, Todd," Annie said as she dropped her hands to her side, exposing the goods she had been previously hiding. He handed me the refreshments then reached into his coat pocket and removed his driver's license and a folded-up ten-dollar bill. I watched closely, confused as to what he was doing. He then placed the items into his back jean pocket and took off his black leather jacket.

"Here, Annie, you can wear this until you get your shirt on." He handed over his coat.

"Why? Deez not nice 'nuff ta show?" She placed a hand under each breast and jiggled them slightly for his viewing. I took a step back, trying not to laugh, and waited for his response.

"I won't lie—I think they are quite nice. But they do draw the attention away from your eyes." He draped the jacket over her bare shoulders.

"Ew 'ike my eyes?" She slipped her arms into the jacket and zipped it halfway to cover herself.

"You have the bluest eyes I've ever seen," he said. Now that she was covered, I was able to focus on the only bare skin I could see—her face. "It's true, Annie, they sparkle from across the room, especially when you smile."

She had a pale complexion; her skin was as fair and soft as baby powder. Her porcelain veneer was framed by her salon-spiraled blond hair that hung an inch above her shoulders. Her lips were petite, with only a sliver of a top lip that she had painted bright red. She was an attractive girl. Perhaps not a traffic-stopping beauty but still attractive. "Oh sanks, guys. I juss wuv you sho much." Her sobs amplified as she fell into my arms.

Finally over her alcohol-induced emotional breakdown, I watched as she stumbled through the crowd to locate her missing clothing. Staggered by the hazy conversation we just had, I took a sip of my drink, watching her bounce off of innocent bystanders.

The warmth from Todd's hand as he rested it on my shoulder pulled my attention back to him. My free hand found its way to the source of the heat wave taking over my body. I intertwined my fingers with his; he pointed to a couple of empty seats by the window. Ignoring the stumbling idiot behind us, we carefully slipped through the groups of people blocking the path and weaved our way to the bare oak chairs.

I plopped down and instantly found comfort in the oversized dining chairs. Wasting no time, my eyes automatically started filtering through all the figures between me and the other end of the house. My emerald scanners shifted back and forth until they found Tara. She was standing out on the back patio beneath the light, making her easy to spot. I strained my eyes in attempt to improve my view to make out the image in front of her. I could see she was talking to someone, but the dark shadow proved to be a mystery. The throw of her head in laughter, told me she was doing fine at fitting in and made me feel more at ease.

Confident she was having a great time, I looked back to Todd, who was staring at me with a serious look on his face. It made me feel as if I had something on my face. "What?" I said, rubbing the bridge of my nose to wipe off whatever was attracting his attention.

"I don't know, I just love to look at you." He smiled. I could feel my cheeks flush with color. My insides warmed with delight as an electrifying chill ran up my back. The only words I could find to respond with were "I love you too."

That was the first time I had said those words. He had said them a few times before, but I could never bring myself to repeat them. As the words flowed from my mouth, I could see his eyes brighten. His hand found its way to my cheek, and he gave me a gentle kiss on the lips. "I love you, sweets. I love you more than anything." He rubbed my cheek with his warm hand.

For a split second, we shared the memorable moment all to ourselves. But the music soon found its way back into my head and took control of my feet. Todd noticed my tapping foot, grabbed me up by the arm, and led me out onto the dance floor. I could hear others in a drunken stupor in the background and the giggling from gossipers surrounding us on the floor. But the only vision I saw was that of Todd's perfect smile and dazzling eyes—a vision I hoped to see before me for the rest of my life. I eventually snapped back to reality as Cassie and Becca jumped in to dance with us.

"It's almost too sad to think this could be the last of these parties . . . I'm gonna miss you guys!" Cassie said.

"We'll still see each other around, I'm sure." I allowed my body to stay in sync with the music.

"Not the same, Clara. It's just not the same," replied Becca as Cassie pulled her away to intrude on someone else.

The crowd gradually got thicker as the party carried us further into the night. Visiting with classmates I knew seemed to speed the hand on my watch by the minutes rather than the seconds. The thoughts of never seeing some of these faces again made me sad, for the most part. Yet honestly, some of those thoughts were coated with the sense of relief.

We were talking to Jessica and Chase when Annie returned. She was wearing her shirt, carrying the leather jacket, as she approached us. At first I thought she was coming to return the jacket, but her face screamed a different agenda. The tears that spilled out of her eyes told me the drama with this lost friend was by no means over.

"What's wrong?" I placed my arm around her.

She wiped her tears. After Todd took back his coat, she settled the sobs long enough to explain. "I'll be fine," she sniffled. "It's just that . . ." She swallowed hard and pushed back some tears. "It's just that I seen Bradley with someone else . . . I know we're not exclusive, but . . . but it still burned to see him kissing your sister."

"Kissing! *My* sister?" I spun her to face me. My hands grasped her shoulders as I stared deep into her bloodshot eyes. "Are you sure it was Tara?"

She nodded while wiping away a few more tears "It was her."

I looked to Todd in almost a panic. "We've got to find her!" My heart sank into my gut, stirring my insides into a near-nauseated state of fright. I pulled him though the crowd leaving Annie to cry with Jessica and Chase. My mind flashed an image of the last place I'd seen her: the back patio. I ran to the door and looked around the yard but saw nothing.

My body's alarm was sounding loudly, and I knew I needed to find her. I examined every detail of the faces that surrounded me in hopes to see hers, but again I saw nothing. Todd pointed out Cindy across the room. She was giggling with some girls from school on the couch in the other room. He took charge and pulled me through the crowd, moving people out of the way. Reaching the back of the couch, I grabbed it firmly and leaned down into Cindy's face. "WHERE IS SHE! WHERE IS TARA?" She jumped up off the couch and stood up to make eye contact. "She's fine . . . oh my god, don't freak . . . she's outside talking with Bradley." She took a sip from her bottle of beer.

"Errr!" I growled, fighting to remain calm. "I *just* looked out there! She's not there!" I looked toward the back door.

"That's where she is, I swear." Cindy smiled, showing no concern as she pointed at the window. Todd was already making his own path through the people once again to the back door. I stayed right on his heels the whole way.

Reaching the door, he swung it open and marched out onto the brick steps. I hardly remember my feet using them to reach the brick-laid patio as I rushed with Todd outside and examined the darkness for any trace of my sister. I gasped for air as a dark silhouette emerged from the shadows across the lawn. The mysterious figure seemed to move in slow motion as the suspense burned through me. Bradley's face soon became visible, and my stomach instantly knotted up.

I ran past Todd to meet up with Bradley. I came face to face with him at the end of the patio near the lounge chairs. The anger within was blaring in octaves too loud for me to ignore. My body was shaking frantically as my mind began screaming the words I couldn't gather to spit out. With my heart pounding, I took a breath and opened my mouth to ask about Tara.

Before the words could roll off my tongue, he smiled his evil smile and stepped closer to me. He leaned down slightly and whispered in my ear, "Like I said." He placed his left hand on my right cheek and slid it softly down my face. "Bradley gets what Bradley wants." His words smoldered like a dagger to my heart, and his touch made my stomach turn. I lifted my right foot and stomped down as hard as I could onto his left foot. He stumbled back limping. "YOU BITCH!"

His holler was music to my ears; his pain pleased me. Still needing some answers, I lunged forward but landed short as Todd stepped in front of me like a shield. "After you apologize to Clara, you better tell me where Tara is, or you're going to experience some real pain."

Bradley was amused at the words and refused to answer the question. He crossed his arms and smirked with a teeth-bearing grin. Todd apparently found the look on Bradley's face to be as creepy as I did, because without warning Todd punched him straight between the eyes. Unprepared for Todd's delivery, Bradley stumbled in a daze. His body collapsed straight back, like a fallen tree. His head landed on the hard brick pavers with a loud thud.

Through the commotion, I caught some movement out of the corner of my eye. Staring into the dark shadows lining the lawn, I could see the glow of Tara's pale bare legs. I stepped over the motionless body on the ground, being sure to grind the heel of my shoe into his hand that laid limp in the grass. I ran beneath the limbs of the oak trees and hurried toward my sister.

Running through the darkness made it difficult to see if she was all right. "Tara!" I yelled in hopes to get a reassuring reply of hope that all was well. Instead, I heard only the breeze rushing by my side as I raced up the incline to the tree she was sitting up against. Todd walked slowly behind me, keeping his distance to allow me to talk to her in private. "Hey." I panted as I finally reached her, and I sat down beside her. I shifted on the cold grass to find some comfort. She remained silent. Her head hung low, bringing my attention to the direction of her stare. That's when I noticed her dirt-covered knees. "You okay?" My skin shivered, afraid to hear otherwise.

"Yeah . . . I feel so stupid though." She wrapped her arms around her legs, pulling them tightly into her chest.

"What happened? Did he try anything?" My hushed voice disguised the rage that was twitching every nerve in my body. Her silence lasted forever. I didn't want to push her to talk, but I needed to know. The stillness was playing havoc on my body. I shifted my position crossing my ankles, but the suspense was building. My palms began to itch; my right foot tapped at the cold breeze.

I looked to Todd, who stood silently in the shadows as I sat by her side and shrugged my shoulders. I knew something was wrong; I only prayed it wasn't as bad as what was rushing through my mind. After what seemed like an eternity, she began to sob and leaped into my arms. Her tears told me more than I wanted to know; my heart sank as I too began to cry with her.

She eventually relaxed enough to tell her story. "Things went too far too fast." She held me tight.

"Did he force himself on you? I'll kill him." I saw red as my hatred for him mounted even higher.

"It *wasn't* all his fault." She pulled away from the embrace, getting control of her sobs and sniffles. "He said all the right things," she explained as she wiped away the tears. "Part of me honestly wanted to experience it with him . . . but by the time I knew it was happening and that I didn't want to . . . I said no." Tara looked out into the darkness. "But it was too late. He was on me, and I was helpless." She paused to wipe her cheeks clean of the tears. "That's not even the worst part." She covered her face with her hands as she began to cry again.

"What's worst than being forced into something you didn't want to do? What could be worse than rape?" I shook my head in confusion.

"The words he muttered afterward." She finally looked up at me. "When he was finished . . . he said . . . 'I will always love you, Clara.' He had imagined I was you. He couldn't even call me by my own name."

I wrapped her in my arms like a much-needed security blanket, and we cried together. I felt awful, and the part of it that tore at me most was I knew something like this was going to happen. His eyes told me he was trouble, yet no one could hear my warnings. *I wanted to scream!* I felt responsible for what had happened but didn't know how to make it right.

The tears finally ran dry, and we sat up to wipe away the dark circles of smeared makeup on our cheeks. "You will press charges, right?" I watched her stand and brush the filth from the back of her dress. Her eyes pierced through mine as I slowly got to my feet as well.

"No! I just want to put this night behind me. Nobody needs to ever know what happened here tonight. Ever!" Her grip on my arm was tight and shaky. "Promise me we will never speak of this. I mean it, promise." Tara's grip tightened.

"Are you sure? I think he should pay for what he has done." I looked to the vacant patio where I had left Bradley.

"No! You promise." She pulled my attention to her.

"Okay, I promise." I nodded hesitantly.

"I want to go home." She released her grip.

"Okay . . . I'll drive." I wrapped my arm around her and escorted her through the side yard with Todd following close behind.

* * *

Keeping my sister's secret was difficult. Growing up we had made many pacts between us and swore to take many secrets to the grave, but this one pained me to keep. The guilt I held was making me ill. I hated the thought of allowing him to get away with it. The nagging of right from wrong versus a pact between sisters—twin sisters at that—was affecting my daily routine, my concentration, and my sleep. Regardless, I had made a promise, and I intended to keep my word, but I also intended to do what I could to make it up to her.

It took a couple of months before we could look at each other without thinking about the dark secret that loomed between us. We eventually put that night aside and started to focus on the fact that we only had a few more weeks together before we would be miles apart. Her leaving for college was a big enough deal without focusing on other issues that only added to the sadness that was collecting between our bedroom walls.

Being apart was going to be a challenge in itself. Life without her by my side was one of those nightmares that I prayed I would never have to deal with. She was my motivation in life. Tara was more than just my sister and my best friend. She was my other half who had been there through my every beck and call.

Chapter 4

A Turn of Events

My feet were dragging with each step as I made my way to the front door. I had no idea that juggling classes, and the new intern job at the *Tribune* would require so much mental, and physical energy. I turned the knob on the door ready to head straight for a hot bath, followed by a crawl leading straight to my warm bed for some much needed sleep.

I walked into the house to find my sister and parents sitting on the couch. The hung heads told me something was definitely wrong and my previous plans were about to change. I took a seat in the green recliner and waited patiently for someone to share the devastating news that had settled heavily in the air.

Mom's eyes were red and puffy; her hand shook as she wiped her tears. My ears were prepared to hear of a death in the family. "Clara." Her voice was weak. "Your sister should be the one to share with you the dilemma she's gotten herself into."

I looked to my sister. The room grew to a chilling silence. My fingers dug into the arms of the recliner, as if to hold on for support. I focused on her face, waiting for the news to be delivered.

Her mouth slowly opened, then she hesitated briefly before speaking in a soft voice, "I went to the doctor today." Her face was as pale as a ghost. She got up, and walked to the fireplace to continue her story while staring at the mantel. Her thumb made its way up to her mouth where she started biting at its nail, something she always did when she was nervous.

I waited through the long pause. Finally she spit out the words that appeared to be caught in her throat. "Clara,"—she turned to face me; her bottom lip quivered—"I'm pregnant." She dropped her face into her hands as tears poured down her cheeks. Mom's face tensed as Tara spoke. Dad's glare weakened my knees. I rushed over and took her in my arms. The lump in my throat was instant and unbearable. The parents seemed more mad than sympathetic, but they didn't know the story. I held her close, partly in attempt to keep myself standing.

My heart cried with hers as I held her tight. If only I hadn't insisted on her going to that stupid party. It was all my fault, and I knew I had to make it right. The wheels in my head began to spin as I fought for the perfect solution. "Maybe you can talk some sense into her . . . she hasn't said a single word since she got home." Dad's voice hovered in the background.

Thoughts of that dreadful night came rushing back. The image of her sitting next to the tree—cold, miserable, and helpless—became unbearable. I whispered in her ear, "I'm so sorry." I rubbed her back, trying to control the anger I held toward Bradley. Her whimpering made my chest ache. My head was throbbing, and my stomach was turning at the thought of all her achievements being wasted by the likes of some arrogant jock.

My vision clouded as I imagined all of her hard work squandered. Then my mind cleared. I pushed her away and wiped the tears from my face. "You can't raise this baby and throw away your scholarship and everything else you've worked so hard to achieve. But *I* can." I placed my hands on her shoulders and allowed our matching eyes of green to connect.

"What are you saying?" Dad sprung up off the couch. "Who says she's even having this child?" His tone rose with each word as he took a couple steps toward us.

"I'm having this baby, Dad!" Tara pleaded as she covered her belly. "I don't think you've thought this through." Dad's shadow casted down on us as he neared closer and spoke louder.

"It's all I *have* thought about, Dad! I haven't thought of anything else since I found out." Her hands clenched at her side as she leaned forward.

"So then tell me, how are you going to raise this child?" His breathing was heavy and the vein on his forehead was bulging.

"I don't know." She relaxed her tense stance and shrugged her shoulders.

"Great! Now that you're talking, how about sharing with us who the father is." Mom leaned forward, now sitting on the edge of the couch. Tara turned her head away, saying nothing.

"You can't raise this child on your own, and I'm not going to do it." Mom crossed her arms. "We can put it up for adoption!" Mom's suggestion sounded more like a command.

"*Quiet!*" I raised my hand to motion them to stop. All eyes were focused on me. "I'm raising this child as my own. As far as anyone is concerned, I'm the one who's pregnant."

"That's absurd!" Dad's eyebrows lowered and his arms flew up.

"This is my problem, not yours." Tara wiped away her tears. I nearly laughed at her response—had she forgotten we shared everything, including problems? I took complete blame for this one in particular.

"Okay. Explain to me how you're gonna raise a child *and* go to school." I crossed my arms and waited for her response.

"I'll just wait and attend school next year." She looked away to avoid eye contact.

"And your grants will be enough for you *and* a child to live on?" I leaned my body into her line of vision.

"I'll have a job." Her voice was shaky and uncertain.

"Right, and while you're working and going to school, you'll be paying for day care. While you're home, you'll be tending to the baby. When will you study?"

Tara's eyes looked through me as she absorbed my words.

"The adoption idea is sounding better and better." Dad paced the floor with nostrils flaring. "I honestly can't even believe we're having this discussion, I thought I raised you girls with more common sense than that." Mom's head hung low and she looked to the floor, but her words were loud and clear.

I stepped forward. "You can call it adoption, but I'm raising this baby! It's not like we haven't changed places before . . . and I am the one who insisted on her going to the party." My stomach churned the second the word *party* slipped out over my tongue.

"This happened at the party!" He stopped in his tracks. "Who's the father?" Dad's face was a shade of red I'd never seen before. Mom's eyes locked onto my sister, waiting for her answer. But Tara said nothing.

Dad was no longer looking to her for answers. His eyes pierced mine like a red-hot laser. "How could you let this happen? Do you know who he is?" His eyes were stern as he took a step toward me. "And where the hell were you anyway?" His last words grabbed hold of my heart and squeezed tight. I had asked myself that same question many times before, but to hear them from him hurt worse than any punishment that could have been dealt.

I swallowed hard. "I never saw him." I looked to the ground, unable to make eye contact with him. "I left her with our friends. I thought she'd be fine." I slowly glanced back up at him. "You're right, though, I should have stayed by her side, then maybe it never would have happened." I looked to Tara. "I'll make it up to you by taking responsibility for that baby."

Her pale face grew red. "You guys talk as if I'm a baby myself. I can take care of myself, it's nobody's fault but my own. I'm human is all, I don't need a babysitter. I messed up!" Tara's body trembled as she raised her voice.

"You can say that again!" Dad kicked the table leg as he passed by it to join Mom on the couch.

"The father's the one who should be taking some responsibility, not Clara. Call him, call him right now!" Mom's shaky finger was pointing toward the phone.

"I can't. I don't know how to get a hold of him." Tara slowly turned to face the mantel again. "I don't know who he is." She lowered her head and her voice.

"YOU SLEPT WITH SOMEONE YOU DIDN'T EVEN KNOW?" Mom was now too upset to shed tears and was yelling in a volume I didn't know she was capable of. Dad wrapped his arm around Mom as he dropped his slowly shaking head. At that moment I felt his heart sink as well. Mom's fist was pressed to her lips. Her hand opened and found its way to Dad's hand on her shoulder. "I just never, never expected that kind of thing. Not from you."

I bit my lip as I was curious to ask if she would have expected something like that from me. Dad held Mom close as she sobbed. I joined my sister at the fireplace. "What do you think?" I laid my hand on her shoulder.

"I think this is the biggest decision of my life," she said in a hushed voice.

"I know. But I want to do this." I nodded.

"You really think we could pull it off?" Her eyes finally met mine.

"Where there's a will, there's a way." The corner of my mouth raised in a half smile. I dropped my hand off her shoulder and looked over to the phone on the end table.

I knew what had to be done; I walked over and picked up the receiver. The echoing tones of each button I pushed bounced off the walls, filling the room with their deafening sound. "Who are you calling?" Dad barked.

I said nothing as I waited for the answer on the other side. Unfortunately I got his voice mail and had to leave a message. "Todd, when you get done, please come by. There's something I've got to talk to you about." I hung up the phone then promptly picked it back up to dial another number. Dad must have thought I was trying Todd on another line because he said nothing. All eyes watched me blankly as I waited for the rings to be answered once again.

This time the phone was answered by an actual person. "Hello, it's Clara," I said as I could see my family leaning in toward me. "I'm fine, but I've got some news." Dad's eyes looked like saucers as they widened in rage, so I hurried my statement. "Grandma, I'm pregnant." Dad's face looked like fire as he yelled for me to hang up the phone. Grandma Marsh insisted on going over the details later and let me go. I hung up the phone, satisfied that I had pushed our plan into action.

"Are you crazy!" He stomped as he moved toward me. "What the hell do you think you're doing?" I pushed my shoulders back as he towered over me. "I already told you I'm raising this child. I am not gonna stand back and let some stranger raise my niece or nephew. It's not gonna happen, and if I'm raising him, then I might as well save Tara's good name in the process. It's the perfect solution. Why can't you see that?" With my chin held high, I rejoined Tara back by the fireplace.

Mom watched the look on Dad's face for a brief moment then looked over to us. "Tara, dear, what's your take on this? Would you be all right if your own child saw you as an auntie instead of Mommy?"

Tara looked to the ground and thought it over then looked up at me with wide eyes. With a subtle nod, she glanced to Mom with an answer. "I'd rather be known as Auntie than not be known at all. I honestly can't be a mom right now, I know that. But I can't deny my child the right to be a child. Clara will make a great mom."

"She can't even keep her room clean, and you think she'll make a great mom?" Dad shook his head in disbelief.

"I think your father and I have a lot of talking to do before any decisions are made." Mom got up, grabbed Dad by the arm, and led him out of the room.

Once assured they were no longer within hearing distance, we sat on the couch. "Thanks for not telling." Tara rested her head on my shoulder. "I surely wasn't expecting this surprise." She sighed. "You sure you're ready to be a mom?" She sat up and looked to me for a reply.

"I'm ready to play the most important role of my life. I'm ready to help out my sister in her time of need." I took her hand in mine. "A mom? Honestly, I didn't think I'd be called that for a while. But yeah, I can do this." My gaze locked onto hers; my insides were no longer flipping. Tara was still pale with uncertainty. "How will we pull this one off?" She sat back in the couch, resting her auburn curls on the large cushions behind her.

"We'll just have to work out the details as we go. It'll work, you'll be miles away at college, no one will suspect a thing. It's perfect." I smiled as I was confident with the plan.

Tara jerked forward. "What about Todd? What's he gonna think?"

I paused a moment as I remembered to add him into the picture. "This will be the ultimate test. We'll tell him everything, and if he runs out the door screaming, then our relationship just wasn't meant to be." I kept a straight face as I tried to convince her I had no concerns about the outcome. "You think he'll run? I don't want to be the wedge that comes between you guys. I'd feel awful."

I had no idea how he'd take the news; deep down I knew there was a chance he'd go his own way and leave me to take on this crazy plan by myself. But a part of me held on to the hope that he'd understand and become the support I desparately needed to make this work. "Hey." I grabbed her arm. "You're my twin. I will always choose you over any guy. You need me, and I'm *not* gonna let you down."

She broke eye contact and looked over my shoulder. "Well, your test is about to begin." Tara nodded toward the front window.

I glanced outside to see the headlights of Todd's faded-blue Chevy step-side truck pulling in behind our little car. As the lights went out, my insides turned into a series of knots that made my stomach turn and the hair on the back of my neck stand on end. I found myself shifting in my seat, unable to sit still as I thought about how he'd respond.

My eyes followed his body as he walked toward the house. He appeared to be walking in slow motion as he passed by the window. The sun had gone down, and the porch light highlighted the puzzled look of concern on his face. His intense stare made it hard to pull myself up off the couch. I forced a smile, took a deep breath, and hurried to meet him at the door.

"Is everything okay? Your message sounded urgent," he said the moment I opened the door. "Yeah, come in. I've got some news that will affect you too. You may want to come in and take a seat before

I tell you the deal." I held onto the door as my knees felt they could give out from under me. "What? Just tell me." He grabbed my arm.

"It's not that easy. Please just come in and sit down." I pulled my arm from his grip and stepped aside to let him pass by.

His motions were slow as he made his way around me. His hesitant movements told me he was confused, and I felt as if I was about to blindside him. I held onto the door a moment longer and considered my options. I could end things and leave him out of the whole thing, but as I caught a glimpse of his awkward smile, I knew that wasn't a possibility; I had to tell him. I quickly closed the door and joined him on the couch.

Before I could decide between the slow and steady method or the quick-like-a-band-aid approach, Tara moved to sit on the coffee table. "Todd, I'm pregnant," she said before I could say a word. His eyes widened as she continued, "Clara has offered to raise the child as her own."

He looked to me with a tilt of the head. "Adoption?" His words were hesitant. I placed my hand on top of his.

"Not exactly." I shook my head and looked back to Tara as she started to explain the situation. "We plan on telling everyone she's pregnant." Todd whipped his head back to focus on her words with his eyebrows raised. "This way, Brad won't know he's gotten the best of me, and I won't miss out on Harvard."

Todd looked to me brightly with a big smile. "You got me. That was pretty good, I'll admit."

I squeezed his hand. "Todd, it's not a joke . . . we're serious. I've already made a call to Grandma Marsh. We're doing this." I tried to look him straight in the eye, but his face dropped, and his focus was aimed away from me. He was pale and speechless; I wasn't sure what he was thinking. He sat like a statue, staring at the wall for a long time.

"I had to tell you, 'cause this will affect you as well." I paused momentarily as I looked at his disturbing gaze of silence. "Since I will be raising this baby as my own, everyone will assume you're the father. So if you don't plan on sticking around, I need to know." The knots in my throat were so large it was getting difficult to speak. "I can leave your name out of it if you wish."

"Why wouldn't I stick around?" He finally spoke. The sound of his reassuring answer dissolved the majority of the tense tissue taking over my insides. I breathed a sigh of relief. "I know it's a lot to ask of you. I didn't know how you'd respond to being a dad is all." I placed my other hand on top of his. "A dad?" His eyes grew large, and he fell back into the couch. He stared up at the ceiling as I watched the color leave from his face. My stomach flipped with panic of raising the baby by myself.

The grandfather clock in the corner ticked loudly inside my head as the minutes of silence grew. I looked to my sister and shrugged. Confusion and concern washed over me as Todd sat motionless. I waited patiently for him to snap from his trance and say something, anything. The longer the awkward calm lingered, the larger the knot in my stomach slowly grew.

Todd eventually pulled himself together after what felt like a lifetime of waiting. His eyes fell to the ground as he slowly rose to his feet. "It's getting late . . . I've gotta go home." He scratched the top of his head as he avoided looking at me.

"Are you okay?" I squeezed his hand.

"I just need some time to myself to think about all of this. I love you, sweets." His eyes found their way to mine for only a brief moment; he released my hand and staggered to the front door.

I felt my world come to a standstill. Beads of sweat collected down my spine. I could see the look of fear on his face as he passed by the window; a part of me crumbled at the thought of this being our demise. The comforting touch of Tara's hand on my back brought me back to a more important issue: the baby. "Should you go after him?" She spoke softly.

"No, I'll give him the space he needs. I owe him that much at least." I stared out the window and watched his truck pull away. As the taillights vanished around the corner, I heard our parents behind me. My once confident attitude teetered with uncertainty.

"We've been talking, and the truth of the matter is, Tara cannot care for this child right now. And honestly, the thought of some stranger raising him just makes me ill." Mom stood with puffy red eyes and crossed arms.

"Are you sure you won't consider an abortion?" Dad interrupted.

"It's out of the question." Tara shook her head.

Mom watched the battle of glares being exchanged between my sister and Dad; she then focused her attention back to me. "Clara, now that you've had a chance to think about this, what are your thoughts?"

I bottled the concerns of my relationship with Todd aside and answered without any hesitation, "I still want to raise this child. My classes will be done by the time he's born, and I'll be working full-time at the paper, where we have an in-house day care. I may be doing this alone, but I *can* do this."

Dad raised his voice to get my attention. "Can't you do this without the lies, can't you just adopt it from your sister?"

I raised my voice to match his volume. "No . . . I won't allow her good name to be dragged through the mud. She has a great reputation around here. I don't intend to let that change. As far as anyone is concerned, I'm the pregnant one. They'd be more likely to believe that anyway."

"What's Todd gonna think of all this?" Mom's arms were still crossed. I looked back toward the window. "I don't know." Plopping on the couch, I explained, "He came by, and we told him every-thing . . . he needs time to soak it all in." I felt as if I were beginning to drown in a sea of emotion; I struggled to keep my head afloat.

"Do you blame him?" Dad sat next to me.

"No, Dad, I don't. But no matter what he decides, I am not gonna change my mind." I looked to Tara, fighting the tears that were close to escaping. "My sister needs me now more than ever, and I won't let her down."

Chapter 5

The Perfect Solution

My alarm filled my head with its annoying buzzing that only reminded me that the nightmare I lived through last night was in no way over. I slid off my bed and scooped up some clothes off the floor as I left the room for the shower. My mind played over the details from the previous night's event. I continued to rummage through all the promises and uncertainties as I moved through the normal day's routine.

By the time I was dressed, I had snapped from my sleepy daze and was thinking a bit more clearly. The reality of the new course my life was taking sank in. Excitement and fear were fighting it out with no sign of a winner in sight. I was eager to make everything right for both Tara and Todd. My mind sizzled with confusion as it came up empty with the perfect plan.

I drifted down the stairs with Todd's reaction burning itself into my mind. The look of bewilderment that took control of his eyes as he heard the word *dad* would forever stay embedded in my memory; accompanied with fear for now and, quite possibly, humor later.

As I approached the kitchen, I could see Tara sitting alone at the table with a glass of orange juice. She looked so sad, so lost. My heart ached as I noted that her usual upbeat innocence had been lost or, rather, taken from her. My teetering mind on how to satisfy both her and Todd was now at ease with the more important mission: helping my other half, my twin sister.

I took a deep breath and bounced up my step as I entered the kitchen. No matter how scared, nervous, or confused I was about the situation, my vow would be to not let her see it. That would have to be the vow; we would never survive this ordeal any other way.

"Morning, sis, how you feeling?" I grabbed a yogurt from the fridge.

"Nauseous. I'm hoping the orange juice stays down, nothing else will." She crinkled her nose.

"Anything you want me to bring home for you after work?" I sat in the chair across from her.

"I'm not ill, I'm pregnant. I can still do things for myself; just not first thing in the morning." She stared into her cup of juice.

"Sorry, just trying to help. You are carrying my baby, after all." I pointed to her belly with a subtle laugh.

"Very funny. Is this the day you'll be telling your coworkers you're pregnant?" She took a small sip, closing her eyes as if to wait for its effects.

"No. I'm gonna wait to see what Todd decides." I pushed the yogurt aside, as my knotted stomach changed its mind about eating. "I'm gonna go. If you need anything, call my cell." I got up, grabbed my keys from the counter, and headed out of the room.

"I'm sure he'll call tonight. He'll come around, you'll see." I stopped momentarily in my tracks as Tara's assuring words comforted my doubts. I nodded slightly as I resumed my motions and left for work.

My mind played Todd's words over and over inside my head all the way to work. I parked in my assigned spot and sat in the car staring at the large green lettering on the side of the building. I wanted to run inside and spread the word that I would be having a baby. I was honestly excited to be taking on such an important role. My body ached at the thought of experiencing it without Todd. I had many dreams of raising a family with him. I dreaded the thought of starting the dream without him.

Ready to call him, I reached for my cell phone. My trembling fingers made contact with the zipper on my purse. Before opening it, I quickly retrieved my fingers empty-handed. I gripped the steering wheel and stared at the backdoor of the old building. I slowly lowered my right hand to the keys dangling from the ignition. I clenched them tightly, unsure if I was going to restart the car or pull them out.

My fingers relaxed slightly and chimed off the musical set as my mind pondered the need to run inside and hide myself in my work or rush home to be alone. As my hand tightened the keys to give them a turn, a loud tapping next to my head caused me to jump. I looked to the window to see Sonya knocking on the glass with a smile. I pulled the keys out and grabbed my purse.

Opening the door, I stuffed my keys back where they belonged. "You scared me." I got out of the car and closed the door.

"Sorry, I didn't mean to startle you. Are you okay? You look worried." Sonya brushed her brown curls from her face as she fought the breeze that was playing with her hair. "I'll be fine. I just have no desire to be here today." I started the walk toward the back entrance.

"You don't want to miss out on today. Kathy's gonna announce who will be covering the movie set on Main Street. That'd be a nice change from the normal assignments I've been getting." Sonya pulled the strap of her large bag back up on her shoulder. "I'm not stressing it. I'm just an intern. I'm not getting anywhere near those stars."

"You might if Patsy gets the assignment. This may be the only advantage of being her understudy," Sonya said as we approached the steps to the back door. "She's very good at what she does. But you're right, she is a real bitch," I chuckled. We were both giggling as Sonja opened the door. Our giddiness halted as our view changed to the harsh makeup-soaked stare of Patsy Vanburg. The fake tan and platinum-blonde bob hair cut made her stand out from a mile away. She squinted her eyes then slowly moved her head back toward Claudia, the editor. I looked to Sonya and covered my mouth in attempt to muffle the laugh as we walked down the hall.

"You think she heard us?" Sonya whispered through her teeth. I shook my head and removed my coat. As Sonya hung up her own coat, I grabbed the time cards.

Sonya clocked in. "Hey, you want to go to the Lemon Tree Café for lunch today?" She put her card away; I clocked in but didn't answer. "We don't have to talk if you don't want to. But if you need a shoulder, I'm here."

I breathed a sigh of relief. "That obvious, huh?" I leaned up against the wall.

"Just a little. You have stress written all over your face." I didn't doubt it; I nodded, afraid that if I opened my mouth, stress-filled emotions would cause the tears to flow.

"So we on for lunch?" Sonya stood near the swinging doors leading to the desks with a smile. I nodded. "Great!" She disappeared behind the large gray doors that blended into the warehouse feel of the old building. I made my way through the doors with a feeling of relief to have such a great friend. Sonya had taken me under her wing and mentored me in the true ways of succeeding in the business. Which had nothing to do with how well you did your job and more on what toes you had to avoid stepping on.

I walked past the row of cluttered desks, smiling at Sonya; who was already busy on the phone as I passed by. I rushed to the back-room, hoping to engross myself in my own work before Patsy came by to stand over my shoulder. She was a great writer and photographer. She was very knowledgeable, and I had learned a great deal from her, but in her eyes, her shoes were much too big for anyone to fill. She was only able to criticize, not praise; she reminded me a lot of Belle.

Entering the backroom, I was happy to see that only Trevor was in the room. "Good morning, Trev." I walked straight to my desk to see what Patsy had on my agenda for the day. "Morning yourself." He grabbed his papers then left the room. I gave a slight wave and took a seat at the desk. I scanned over the chores on my list. Halfway down the schedule, the door slammed. I jumped; my startled hand knocked my pen onto the ground. I quickly looked up at the door. Patsy's bright red lips were pressed tight. Her tan face was crinkled like old leather. Her eyes glared in my direction; I broke the intense stare by leaning down to pick up my pen.

My mind instantly recalled the conversation with Sonya, and I started thinking of excuses to cover my butt. "I'm sick of losing out to all these inexperienced teenyboppers!" Patsy placed her hands on her hips. I sat upright in my chair, trying to control the smile that was ready to emerge as I felt relieved it wasn't me she was angry with. My shoulders relaxed. "I'm sorry."

"Don't patronize me!" Patsy stomped her navy heel into the ground. "I know you're on her side." She shook her finger at me.

"Whose side?" I stood up and placed my hands on the desk. "I'm not on anyone's side." I felt I was in the middle of some petty high school game.

"Sonya's." She took a step forward. "You know, your little buddy. She got that assignment. Don't even tell me you didn't know." Patsy was grinding her teeth as her nostrils seemed to flare.

"I didn't know." I removed my hands from the desk and stood up straight. "I don't think she even knows."

"I seen you guys laughing at me. You can stop the act, I'm not stupid!" She crossed her arms.

"There's no act. We weren't laughing at *you*. Sonya hasn't heard a word." Her glare burned into me with force. I nearly screamed out my true feelings, but as I thought about how much I needed this job now, I sat down. I lowered my voice. "Patsy, I have no reason to lie to you. I promise, no one has talked to Sonja, she knows nothing." I watched her face relax. "Is Kathy here already?" I looked at the clock on the wall as the big hand met the small hand on the eight; Kathy hardly ever came in before ten.

"She's not here. Claudia heard her talking last night about it being between Sonya and me." She turned and started to walk to the other desk. "When we saw you two this morning, we just assumed." She sat at the desk and thumbed through the pile of papers to avoid eye contact. Shaking my head, I picked up the phone and dialed to start on my to-do list.

"It sounds like this assignment means a lot to you. I hope you get it." I hit the last number and waited for an answer.

"Whatever. You're all against me, I just know it. All these new-bies wanting my job, I know how it is." She slammed a drawer. I ignored her ranting as I ordered the needed supplies. Once I hung up, I crossed off the first item on the list with a red pen. "Forget that blasted agenda. Go in and finish those rolls of film in the darkroom."

I nearly smiled at the request. She never let me in there without me having to beg first. I kept my composure, even though my nerves were dancing with delight. I grabbed the rolls and escaped to the best place in the building. I closed the door and did the happy dance. I was finally in a nice, quiet place to hide from the chaos that was life.

I took my time, but all good things have to come to an end. I finished the pictures with Todd weighing heavily on my mind the whole time. With the decision made that I would call him on my lunch break, I opened the door and stepped out into the office. My eyes gravitated to a bouquet of radiant colors sitting on my desk. My feet froze where I stood. I stared at the beautiful arrangement of flowers.

"Why didn't you tell me?" Patsy tapped her pen on her desk. Patsy's words broke me from my trance and I started to walk toward the brilliant colors. "Tell you what?" I nuzzled my nose inside a lily and inhaled its sweet scent. The pale pink card was pinned to a yellow ribbon without an envelope. Patsy didn't answer, but I soon knew what she was referring to. The card read:

Clara: Yes! I'm ready to be a daddy. I love you! Todd.

"You shouldn't be in that room with all those chemicals if you're pregnant." I slowly shifted my eyes in her direction to see if she looked mad. She had her focus glued to her computer screen with a relaxed look on her face that showed no emotion. "Just as well, we're going strictly digital anyway." She turned off her computer and leaned back in her chair. "The photos taken from the 35mm backup's can be developed by me or Trevor, for the time being. Congratulations— that is, if you plan on having this child." Her lips were pierced together and her arms folded in front of her.

I flinched at her last sentence. "Yes. I'm having the baby." The room grew cold. I felt out of place and uncomfortable. Breaking away from her cold stare, I moved across the floor to the door. "Where are you going?" She leaned forward. "To the bathroom." I pointed toward the door. She nodded as if to give me permission. I opened the door and met Claudia face-to-face. I jumped back. "Oh, sorry." I leaned against the open door.

"Yeah, whatever." She pushed her plump body through the doorway. "It's time, she's called a meeting."

Her words were the last thing my mind was focusing on as I slipped through the door. Anxious to speak with Todd, I disregarded the invite to the meeting and rushed down the hall to the restroom. I pushed open the blue door; its peeling paint on the exterior was an indication to the dated decor that appeared on the other side. As I walked across the dingy white tiles, I pulled my cell phone out of my pocket and dialed Todd's number. Washing my hands in the rust-stained sink, my body shook with anticipation for him to answer my call.

"Hello?" His deep voice sent my nerves dancing down my back.

"Thanks for the flowers, they're beautiful." I turned off the water.

"You got them already? Wow, that was fast." He sounded surprised.

"Do you mean it?" I dried my hands off with the harsh paper towels.

"Once the initial shock wore off, I did some thinking. I want to have a family with you. Of course, I would rather it be *our* family and not one that I feel has been pushed onto me. But I also know that your ties to your sister run deep, and there is probably no talking you out of this."

"Are you trying to talk me out of it right now?" I glanced toward the bathroom stalls. All three doors were open.

"No. That would be a waste of breath," he said.

"You're right." I nodded. "What I *am* saying is that I understand where you're coming from. Even though this isn't how I had imagined things, I can't abandon you when you need me most. And truth be told, the more I thought about being a dad, the more I found myself liking the idea."

"So you're excited?" My eyes brightened.

"I don't think I'm there yet. But I think I could be, yeah."

"I love you. I'm relieved to be doing this with you by my side."
I crumpled up the brown towel and threw it into the trash.

"I will always be your partner in crime."

His words were exactly what I needed. "Thank you. That means
a lot. I wish I could talk more, but I've actually got to get to a meeting. I will see you tonight." My body relaxed.

"Sounds great, I love you, sweets."

"I love you too, rebel, bye." I hung up the phone and ran out
the door.

As I returned to the main office, I could see everyone sitting
on the front of their desks facing Kathy at the front of the room.
She hardly looked like the boss type with her casual jeans and white
T-shirt. The bright-red blazer dressed up her outfit a little, but it
seemed a bit much against her tightly permed burgundy-dyed hair.

"Hello, Clara. Nice of you to join us," Kathy said with a smile
and a wink.

"Sorry, Ms. Warner." I smiled sheepishly, as all eyes shifted to
watch me join Sonya at her desk.

"Well, you can expect her many late arrivals and dives to the
bathroom. She's pregnant!" Patsy blurted with an evil smile. My eyes
widened, my mouth dropped, and my body temperature rapidly
increased.

Sonya hit my arm with the back of her hand. "Why didn't you
tell me?" I shrugged as everyone still looked in my direction.

"Is this true?" Kathy tilted her head slightly.

"Yes." I nodded.

"That is good to know. Congratulations. This does, however,
change some things." She picked up her folder and wrote down a few
notes as I feared my job was on the line. "I'm happy for you, Clara,
and can't wait to watch you grow. However, I will need a reliable team
to cover the Main Street story. So I will be giving that assignment
to Sonya and Trevor. Sonya, I want around-the-clock coverage—if
they're filming, you're there. Get interviews from everyone. The public wants to know everything, it's your job to get it." Kathy looked
back to me. "Clara, how you doing with smells, are you nauseous?"

"I feel fine. Not really sick at all." I smiled, relieved I wouldn't have to worry about that part of it.

"Good, you and Patsy can cover the arsine fires that started last night. Get me some good photos, Clara," she said, looking back at her folder.

"I will," I said as Sonya squeezed my leg. "Well, that's it. Go back to work. Oh, and Keith, I want to see your story for tomorrow's paper in my office within the hour." She pointed him out at the back of the room then turned away.

As soon as Kathy disappeared in her office, Patsy stormed off and slammed the door to the photographer's station. Seconds later, we heard a scream and what sounded like breaking glass. "Wow, she's mad." Sonya stared toward the crashing sounds at the back of the room. "Why didn't you tell me?" She looked back to me with her head tilted.

"I wasn't gonna tell anyone for a little while. I'm still absorbing the situation myself." I stood up to get back to work.

"I can understand that. Are we still on for lunch?" Sonya sorted some papers on her desk.

"Yeah." I stared at the door leading to my desk. "Hey, congrats on the assignment." I said as I focused on the yells and crashing coming from behind the door. "I think I owe Patsy and her big mouth a big thank-you."

Sonya chuckled. "You might not want to do that just yet." I flinched at a loud crash that echoed off the tall walls. "You may want to avoid going into that line of fire yourself."

I nodded. "Sad thing is, she shot herself in her own foot with this one. But you know how those reporters are, they can't keep a secret for nothing." I grinned with a friendly wink.

"Funny." Sonya grabbed some papers from her desk and handed them to me. "Here, take these to Trevor. He's getting the photos together for tomorrow's paper."

"I can do that." I smiled and took the papers from her hand.

Walking past the vacant desk that Patsy usually occupied as a reporter, I crossed my fingers that she would be sitting there when I returned. I took my time to make the delivery to assure Patsy could get over her tantrum before I returned to my desk. The moment I turned to walk down the hallway to Trevor's workstation, I was overwhelmed with the laughter from the day care. I quickened my steps to the half-door that kept the happy children from roaming the halls. As my eyes were drawn to the picture-perfect scenery inside the small, brightly colored room, my steps slowed.

My attention was drawn to two little boys that were stacking large wooden blocks while a third pushed his miniature car through the openings. Sitting up against the bright yellow wall was a little girl brushing her dolly's hair. I smiled and placed my hand on my belly. I never thought about having kids, but as I watched the kids play, my insides tingled with delight. I was excited to be having a child; my only regret was that I wasn't the one that was actually pregnant.

My feet eventually carried me away from the view of children playing and down to a small room at the end of the hall, where I found Trevor slumped over, concentrating on the lineup of pictures he had sprawled out on the table. His eyes were stern in concentration, making him look twice his age. Trevor was an attractive guy, with broad shoulders and dark eyes, only a few years older than me. He was quiet and kept to himself; he took refuge in the old empty room the day I started working here. He said he needed peace and quiet in order to get his job done.

"What are you doing in here?" He looked up from his table. "Sonya asked me to deliver these papers to you." I handed them over to him. He quickly snatched them from my grip and thumbed through them. His glare shifted up from the documents in hand. "She gave you these?" His tone was covered with anger. I nodded. "These are the ones I've already rejected! Is she messing with me, or you?" He handed them back to me. "She must be messing with me." I looked down at the papers. He sighed. "Nice, I don't have time for these games." He turned his body and went back to his pictures.

The room appeared to grow colder with his presence. I rubbed my shoulders to find some warmth and then turned to head out the open door. As I stepped out into the hallway, I heard his voice. "Congratulations on the baby." "Thanks." I looked back to see him staring down at the table. I opened my mouth to say something more but couldn't find any words. Wondering why he seemed so mad all the time, I continued out the door and down the hall.

Rounding around the corner, I could see Patsy's desk was still empty. My shoulders dropped. I walked between the rows of desks that filled the room with loud tapping from the busy fingers typing at their computers. Sonya looked up as I approached her desk and smiled brightly. "You missed it. Kathy came out to talk over some details with me on the story and heard Patsy throwing her fit." Sonya looked back toward the open door at the back of the room. "She was escorted out by Kathy, I heard her say something about a much-needed vacation and a leave of absence."

"No way." My mouth dropped. She nodded with a smile that beamed from ear to ear. I shook my head slowly "I always miss the good stuff."

I laid the papers on her desk. "You already know he didn't need these." I smiled.

Sonya nodded with a wink. "Thought you could kill some time before going in to face the music with Patsy, but I guess you've dodged that bullet."

"Trevor wasn't amused." I shook my head and pointed toward the hall leading to his dungeon of an office.

"He'll get over it." She placed the papers back in the outgoing bin on the corner of her desk.

"True . . . I'll see ya at lunch." I laughed as I walked away.

The thoughts of the scene I missed played in my head. My mind was amused by the thought, but my heart was disappointed I missed it. I reached the doorway and stopped in my tracks. My heart grew heavy at the sight. The desks were clear of everything except the computers. Everything that once cluttered the desktops was now scattered on the floor. My jaw dropped as my eyes were pulled to the dark spot on the wall next to me. Water rolled over the faded powder-blue paint and collected as a puddle under the mangled lilies that lay in a pile on the floor. Shards of glass and orange-striped petals covered the dingy gray carpeting.

Todd's card was on top with his assuring words still pinned to the ribbon. Only now, the ink was smeared with droplets of water. I kneeled down and removed the pin from the card.

"I'm sorry, Clara." I slowly looked behind me with card in hand. Kathy was standing in the doorway. "Don't worry about cleaning it up, I have a crew on the way. I'd hate for you to get cut by the glass." She extended a hand down to me. "Come on, I'll see to it that they save the flowers."

My emotions were numb. I stared blankly at her hand then took hold and allowed her to help me up. Once on my feet, I let go of her hand and looked over the mess. Spotting the bright-yellow paper of my agenda, I stepped through the sea of debris and picked it up. "What are you doing?"

Kathy's head was tilted to one side. "I'm getting back to work." I held out the list.

With a smile, Kathy extended her hand for the paper. I handed it over then watched as she tore it up into little pieces. My eyes widened, and I swallowed hard. Kathy threw them into the air. The yellow pieces fell to the floor like confetti. "You won't be needing that." She was no longer smiling as she made eye contact with me. "You're no longer working under Patsy. You're our newest photographer, and I need you to get busy on those shots of the arson fires."

"Really? A full-time position?" I tried controlling the large smile that was taking over my face.

"Only if you want it." Kathy's smile returned.

"Yes, yes I'll take it." I grabbed her hand and shook it.

"Great, we'll discuss your benefits and pay later. Right now, I want you to get to work."

Chapter 6

Taking It to the Next Level

I rolled over. My eyes instantly locked onto the bright-red numbers of my clock. The alarm was due to sound in two minutes. Staring at the time, I debated whether or not I should rest until the clock could do its job or not. My comfortable body opted for the rest, but before my eyes could close, the subtle movement of Tara drew my attention in her direction. She was still sleeping and looked so peaceful; I hated the thought of waking her. I quickly turned off the alarm and climbed out of bed. I grabbed my clothes and quietly slipped out of the room to take a shower.

As I slowly closed the door behind me, Mom came up the stairs. "Morning, Mom." I slowly stepped away from the closed door.

"She still sleeping?" She took a sip from her steaming cup of coffee.

"She looked so peaceful I didn't want to wake her." I held my clothes close to my chest.

"What time is the ceremony for Todd's new studio?" Mom ran her fingers through her red hair.

"I'm supposed to be there at ten. Are you going?" I held my bundle of clothes tight with one hand as I covered my mouth to cover a yawn with the other.

"I think I might. Your dad was talking about going too." Mom paused with a yawn. "Oh, now you got me doing it. Go get in the shower," she chuckled as she motioned me toward the bathroom. With another sleepy yawn, I continued down the hall. I rubbed the sleep from my eyes and locked myself in the small bathroom.

Once I was cleaned and dressed, I opened the door and walked out into the hall. As I stepped out on the pale-blue carpeting, I spotted a blur that appeared to be Tara rushing toward me.

"Move, move, move!" Tara pushed me aside and darted inside the bathroom, slamming the door behind her. I stared at the closed door for a moment, feeling helpless. I knew she was experiencing morning sickness and desperately wished I could do something to help her. I knew there was nothing I could do. If only there was a way to trade places completely, I'd do it.

I grabbed the doorknob.

"Go away!" she screamed from the other side. With feelings of guilt, I let go of the handle and slowly walked down to our room. I applied my makeup and started primping my hair when Mom hollered up the stairs. "Clara!"

Peeking my head through the doorway, I yelled back, "What?"

"Todd's here!" Her words traveled up the stairs.

My eyebrows drew together as I went over the original plan for the day. I knew we had decided that I would meet him there. Wondering why the plans had changed, I walked down the stairs while putting in my earrings. I caught a glimpse of Todd sitting in the recliner as I neared the bottom step; I couldn't help but smile. The mere sight of him made my chest ache as my heart pounded faster.

His bright eyes found their way to mine; his smile made my throat tighten. "Did we have a change of plans?" I caught my breath and stepped off the last step. He stood up and looked to Mom; who was standing in the doorway leading to the dining room.

"Something like that." His eyes now focused on me. His lips turned up into a smile, and the adorable dimple on his right cheek made me melt.

"Well, I'll just grab my jacket and we can go." I started toward the entry closet.

"Let's wait a minute, your dad wants to follow us." He walked over and took me by the hand. I followed his lead to the couch and sat next to him. My mom stared at us lovingly, perhaps a little longer than usual. Todd's focus was fixed on the fireplace as we waited. Dad joined Mom by the doorway leading into the living room. "Okay, I'm ready." Dad nodded.

I stood in unison with Todd. He took my hand and turned to face me. My stomach tingled as his gaze held me captive. "You know, I've been thinking." He grabbed my other hand and held them tight. My knees grew weak. "Since we're gonna be a family, I'd like you to move in with me." He released one of my hands. My heart leapt.

"I'd like that." My words were soft, even though my insides were racing with excitement.

He kissed me softly on the forehead. He then wrapped his arms around me and whispered in my ear, "Would you like to be my wife too?" My eyes shifted to my sister smiling on the staircase. Once the words soaked in, I kissed him on the cheek, then whispered back to him, "I'd like that."

He stepped back and lifted a ring box up between us. My heart fluttered as he opened it, exposing the sparkling princess cut that sat high upon a band of gold. He removed the ring and placed it on my shaky finger. A tear rolled slowly down my face as he embraced my trembling body. It was all so surreal; it felt like a dream. A dream I hated the thought of waking up from. I held him close with my eyes closed. His deep voice comforted my dazed mind. "I love you, sweets."

"I love you too, rebel." I nestled my head into his broad chest, forgetting that we weren't alone.

"Okay, okay. Let me see the ring." Tara hurried down the stairs. I released my grip and wiped my eyes. With a large grin, I extended out my hand and let Mom and Tara admire the gleaming rock on my finger. "It's so beautiful!" My sister hugged me tight. "I'm so happy for you." She released her hold.

Mom stepped closer to me and grabbed my hand. My stomach knotted as I waited for her response. "Congratulations, sweetie." She looked at the ring and squeezed my hand.

My attention shifted to Dad, who was standing in the entry to the dining room. With a smile, I pulled my hand from my mom's. I took in a deep breath and directed my nervous body toward him. I held up my hand flashing him the ring as he slowly lifted his focus from the floor. I smiled sheepishly as his face showed no emotion, just a blank stare. I wiggled my fingers and grinned big. A corner of his mouth lifted, and he stood tall.

I ran into his arms. "I can't say I'm happy." He pushed me away. My smile dropped. "I will congratulate you, but I don't like that my babies are growing up." My smile reappeared. "I'm not going far, Daddy." He pulled me close for another hug. "You leaving at all . . . is too far," he sniffled, then changed the subject. "We should probably get going if we're going to make it on time."

"They can't start without me. But you're right, we better get . . . so, sis, will you be coming?" Todd looked to Tara, whose face lit up.

"Hmm, sis. I do like that. But I'll have to catch the next one. My stomach won't be ready to leave the house for at least another hour."

* * *

With the summer coming to an end, Todd and I planned a small ceremony in the backyard. Our exchange of vows took place the day before Tara was due to leave for college. I blamed the lack of nerves to the fact that everything happened so quickly.

With my drive tunnel-visioned onto the protection of my sister and her need for me, I was unable to fully absorb the event's whirl-wind of emotions. Ideally this was a day I had dreamed of since I was a little girl. It was supposed to be a day that would fill my heart with cherished memories. The day that I had dreamt of time and time again had finally arrived. Although things were not set up as glamorous as I had imagined, it seemed perfect all the same.

The vision of seats filled with all my friends and family dressed in their Sunday best was replaced with a few simple chairs, set up facing the flower garden in the corner. The only faces to be found looking back at us to witness our blessed day were those of our parents.

Todd's parents sat tall and proper, wearing matching outfits—dark-blue jeans and shirts of the same shade of maroon, which fit snug around their massively sculpted arms. My dad wore his usual suit and tie—not sure I'd recognize him in anything else. My mom wore an elegant pink-and-white floral dress that buttoned up and front and flowed down to her ankles. The two couples were complete opposites, yet their assuring smiles made them a perfect match. Their sparkling eyes of approval made the image before me more perfect than anything I could have ever dreamt up.

Tara was at my side as my maid of honor, while Todd's best friend, Bobby, was standing as the best man. I was pleased with the casual setting and small party. I was wearing a comfortable white summer dress, while Todd wore his best black jeans and a light-blue shirt. No stuffy altar, no expensive flowers, no uncomfortable clothes—no way could it have been any more wonderful.

With words spoken to unite us, we stood before the minister, who happened to be a close friend and neighbor. I gazed helplessly into Todd's eyes with butterflies dancing in my stomach. The moment felt surreal as he placed the ring on my finger, yet as the symbol of love was slid into place, I felt complete. My eyes filled with tears of happiness as I melted into his stare; it was truly a dream come true. "You may now kiss the bride." Mr. Roberts's words broke my trance as he closed his bible.

Todd placed his hands softly on my cheeks, leaned in, and kissed me quickly on the nose. His weak display of affection caught me off guard. I watched in disbelief as he dropped his hands and stepped away. His sheepish grin told me he was proud of himself, a feat I was not about to share his pleasure in, so I grabbed him by the shirt and pulled him to me for a real kiss.

Sounds of clapping and cheers filled my ears as I delivered a kiss that made my own knees buckle. We unlocked our lips and looked to Tara and Bobby, who were causing the loud scene of celebration. I smoothed the wrinkles out of Todd's shirt that my tight grip had created then took him by the hand. "Congratulations, Mrs. Rivers,"

Mom said, wiping her cheeks with a wadded-up tissue. My heart bounced with excitement at the sound of my new name as everyone else mimicked Mom's words.

I had doodled his name with mine on my notebook many times in class, but hearing it struck a new kind of happiness. For a brief moment, I forgot about everything else; my mind was on the magical feeling of spending my days with my perfect companion. In my daze of contentment, I barely caught my sister as she fell into my arms. Nearly throwing me off-balance, I grasped her in a brief embrace before she stepped back. I could see that she was happy for me, but her awkward smile also told me she was envious. "Are you okay?" I grabbed her hands and gave them a squeeze.

She nodded. "Yeah. This is your day, and I'm happy for you, I am." She wiped away the moisture from her face.

"I know you are." I went to give her another comforting hold, but Mom jumped in and grabbed both of us. After a short huddle, she released us. "I can't believe my girls are all grown up." She wiped the tears from her face with the back of her hand.

"Hey, sweets." Todd placed his hand on my shoulder. "Did you talk to your sister about the car?"

"I already said I didn't need it," Tara interrupted.

"That's just it, neither do I. I'm going to be driving the Chevy, and we figured you might as well take it and use it for your appointments."

"I think that's a great idea." Mom nodded.

"I guess it's settled then." Tara smiled. "I probably should start packing it with all my stuff." She looked to the house with a blank stare.

"Yeah, I've got to get the rest on my things to take over to Todd's too."

"You mean *our* place," Todd interrupted.

"Yeah, our place." I felt my cheeks brighten to a deep shade of red.

Todd's parents broke away from my Dad, who was talking their ears off.

"This is the happiest day for me." Todd's mom, Hannah, placed her hands on my shoulder. "I couldn't have asked for a greater daughter."

"Thank you." I grabbed her hands still resting on my shoulders as my insides danced to her words of approval. Tara rubbed my back for a brief moment as she walked away with Mom by her side.

Hannah removed her hands. "These last few months have sure been eventful." She tightened her grip on my hand, nearly causing my knees to buckle from the pain. "Your relationship is strong." She let go to flex her already-bulging arms. "I know you guys will make a beautiful family." She slapped me on the arm, nearly pushing me over.

I widened my stance slightly to better my footing, just in case her strength found its way to my arm again.

"I think so too." I smiled.

"Your sister is very lucky to have such a loving and understanding couple on her side." She watched Tara setting food out on a picnic table. "And I'm lucky to be able to start shopping for a grandchild." Her face brightened.

I recognized that same look of sheer excitement from the time we had told her the news. We had told them the whole story and why we felt we needed to be there for her to raise the baby. I was so afraid of their reaction. But Hannah never showed any concern for how we'd pull it off. She was far too excited about being a grandmother; it was comical to see a musclebound lady who looked so tough get all weepy and excited like a little kid. As for Todd's dad, Drake, neither of us knew what he thought. Drake was a quiet man and tended to keep his comments to himself.

"Just wait until you see the little booties I picked up the other day." Hannah grinned and brought her focus back to me. "They are so cute. They're white, so they'll be perfect for a little boy or girl." Her face lit up as she indicated with her fingers the size of the booties.

"It sounds like I better hurry and get the nursery ready." I tried not to laugh at her excitement.

"Oh yeah! I've seen the cutest teddy bear border, have you decided what you'll be doing the room in yet?"

"I really haven't put that much thought into it. I figured we'd get all my stuff settled in the house first then work on the baby's room later."

She stared at me blankly for a moment before responding to my plan. "Yeah, I guess that'll work. Just let me know when you're ready to do some shopping. I'd love to go." My view caught Drake working his way toward us. His arms were large and extended out away from his body. I held back my urge to giggle at his bodybuilder strut.

"Clara, I hear you still have some packing to do here. You need me to move anything for you?" He rolled his shoulders.

"No, I've just got clothes left." I looked up to my bedroom window. "I should be able to get those today. Thanks for the offer though."

"Welcome. If you need help, don't hesitate." His eyes left mine to look over my shoulder.

I turned around to see Mom approaching us. "I have a lunch prepared, if everyone is ready to eat." Mom pointed toward the tables set up on the patio.

Drake didn't wait for her to finish talking and rushed to the display of food. Hannah walked with Mom back to the house. I stood and watched the two different families coming together as one; it made me beam with pride. I met the stare of Todd from across the yard, which automatically lifted the corners of my mouth. He slowly raised a hand, and with one finger, he motioned for me to join him by the birdhouse. My eyes remained locked on his as I walked across the freshly mowed lawn.

"Come here, sweets." Todd winked; I dissolved in his arms. "I just wanted to tell you how beautiful you look today."

I could feel my face warm with his words. "You're looking pretty handsome yourself." His eyes left mine for a brief moment as he looked up toward the family. He pulled me closer and kissed me passionately. My toes curled as my mind absorbed that perfect moment.

Chapter 7

A Fond Farewell

The day of Tara's farewell party arrived. A crowd of nearly two dozen showed up at Zippy's to say their good-byes. "A pizza parlor would not have been my first choice to have a party." Belle approached the table with her most common sourpuss pucker.

"It's not just any pizza place, it's the best in the state." I stood and pulled out her chair.

"Pizza's pizza, dear, no matter how you slice it." She wiped off the seat with a white hanky from her pocket before sitting gracefully at the bulky wooden table.

Shrugging off Belle's criticism, I sat back down; she was the last to arrive. Everyone was now sitting around the large banquet table talking amongst themselves. Smiles surrounded us with joy to be spending these last moments with Tara—well, except for Belle, whose smug frown stuck out in the crowd. Tara looked around the room; her roll of the eyes told me noticed the black sheep in the room as well. I smirked to myself as Tara's focus landed on me. Without hesitation, I responded with the nod of approval she was seeking.

"Thank you all for coming." Tara stood. Her long red tank top covered her slightly bloated belly. "For those of you who don't know already, there is great reason to be here to celebrate today." She paused as everyone hushed to hear her speech. "This isn't just my farewell party. It's a congratulations party for my sister, her new husband, and the baby they will be having in the spring."

Most everyone had already heard the rumors of pregnancy, but the mention of a husband sent a wave of gasps and sighs across the table. Tara smiled and sat back down. She had started the first stage of the master plan. With the damage done, I watched as she sat back to admire the reactions it had triggered.

"There was a wedding?" Belle's tone brought everyone to a hushed silence. You could have heard a pin drop in the tension-filled room. My knees went weak as her words seemed to wrap around my throat; her nostrils were in a flare as she clenched her napkin tightly. "We had a small ceremony yesterday at the house." I forced the words and a grin, as her stare gave me chills.

"Was there a reason you chose not to have family there?" She took a small sip of her water. "You shouldn't be so ashamed of your irresponsibility."

I squeezed Todd's leg under the table as I bit my lip. My mind scrambled as friends and family stared with dropped mouths at Belle's words. I struggled to find words to remedy the situation but couldn't. My stomach fluttered until I saw my dad lean forward and look at Belle. "Mom, this is Tara's day." My shoulders eased as he had come to my rescue like usual.

"I know. I just don't like surprises is all." Her lips pressed together into a straight line, as she snubbed up her nose.

I was speechless; the words that kept rolling down my tongue were not appropriate and could have made the scene a lot uglier than it already was. I choked back all the temping inappropriate statements and kept my mouth shut. Flustered, I looked to Todd for support; he kissed my forehead. "I love you." His whispered words of affection rested softly on my ears and tugged at my heart. His warming tone gave me strength and allowed me to find the humor in her pouting stance.

She was still looking up at the lights on the ceiling. Her nose pointed upward as she breathed heavily with arms folded. Belle reminded me of myself when I was three and was told no. I no longer had to control my slip of harsh words; I was now holding back the laughter that begged to escape.

"Pizza's here!" Tara's announcement was a relief as she pointed toward two waitresses who were each carrying a large pizza to the table. The aroma of the greasy pepperoni filled the room. I looked to my sister and saw her rosy pink color change to a pale white in a matter of seconds. I knew she was going to take off running to the bathroom at any moment. Knowing I had to do something, I quickly stood up, holding my belly with one hand and my mouth with the other and ran from the room. I rushed to the bathroom with Tara right behind me.

As soon we were inside the restroom, I locked us in, and my poor sister ran for the only stall. With the door open, I could see her head drop to the toilet. "Do you think anyone noticed it was really you who was sick?" I asked as she continued to relieve herself of her previous meals. Feeling helpless, I turned my attention to guarding the door, even though it was locked.

Once she finished, she slowly gathered herself and got back up on her feet. She walked across the grey speckled flooring, wiping her mouth. "When I ran by them, they were all looking at you. I think we're good." She stood before the mirror staring at the reflection. "Too bad my face is blotchy and pale." She slapped herself lightly, reviving some color in her cheeks.

I stood beside her and glanced at the view. I could see exactly what she was talking about. Leaning down, I splashed water on my face. My cold wet hands rubbed my eyes briskly until they were puffy and red. "How's that?" I ruffled up my hair.

"That's dedication." Tara pulled a face powder compact from her pocket and touched up her cheeks and eyes. With a new layer of color, she admired her profile. "Looks a little better. I guess if anyone asks, I can blame it on sympathy pains."

"That might work." I looked to the door then back to my sister. "You okay? Ready to join the party?" She primped with her hair a moment before responding.

"I think I'll be all right. But I am definitely staying away from the pizza," Tara said. I chuckled slightly as I unlocked the door. We proceeded back to the party waiting for us in the private room at the end of the restaurant. Thoughts of our plan being foiled before it even got started entered my mind sending my stomach into a whirlpool of nerves. My fingers trembled as I grabbed hold of my sister's hand before entering the room of silence.

A smile spread across my face as all eyes fell upon me the moment we stepped through the door. Tara slipped away, allowing all focus to stay on me as she found her seat at the table. Todd stood and extended his hand out to me. "You okay, baby?" I swallowed hard and nodded. My subtle response was enough to bring the silent room back to normal. Noise of ice cubes dancing in glasses as people took drinks and a mixture of conversations stirred in the room.

Todd pulled my chair out, and I pushed the plate of pizza away from me to stay in character of the pregnant sister. "We're gonna miss you, T. M.," Cindy said as she held up a glass of soda in a toast. "Clara, I am so happy for you and Todd." She paused briefly as her bottom lip quivered in response to the moisture collecting in her eyes. "And I think I speak for everyone when I say congratulations."

The plan was in motion, and things were playing out perfectly. It was apparent that no one suspected a thing. We withheld our sighs of relief as we mastered the first hurdle of convincing friends and family. After all the exchanges of memories and bids of farewell, Tara left to attend college, and Todd and I continued the charade as the perfect family.

* * *

The next couple months went by faster than I had expected. I filled the void of my other half being hundreds of miles away, with the preparation of the path my life was taking. By the time Tara was five months along, Todd and I were preparing our small single story home for the new arrival.

I was bolting together the white crib I had purchased for the nursery when the doorbell rang. Dropping the tools to the ground, I rushed to answer my visitor. I opened the door to find a delivery man waving as he walked back to his van. Waving back, I stared at a package he had left on my front step. Picking up the medium-sized box, I was ultimately surprised by its light weight. I shook it gently, trying to guess its contents as I carried it inside to the kitchen table. The return address, written in red marker, was from Tara.

Anxious to tear into the box to see what she had sent me, I grabbed the closest knife. I carefully slid the blade across the tape. My heart raced as if I were a little kid on Christmas morning. Finally pulling back the flaps, I could see a strange-looking pillow. I removed it from the box. My mind was baffled by the strange looking contraption at first, but as I held it up, I could clearly see it was a pregnancy belly. It had three pads that could be tucked inside the stretchy flesh-colored band that allowed you to adjust your size accordingly. I laughed out loud, even though I was the only one to hear my amusement over the new garment.

A card at the bottom of the box grabbed my attention. Reading my name on the front of it, I quickly retrieved the note from the package and removed it from the envelope:

Clara,

Call me if you are interested in knowing the sex of your baby.

Hope the gift I sent is helpful.

Lots of love,
Tara

I carefully placed the card back inside its envelope and stuck it in the top drawer. Pondering over her note, I lifted my shirt and tried on my baby belly. I clasped the row of hooks on the back. After shifting the garment into the proper position, I placed one of the pads inside the empty pouch in front. Dropping my shirt to cover the belly, I was impressed with the looks of my new bump.

With a smile on my face, I grabbed my purse from the table and darted out the door. It would be a couple hours before Todd would be done teaching, which gave me plenty of time to do some shopping. I couldn't wait to buy some maternity clothes to accent the new addition to my belly. Looking the part gave me an instant push into the reality of it all, and the smile on my face was unmanageable.

After gliding through the "motherhood" shop at the mall and acquiring an armload of new outfits, I changed into one of my peasant-style mommy-to-be shirts and hurried through the rush-hour traffic to catch up to Todd as his class ended. I pulled into the parking lot in front of his newest studio and adjusted my belly before getting out. Inhaling the fresh air of the chilled autumn breeze, I quickened my steps to the door.

Opening the large glass door, my ears filled with the echoing hollers and yells that followed each enthusiastic punch and kick. The sounds bounced off the tall white walls and roared loudly at those who entered. I found a seat in the row of proud mothers and rubbed my belly with thoughts of motherhood streaming through my mind.

I watched Todd proudly as he stood before his class and instructed them through his routine of grunts and jabs. After a loud and energetic performance of commands, his arms finally met stiffly by his side, and he bowed before his class to excuse them for the day. Once he spotted my presence, I stood up and grabbed my belly.

His smile showed his approval as he walked across the floor. "Brian! Good job today, you looked great out there," he said to a little black-haired boy as he wrapped his arm around me. The little boy grinned brightly but said nothing as his cheeks turned a delightful shade of pink. Todd kissed me softly on the forehead before releasing his hold on me. He then followed behind the words of encouragement being spoken by the moms, as they escorted their little fighters out the door. He locked up behind them and turned off the open sign.

Before he could turn around to face me, I asked the question that had been plaguing deeply on my mind. "Do we want to know the sex of the baby?" We'd been pretending for so long the question felt natural, as if I were the one carrying our child. I already knew what his answer would be, since we'd been waiting for this moment for what seemed like a lifetime. It was all I could do to keep from getting overexcited and jumping into his arms.

My enthusiasm took control of my face as he quickly spun around to look me in the eyes. The look on his face was almost comical; his eyes widened like an excited child. "Do we know?" he said, nearly shaking out of his skin with excitement. "I'm not sure, her note wasn't clear. I was waiting until I was with you to call her."

"Well, call her, I want to know!" He rushed to his office; the canvas of his white uniform brushed together loudly in his hurry for the phone. I had to speed up my pace to keep up with him.

I was only a few steps behind his stride, but by the time I entered the office, he had already reached the phone. He held the receiver to my face and waited for me to dial. Absorbed in his exhilaration, I took it from his grip and dialed the number. He hit the speakerphone button with one hand and rubbed my fake belly with the other. "I've been waiting for your call," Tara answered, her voice filled the room.

"I got your package today. It's pretty cool, I'm wearing it right now. It's a little scratchy though." I scratched my left side.

"Fits all right and looks like the real thing, then?" Tara said as I watched Todd bite at his pinky nail.

"Oh yes, you did good. I had no idea they made such a thing." I grabbed my belly.

"So are you interested in knowing what you're having? Because I know what it is." Tara sang the last sentence.

"*Yes!*" Todd placed his hands on either side of the phone, bracing himself over the speaker.

"Clara, you want to know too?" she said. Todd still braced on the desk, waiting to hear the answer.

"Yes, I do." I laid my hand on Todd's back and stared at the phone with him. After a brief pause—no doubt to add to the suspense—she made her announcement. "You guys are going to be the proud parents of a precious little girl. I do, however, have one request."

My head tilted in curiosity. "What's that?" I asked, still absorbing the information she had just thrown our way.

"I'd like to name her." Without an answer for her, I looked to Todd. He nodded then answered for the both of us.

"Fair enough, but we have to approve, and I would like the middle name to be after my grandmother, Jessamond Marie." Todd added his own request without hesitation.

"Done," Tara said.

"So do you have a name already in mind?" The question slipped out as a natural response.

Her sweet, subtle giggle danced from the speaker. "Yes, actually I do." Her laughter stirred a mixture of emotions within me. I wasn't sure if she was amused that I was enquiring or if the name had a laughing quality about it.

"So will you be sharing your name choice with us?" I asked, trying to hide my hint of concern.

"I'll tell you her name in a couple months, when I know for sure. Bye for now, love ya." Her good-bye was rushed and left no time for our response.

After she had hung up, Todd pushed the button to turn off the speaker. "Wow, I can't hardly believe it, a girl." His eyes lit up. "We're actually going to be a family," I said as the images of a baby girl began to take over my thoughts. He pulled my back close to his chest and wrapped his arms around me to rub my poly-cotton-filled bump of a belly. "And we're having a little princess." He kissed the top of my head. The vision of a little girl to call my own brought a joyful tear to my eye.

In that moment I think we both forgot that I wasn't the one that was pregnant. The excitement ran though my body, sending uncontrollable chills through my veins. I could hardly wait to fill her closet with frilly outfits and decorate the nursery in shades of pink. I spun around to face him. "We've gotta go shopping!"

Chapter 8

The Next Phase of the Plan Begins

I stood staring at all the hard work that went into the arrangement of the baby's room. Various hues of pinks and purples awaited the arrival of the new baby girl that would soon sleep soundly in the white crib positioned perfectly at an angle in the corner. I smiled with delight at the cuddly pink-and-white teddy bear sitting on the bookshelf overlooking the crib. The delicately painted rocking chair was covered in a multitude of pastels. The vision of the countless nights that I would spend rocking my little girl to sleep warmed my heart.

My eyes were forced to focus back on reality as the phone rang, pulling me from my daze. I darted down the hallway to answer the rings coming from the kitchen wall.

"Hello," I gasped.

"Hey, Clara," Tara said from the other end as I stared at the pile of dishes that needed to be put away.

"Sis, how you feeling? Are those kicks still keeping you up at night?" I picked up a glass from the counter to put it away.

"She's very active, and I think she may have her days and nights mixed up," Tara sighed.

"So are you getting bigger." I grabbed a pan from the pile of clean dishes.

"Oh boy, it's getting harder to hide the bulge, and my chest is huge. Though I do wish I could keep *them*, they're nice," Tara chuckled.

"Did you call to brag about your massive boobs?"

"No, not exactly. I did call with some news though."

"What's up?" I grabbed a soda from the fridge.

"I had a doctor's appointment today. And we scheduled a cesarean for the start of spring break. So I thought you might want to come up for a visit." Tara nearly sang her request.

"That's only two weeks away! Wait! A cesarean? Won't there be a scar?" I said, overwhelmed with panic and excitement. "Relax, Dr. Hale has assured me that it'll be a bikini cut and no one will ever see it. Not that I ever showed my belly before anyway."

"This is perfect. I'll come see you, go into labor, and return with a baby. No family to hover and get in the way. Sounds like a great plan, you still okay with this?" I mellowed my excitement to allow her to voice any concerns. "I'm fine and looking forward to this being over. I'd like to have my old body back, I miss seeing my feet."

"Well, all except for the chest, you're hoping they'll stay right?" I giggled.

"Right, maybe I'll talk to the doctor about that while she has me under the knife—you know, a two-for-one deal," Tara laughed.

"Funny! Wow, I have so much to plan and arrangements to make. I can't believe it's already here," I said, thumbing through my address book for my boss's home number. "Well, I do have something to give you now. So you won't have to wait."

"What are you talking about? What can you give me over the phone?" Confused, I paused with my finger on the number I was looking for.

"Oh, just the baby's name. It may take some getting used to, but I think you'll love it as much as I do." Her voice squeaked with joy.

"Don't keep me waiting. What's her name?" I listened closely.

"Suzette Jessamond. I'd like it if you called her Suzy."

"Suzy Jessamond Rivers. I can get used to that. I love it, and so will Todd." I played the name over in my mind. "I've got to go, see you in a couple weeks."

She ended the call. "I love you, sis. Bye."

I hung up the phone and imagined my nursery. A wave of chills tickled my body at the thought of the room being occupied with the cries of a child in only a couple of weeks. My fingers fumbled over the buttons as I dialed the phone to schedule my vacation.

After making my arrangements with work to take a much-needed break, I added the final layer to my belly and then hurried off to class. It was all I could do from telling all my new friends that I would be leaving to have my baby. The joyous image of what I'd be coming home with performed over and over, making it difficult to pay attention to the discussion on contrasting that was going on around me.

The next two weeks crept by as we awaited the day we'd leave to watch our child join our family. Plans were set into motion as we told friends and family we were going to Cambridge for spring break. The only ones we could express our excitement to were the parents. My mom wept as she realized she wouldn't be there to see her first grandchild born but thought it best to stay home and not stir up any suspicion.

* * *

The alarm rang at 5:00 a.m. on the Friday morning we were to head out. We both jumped from the bed. Neither of us had slept a single wink all night, and my stomach was swimming with excitement. We quickly showered and ran out the door for the long drive ahead. Our bags had been packed for over a week and were already sitting in the trunk of our new family ride, a 2001 blue Chevy Malibu LS.

It was barely after noon when we arrived at the hospital. The butterflies in my stomach were a-flutter as we maneuvered though the halls that would lead us to Tara. When we found her room, my body paused at the doorway. She was staring blankly up at the television on the wall while flipping through the channels with the remote attached to the bed railing. Aside from the basketball-shaped bump under the sheets, she looked like the same old Tara. "Good morning, sis," I said as I rushed to her side.

"Hey!" Tara rubbed my shirt-covered pillow of a belly. "You don't need to wear this here," ahe laughed.

"I know, it's a habit. I feel naked without it." I grabbed it and looked down, almost sad that I wouldn't have to wear it anymore.

"You do realize that after today, you won't need it. Is that okay?" Tara poked my shirt, as if I were the Pillsbury Doughboy.

"Yes." I nodded and took her by the hand. Todd placed a chair behind me. "How you feeling?" I sat down.

"I feel fine. I'm tired and uncomfortable, but fine." Tara looked away.

Her lack of eye contact worried me. "It won't be long now, and Suzy will be home with family who will love her and take good care of her. And you'll be able to start living the college life." I pulled the chair closer to her bed.

"Yeah. I know," Tara said with tears filling her eyes.

"What you're doing is okay. You needn't feel guilty. I promise to never let anything happen to her, to provide her with more love than she could ever possibly need," I said, still holding her hand.

"I don't doubt that for a minute. You guys are going to be the best parents she could even have. But I still feel guilty. This should be my responsibility. It's greedy of me to pursue what's best for me and ignore her needs." Tara squeezed my hand tightly.

"But you *are* thinking of her needs. We'll be able to provide for her so much better than you could right now. You'll be a part of her family. You'll be able to love her and spoil her without the worries of her feeling your resentment later."

"I know. I know all of that, and I know if I keep her, I'll have to drop out. I would eventually resent her as I wonder what my life would be like if I had followed through. I know all of this. I can't provide for her right now, I can barely provide for myself. I just feel like a ball of emotions, every one of them as strong as the next. Does that make any sense, do I make any sense?" Tara shook her head as she wiped away the tears.

"Perfect sense." I stood up and kissed her forehead. In an attempt to reduce the tension in the sterile room, I helped her find something to watch on the multitude of channels that seemed to be airing shows of nothing. Settling on the comedy channel, we sat impatiently for the doctor to arrive.

It was nearly 1:00 p.m. when Dr. Hale entered the room. She was tall and slender and carried the aroma of vanilla. Her dark hair was pulled back into a tight bun, allowing her streaks of gray to show. "How are you feeling today, Clara?" she said, catching me off guard that she would care about me when my sister was the one about to undergo the surgery.

Tara quickly squeezed my hand then answered the question herself. "I'm ready to do this. I'd like to meet the little monkey who has been climbing up and down my ribcage for the last few months." After a subtle chuckle from her physician, Tara introduced us. "This is my sister, Tara. And of course that's my Todd behind you."

I nearly laughed as Todd's eyes brightened with surprise to her introduction. I was choked up and not sure how to react. Luckily the doctor spoke first to break the bizarre pressure that had built a barrier around me. "Twins pregnant at the same time, I don't see that very often." She extended her hand. "It's nice to finally meet you." I shook her hand.

"You too," I spit out some words as she turned to face Todd.

"It's nice to finally meet the father, I've missed you at the appointments."

Falling into the story, he stood up and answered briefly, "Yeah, but I wouldn't miss this for anything." He smiled and extended his hand for a shake.

As she took hold of his offer, she said, "Well, why don't you go ahead and give her one last hug." She dropped his hand. "Then I'm gonna have to have you two head on down to the waiting room."

Without hesitation, Todd rushed to her bedside and leaned down for a big hug. He took her hand and kissed her fingertips. He laid his other hand on her massive belly. "I'll see you soon, Suzy."

I stood up and bent down for an awkward hug caused by my bumper of a belly. "I can't believe this is it. I can't wait." I held her briefly then joined Todd by the door. We slowly left the room as instructed to find the waiting room. It didn't take long for us to find the other families that were pacing the floor down the hall.

We sat in a couple of empty chairs near a vending machine and stared intensely at the doorway. "Your sister sure took the whole trading places seriously," Todd whispered as his eyes remained glued on the hallway. The large blond-haired lady sitting across from us lifted her head from the blue blanket she was knitting with a smile. I returned the nice gesture, then once she resumed to her project, I responded to Todd's comment, "I think she did that for the birth records."

"Yeah, that makes sense. Did you want something to eat? I think I have some quarters." Todd shifted in his seat and dug around in his front pocket for the loose change.

"No thanks, I'm fine." I laid my hand on his arm to mellow his nervous actions. He removed his hand from his pocket and placed it on my knee. His knees began to shake as he started to bounce his feet.

Moments later, we had a change of view. A short nurse wearing green surgical scrubs stood in the doorway looking at the names on her chart. "Mr. Rivers?" a surprisingly loud voice boomed from the petite-sized lady. Todd's legs became still. "Is she okay?" I stood up.

"She's fine. Are you Tara?" She looked to her chart again and back to me.

"I am." I walked over to her with Todd close behind me.

"Clara is ready for you guys to join her in the operating room, if you wish to do so."

I looked to Todd, whose face was flushed. "We'd love to," I answered for the both of us. The nurse pointed back toward the room where we had originally left my sister. "Great, we have some scrubs waiting for you in Clara's room."

Reaching the open door to the vacant room, the nurse stepped aside and leaned up against the wall. We entered inside and found the pile of green clothes lying on the bed. I closed the door as Todd immediately started putting on the extra layer of clothing. By the time I waddled to the bedside to grab the other pair of pants, he was already dressed. "You know, you look pretty sexy as a doctor," I said as I pulled the baggy scrubs up over my belly.

Todd picked up the other shirt and wrapped it around me; I slipped my arms in. "Maybe they'll let us just borrow these uniforms for a night or two." He winked with a mischievous smile. My giggles echoed off the bare, sterile walls of the room. He pulled me close and tied the strings to my shirt behind me and kissed me softly on the lips. "Shall we go see our baby?" He released his hold on me. "I'm ready," I said.

We unlocked our hands before stepping out into the hallway as the non-couple we were pretending to be. The nurse's sparkling eyes greeted us before leading us down the bright hall that echoed with each step we took on the grey-and-white floor. It was hard not to take hold of his dangling fingers as they swung nervously by his side. But I kept my eyes on our guide and followed her as she led us around a corner.

The short hall led us to a set of double doors. The nurse pushed a button on the wall. I could see a short, plump receptionist waddling away from her spot at the desk through the pair of long narrow windows on the doors. The lady with the burgundy poodle-cut hairdo opened the door with what appeared to be a forced smile.

I returned the gesture with a nod and entered in past her. We continued down the hall and stopped at another set of double doors. "Wait here for a minute." She slipped in through the doors, leaving us to stay in the empty hall. The wait was agony. My vision was starting to blur from staring at the door for so long when she finally peeked her head out "Come on in, we're ready for you." The spinning in my stomach weakened my legs as Todd and I entered the room.

All that could be seen of Tara was her stress-covered face. The rest of her body was tented off in green sheets. Her doctor was prepped in her surgery scrubs, while aids in uniform stood on either side, waiting to assist the doctor in delivering our Suzy.

My heart sank as the reality of parenthood was put aside and my emotions tuned in with my sister's predicament. My eyes filled with equal portions of sorrow and pride for what Tara was doing. What an amazing gift she was about to give. I felt honored to be a witness of her bravery. I approached her with Todd close behind.

"Oh, I can't believe it's time." My hand covered my mouth to conceal my unsteady emotions.

"This is not a time for tears. It's supposed to be a happy occasion." Tara's voice was weak with exhaustion, physical and emotional.

"These *are* tears of joy," I said as I brushed her hair from her face with my unsteady hand.

All thoughts were interrupted once the surgical tools were handed over the large iodine painted stomach. My throat tightened, and my focus locked onto Tara, whose eyes were squeezed tight. I could only imagine the thoughts and emotions that were traveling through her mind. I placed my hand on her shoulder, her flushed cheek pressed securely against my fingers. I glanced behind me toward Todd. His stance lightened my mood as I tried not to find humor in his reaction; he was hunched over with white knuckled hands grasping his slightly bent knees.

The color had escaped his cheeks, and the brilliant flicker that usually highlighted his eyes had been replaced by a blank, lifeless stare. My brave, strong hero was showing signs of weakness, and it made me love him even more. "Are you all right?" I held back the slight giggle that rested in my throat. Raising his hand, he nodded. A nurse rushed to his aid. "Would you like to step out to catch your breath?" She placed her hand on his shoulder.

He shook his head and looked back up at the doctor, who was moving her hand steadily across the belly. I knew she had to be making the incision. I forgot about Todd's shaky knees and concentrated on the miracle that was taking place. My knees wobbled a little as the reality of taking baby Suzy home with us forced me into realism. I felt a hand grip my shoulder firmly. I turned to see Todd by my side. "Feeling better?"

His coloring was a little closer to normal. "I'm fine, I don't want to miss this."

Supporting each other, we stood in awe. Tara kept her eyes closed with her face pressed firmly against my hand. Todd's grip tightened once the doctor lifted her hands onto Tara's belly with the baby. Dr. Hale propped Suzy up so we could see her. "It's a girl, a very healthy and beautiful little girl."

She was the most beautiful thing I had ever seen. She opened her eyes wide and then let out a cry that was music to my ears. Tara opened her tear-filled eyes. I kneeled down and whispered in her ear, "Sis, she looks just like you."

Nurses scrambled to bathe Suzy and check all her vitals, while Dr. Hale worked on Tara's stitches. "Seven pounds, twelve ounces. Nineteen inches long. Good job, Mom, she's perfectly healthy," a nurse announced.

I started to stand up straight, when Tara whispered my name. I turned my attention back to her smiling face. "Clara, I want *you* to hold her first."

I hesitated momentarily, and then asked, "Are you sure?"

She nodded her head with subtle ease. Her cheeks glowed bright pink as they grew into a smile.

The nurse approached us, carrying a bundle of blue-and-pink stripes. I reached out and relieved her of the precious little package. My insides trembled as the newborn looked up at me; her eyes gazed into mine. In that split second, nothing else seemed to matter. All troubles seemed to vanish; everything else became so minor. Suzy had captured my heart, and she was all that appeared to matter. I would do anything for her, and I honestly believed she knew it too. I shed a tear, assuring the devotion I had for her as my heart leapt, grasping the concept of love at first sight.

Feelings of guilt rushed through my veins as I wanted to hang on to her forever and never share her dark hypnotic eyes with anyone else.

Todd peered over my shoulder and rubbed her petite little cheek with his finger. "She's so beautiful. She looks just like you."

My smile grew, and I giggled with delight. It felt like a real family. My grip tightened and I dreaded having to give her up, even for a second. I looked up as a hand wrapped around the blanket in my arms. "Should we let the mommy hold the baby now?" The nurse removed her from me. I was speechless but gave no resistance, even though my insides wanted desperately to scream out "*No!* She's mine." I grew numb as I watched Suzy being placed in front of Tara's emotion-filled face. Her tears made mine flow faster. "You did a good job, sis. She's perfect." I found words of comfort at the last moment.

The nurse spoke up before Tara could respond, "We're gonna get Mommy and baby cleaned up and settled back into their room. Why don't you guys go ahead and derobe and get a bite to eat. You'll be free to visit them back in their room in about an hour."

Chapter 9

Rollercoaster of Nerves

Naturally I hated the idea of leaving; it took all my strength to move my body out the door. I never could have done that much without the soft nudge of Todd; he placed his hand on the small of my back and pushed gently to guide me through the exit. My stature remained calm, although my insides were kicking and screaming with every inch I put between Tara and myself.

Once out the door, my feet anchored themselves in the hall, and my eyes fixed onto the door. Todd's arm wrapped around me and pulled me close. "Let's get something to eat." His voice soothed my heart momentarily, and I nodded in agreement.

We found our way through the halls back to her room and disrobed. The relief I thought I would feel was replaced with a surreal atmosphere that made me feel like I was floating on uncertainty. My mind was filled with a dark fog that screamed I was selfish for wanting to raise Suzy as my own. As the new phase of the plan was staring me directly in the face and I could feel Tara's mixed emotions of carrying through with the next phase, I was scared, and that left me full of guilt.

Todd's face was still pale as he opened the door. "I wonder where we'll find some food in this place?" He looked down the hall. "We could let our noses lead the way," I said as I brushed by him out into the hallway. His smile was always a security for me, and today it was no different. I felt that no matter what happened, he would still be my shelter, where I could find comfort and security. Today held our future in its hands. The importance of the day's events and what my sister would say or do next would affect us in a great way; today, we needed each other's support more than any other day in our relationship thus far.

I pointed at a sign on the wall that answered his question, and we followed the arrows guiding us to the cafeteria, where we settled on a couple of sandwiches. My nerves were on edge as I picked at the roast beef that was escaping out from under the bread. My stomach was grumbling, but Suzy's cries were still playing in my mind. Her musical whimpers were much louder than the sounds of hunger, and they were all I could concentrate on.

I wanted to rush back to her room and scoop Suzy up in my arms and never put her down. "I can't wait to get her home." I took a bite of the sandwich. Todd nodded and then took a sip of his soda. "How do you think your sister's doing?" His brows dropped in a look of concern. "You think now that she's held Suzy, she'll be able to go through with it?"

I nearly choked as he spoke the words I'd been pushing to the back of my mind since the doctor uttered the words *It's a girl*. I took a drink of soda to help the lump in my throat dissolve. "I'm hoping that everything is still a go. I hate to think it'll be different now. But whatever Tara decides, we need to be supportive." I nibbled on some of the bread.

His eyes were burning into the side of my face. I knew he was waiting for a more assuring response, but that was all I could offer him. His eyes eventually dropped back to his plate as he picked at his meal. I ignored his look of distress and continued to eat as I pushed the negative thoughts aside.

"I can't really eat. Should we go and see if she's back in her room now?" Todd said as he pushed his plate toward the middle of the table. I took one last bite and abandoned the half-eaten meal as I stood in agreement. I adjusted my itchy oversized belly then paused as it occurred to me that this was going to be the last time I'd have to wear it. I honestly did love playing the pregnant sister role, and part of me was going to miss wearing the bump. But another part of me was actually relieved to be putting the uncomfortable garment away. "It's going to be weird to be able to see my feet again." I leaned forward to look down.

Todd's eyes brightened back up for a moment as he let out a slight chuckle. "Let's stop by the gift shop and see if we can find something for your sister and Suzy." His hand rested on my lower back. "We can do that." I rested my head on his chest for a brief second for a quick boost of comfort, before following his lead through the halls.

The gift shop was small, with very little to choose from. I stood near the door and scanned over the items that were displayed neatly on four small shelves that lined the outer walls and the glass case that sat in the middle of the floor. Todd instantly migrated toward the shelf of pink.

He waved hi to the young lady that was running the register up against the back wall. Her long black strands fell forward as she sat in a slouch on her stool. Her nose was in a magazine, and her hand was too busy to return the nice gesture. My eyes fell upon a bracelet that was nagging for my attention in the glass case. Without stopping to check out its details, I walked to the checker dressed in dark attire that displayed a presence of gloom all around her. "I would like to see the bracelet inside the case." I pointed to the middle of the floor.

Her eyes slowly lifted up from the magazine she was reading and looked around me to the case. "Which one?" she said with a tired and irritated yawn. Ignoring the poor manners of the immature teenager, I walked over to the case and pointed to the one I wanted. The sound of dragging feet raised the hair on the back of my neck. "Which one?" the mumbling voice asked again.

I squatted down as best I could with the huge belly still on. I tapped on the glass in front of the silver bracelet with small heart charms dangling from its links. "I want that one. Do you have a box?" She stood behind me as I slowly rose back to my feet. "That bracelet is forty-five dollars." She twirled her hair, making no attempt to move toward the item in question. Slightly irritated, I reached into my pocket and pulled out my coin purse. I opened it up, pushed my driver's license forward, and pulled out a fifty-dollar bill. "Will you get the bracelet out for me now?" My voice rose higher than I had intended.

"Is there a problem here?" Todd rushed to my side and wrapped his arm around me.

"No, sir, I was just about to get a box for the lovely bracelet she picked out." I couldn't control the daggers that were shooting from my eyes as I watched her walk back to the counter.

"What did you find?" Todd pulled me close.

I pointed to the bracelet in the case. "When we were kids, Grandma Marsh had a bracelet almost identical to that one. Tara would go and find that thing every time we'd go over to visit. I couldn't count the number of times she got in trouble for taking it without asking. A few years ago, Grandma went to the beach and lost the bracelet. Tara was devastated—she had hoped she would get it someday." I admired the similarity to the one Grandma Marsh had worn a few moments longer. "It's just too perfect." I looked to his hands to see if they contained a gift for the baby. "What did you find?"

Todd held up a sterling silver jewelry box. The box was about three-inch square with two hearts carved into the top. He opened it; inside there were two matching heart necklaces. "It says the mother is supposed to wear one, and the baby gets the other when she gets older. But I thought maybe you and your sister could wear them, and Suzy could have the jewelry box."

"Because Suzy will always hold our hearts?" I said as I pulled one of the sterling chains from the box.

"Is it too corny?" His shoulders shrugged.

"No, I think it's great." I carefully placed the necklace back inside.

The clerk finally arrived with a jewelry box and removed the bracelet from the locked case. "Will that be all, miss?" Her voice was sweet and phony.

Todd grabbed the box. "I want this jewelry box too, you can just wrap some tissue paper around it, if you have any."

I stood aside as he paid for the gifts. As she handed him the change, I heard her wish him luck with his emotional pregnant wife. Though it was impressive to see her actually crack a smile, I wanted to slap her. Todd placed his change in his pocket. "Thanks, and good luck finding a personality." I was shocked by his response, but it saved me from having to make a scene. He threw me a wink then wrapped his arm around me. "I love you, even if you are emotional." He gave me a squeeze.

The walk back to the room was a short journey, but my feet were heavy with anticipation. The room seemed to grow further and further away as we approached its partially opened door. Finally reaching our destination, I paused momentarily. I took a deep breath in an effort to prepare myself for whatever was to happen next. I wanted to grab Todd's hand but strained to keep up the charade as we walked in as the characters she had assigned us as.

My smile was forced as I neared her bedside. My rapidly pounding heart drowned out all other sounds. Her appearance was drooping with exhaust and bright with color. The screeching sound of the chair on the white linoleum floor as I pulled it close returned me back to reality and I could hear everything around me once more. I quickly sat down and handed over the plain white gift box.

"What's this?" Tara shifted her body up as she reached for her gift.

"Just a little something. Open it." I watched her face as she slowly lifted one corner of the box, as if she expected something to fly out of it.

Her eyes soon widened, and she ripped the lid off. Her face glistened with approval. "It's just like Grandma's." She held it up.

"Not exactly the same. The links are wider, and I think there are more hearts. But it's very close, do you like it?"

"I love it." She placed it on her arm, then reached out for me to clasp it for her.

"Fits you perfect. I'm happy you like it." My smile relaxed and I exhaled through the awkward fog that was surrounding me.

"We found something for Baby too," Todd said as he walked to the opposite side of the bed. He placed the tissue covered present on the bedside table and wheeled it over her much smaller belly.

She removed the thin white paper and picked up the shiny box. Her finger traced the engraved hearts on the top of the box.

"Open it." Todd sounded like an excited little kid. His eyes lit up as she opened the lid and pulled out a chain. "They match." He pointed inside. "There's one for you and one for Clara."

I could see the smile on Tara's face as she looked up at his gleaming expression of satisfaction. "We'll never take them off," she said as she handed me the one she had been holding and then took the other out for herself.

The sound of footsteps echoed through the room, shifting everyone's attention to the door. My heart sank as I saw an unfamiliar-looking nurse waddling in carrying Suzy. She was snuggled tight inside a blanket like a burrito. "You ready to feed your hungry little girl?"

Tara quickly responded with the shake of the head. "I'll be bottle-feeding. So I think Dad would like to be the first to feed her."

"You're not planning on breast-feeding at all?" The nurse laid the motionless blanket bundle inside the clear plastic bassinet at the foot of the bed. "No, formula will do just fine." Tara looked to the bassinet, avoiding eye contact with the nurse.

"If you're sure, then I will go ahead and get a bottle ready." The nurse stood at the doorway for a slight second, as if waiting for a response, then slowly carried her plump body out the door.

Once the nurse was gone, my eyes fell upon the wiggling grunts coming from the little bed only a few yards away from my fingertips. The cries of hunger increased, and the subtle movements of the blanket became more active. I rushed to her side and scooped her up. I held her close and rocked her slowly from side to side until the loud sounds mellowed. "You're a natural." Tara's voice settled in my ears, but my daze was fixed on Suzy's crimson frown. The nurse soon returned with the bottle, and I was forced to release my grip and let Todd experience some of the glory of parenthood.

The small bundle was placed in Todd's large arms, which appeared to be shaking slightly. His eyes were like saucers, and his grin held a hint of fear that came off as a forced smile. His eyebrows lifted as he sat back in a chair and positioned the miniature bottle.

I stared at the two of them as if I were admiring a prized painting. Todd's shoulders dropped, and his face relaxed as the fussing of his daughter turned into loud slurps. The moment was one I was proud to be a witness to.

"I can tell my Suzy's going to be in great hands. You guys will make wonderful parents." I breathed a sigh of relief as she spoke those reassuring words that allowed my heart to beat at a normal pace again.

It was official; I was a mother. The overflowing emotions escaped in a form of a tear that ran down the left side of my face. "Should we call the folks back home and give them the great news?" Tara reached for the phone on the nightstand.

"I think Todd should be the one to call." I dug through my purse and located my cell phone.

"I can do that." He stood up, still balancing baby and her bottle. "I'll trade you." He said, barely lifting his focus from the tiny person in his arms. I quickly snapped a picture with my phone and then slipped it in his pocket.

Taking her into my arms felt perfect. I couldn't imagine her being anywhere else but next to me. I barely noticed that Todd had left the room. I sat down and held my breath as I hoped this moment would last forever.

"She's a lot smaller than I thought she would be." Tara broke my trance. "I often thought I was carrying around a baby elephant, with all that pushing and constant pressure." She took a sip of water.

"She's definitely not a baby elephant." I laughed.

"That's a relief for us both," Tara said as she stared at the baby in my arms.

"Do you want to hold her?" I almost wanted to retract the words as they fell from my lips. I already loved this baby more than I ever thought possible. I did not want her to take away my dream. But I didn't want to take away this moment from her either. I stepped forward and lifted Suzy enough for Tara to see the precious life inside the blanket.

"Maybe I should." She extended her arms. I smiled big to cover the awkward silence as I placed Suzy in my sister's arms. I shifted slightly in my shoes as Tara stared intensely at the new-born. "I will always love you, little one," Tara said. "But as I stare at your olive-toned face and dark-colored eyes, I know I'll suit you better as an auntie. You look just like your daddy."

Chapter 10

Reality Kicks In

The night had been a restless one; with little sleep and excessive tossing and turning. My body was giddy with excitement, even though the dark circles would lead one to believe otherwise. Todd spent most of the night at the small round table tucked up against the window watching the television. "Did you get any sleep?" I stretched my arms before allowing my feet to touch the light-blue wall-to-wall carpeting of our hotel room.

"No, my mind was too busy, couldn't really sleep." His eyes were still glued to the news.

Anxious to get back to the hospital, I forced my sleepy legs to support my body so I could get into the shower. The vivid white bathroom was fairly small, consisting of just a stand up shower and a toilet. The sink and mirror were located outside the bathroom door with the closet. My mind was overwhelmed with the events that were due to follow with Suzy having finally arrived. I hardly noticed the awkwardness of the small cubicle of a shower, and the three streams of water that pushed out in such force they pierced my skin like little needles.

I finished up my shower, quickly dried off, and threw my hair back into a messy bun. My cotton belly was strapped into place, and my purple maternity top was layered over my large plum-like bump.

I stepped into a pair of MaMa-2-B jeans and primped in front of the mirror that displayed the empty closet behind me. I covered my face lightly with some color and polished my lips with a shiny gloss.

"Ready if you are?" I stepped out of the closet.

"I'm ready." Todd rose to his feet and turned off the TV.

"I'm kind of nervous. Is that weird?" I said as I smoothed the front of my top with my uneasy hands.

"What are you nervous about? You think she'll change her mind still?" He stopped in his tracks and looked to me for an explanation.

"No, I know she has set her mind to this. Suzy is ours. *That's* what I'm nervous about. I've been so excited and ready for this day for what seems like forever. But now that it's here, I can't help but have some questions and concerns. Like what if she doesn't really like me as a mom? What if I'm not a good mom? What if this was a bad idea and we're making a mistake by taking her from Tara?"

"Whoa, relax." Todd wrapped his arms around me. "We've been planning for this, you *are* ready. You are going to make the best mom in the universe for Suzy, and Tara will be a great aunt. Your sister has already said that her career is what she wants to focus on. She's already resenting Suzy with the memories of that night. This is the best thing for Suzy and she's going to love you—how could she not?" His lips pressed against my forehead in a soothing kiss of reassurance.

"Right. You're right. You're always right." I studied his steady, secure stare and tried to mimic his confidence. "Suzy is a lucky girl to have such an amazing person in her life, and so am I."

His hands rested firmly onto my bogus baby belly. "I'm sure gonna miss this bump." His slight chuckle lightened the mood.

"Okay, let's go get our girl." I said as my shaky legs became more stable.

The ride to the hospital was a quiet one. The radio was playing, but my focus was on mute as I stared at Todd's white knuckles gripping the steering wheel. I gazed into the backseat and imagined a sweet baby wrapped in pink, sleeping in the car seat. The butterflies that had taken over my wave of nausea slowly escaped as we pulled into the parking garage. "Everything's going to work out just fine, isn't it?" I placed my hand on his leg and waited for him to make eye contact.

"It always does." He parked the car then gave me the awaited smile. His eyes twinkled as he looked into mine.

My confidence had returned due to reassurance I found in Todd, and my momentary relapse of uncertainty was again tucked away. A smile took over my face as I nearly stumbled over my own feet getting out of the car. I felt like an excited little kid again, and I couldn't wait to see that precious little girl that I could call mine.

"Well, Mom, are you ready for this?" His words sent chills of delight down my back.

"I'm a mom." Tears filled my eyes with joy.

"Yes you are, and you're going to be a great one." His arm pulled me close.

"Well, Daddy, how are you doing?" I leaned against him as we stepped into the garage elevator.

"I'm all right, but I'll feel better once she is home sleeping in her own bed," he confessed.

We walked into the facility with more certainty than we had the day before. We went straight to the nurses' station and asked if my sister was awake and ready for visitors. The nurse buzzed us through the closed doors, and we strolled the halls to Tara's room with shoulders back and embarrassingly huge smiles. Upon entering the room, my attention quickly searched the area for the blanket bundle that was sure to be swaddling my Suzy.

"Good morning," Dr. Hale greeted as we entered the room.

"Good morning, Doctor," I said as I walked toward Tara's bedside. She looked amazing as she sat up in her bed holding her baby close.

"You guys are here just in time to help her with her things." Dr. Hale focused on her clipboard.

"Does that mean that everything has checked out, and I can go home?" Tara looked around me to see the doctor standing near the door.

"That *is* what that means. The nurse will be in shortly to have you sign a few papers, then you and Baby are free to go."

"I'll start taking your stuff out to the car." Todd picked up the complimentary diaper bag from the hospital. "And I'll bring in the baby carrier." He looked around the room in a daze before leaving with the bag in hand.

Dr. Hale dropped the clipboard to her side. "All right, I'd like to see you next week for a checkup. Call my office to schedule an appointment."

Tara's attention dropped to Suzy's face. "I will, thank you." She slowly looked back up to the doctor and smiled weakly.

"Any questions?" Dr. Hale looked to me. I shook my head as I watched her eyes shift down to my belly with a smile.

As soon as Dr. Hale was gone, Tara handed Suzy over to me. "So, Clara, when are you gonna have your cotton baby?" She patted my belly.

"As soon as we get back to the hotel." I said as my concentration stayed fixed on Suzy's precious little features. I found myself mimicking her subtle facial expressions as she tried to fall back to sleep. I was in complete awe, simply amazed at how something so tiny could have such a big impact on me. She was already tugging at my heartstrings, as if I were her little puppet. I was anxious to see where she'd lead me.

I found comfort in the chair next to the bed where I could gently rock Suzy to sleep. As she fell into a restful slumber, a short nurse with straight black hair entered the room with papers in hand. "Grand mornin' to ya, dear. I'm Irene. Ya ready to get that there wee one home wit' ya?" The Irish accent was thick and brought a smile to my face.

"I am indeed," Tara said with an uncontrollable hint of the same accent.

"Sign these here papers an' that wee colleen will be grand to get wit' ya." She handed over the stack of forms then took a peek at the sleeping baby. "She's a beaut, a real keeper that un." She pulled the blanket away from Suzy's olive-colored chin to get a better look; which made the baby squirm a little in my arms. "Yar gonna want a bottle wit' ya, she's 'bout ta scream 'er bloody head off fer a feedin', trust meself 'ers 'bout ta wake." Nurse Irene rushed from the room.

By the time the paperwork was filled out, Todd had returned to assist us in our escape. A tall, slender male pediatrician came in for one last exam of the tiny patient and then watched us carefully as we redressed her and placed her in to the carrier. "Very good. But I want to show you a little trick to help support the baby's head even better." The doctor laid out one of Suzy's baby blankets on the bed then rolled it up into a long plush tube. He then tucked the middle of it in between Suzy's head and the built-in head support that framed her in the carrier. He proceeded to tuck the rolled-up blanket around Suzy. By the time he was done, she was well supported inside the carrier.

"That's better. Now she won't be wobbling around in there like a little bobblehead." The doctor winked as I chuckled at his choice of words.

"That is pretty clever," I said, looking at Tara, who was still sitting at the edge of the bed.

"Yeah, we'll have to remember that one." She smiled and then grabbed her belly with a slight cringe.

"Hurt to smile?" I reached out my hand to help her up.

"Very tender. I hadn't realized that everything you do is connected to your stomach muscles."

Nurse Irene returned with a wheelchair and helped me slowly move Tara with ease into the chair. "I've never been so excited to be going home." Tara adjusted the waistband of her sweatpants so they didn't apply pressure on her stomach.

"That's cause yar a new ma, things'll be quite different at yar home, trust meself. Tara, pet, do me a favour an' get yarself a routine, dearie. It'll make adjustin' to the needs of this here rosy-cheeked critter much easier." She adjusted Suzy's blanket. Tara rolled her eyes as the nurse delivered her words of wisdom.

"Yas, all is grand, go on and go get ma and bebe home wit' ya. Drive careful, I would like 'em to arrive home safe wit' ya, that I would." She handed the carrier to Todd.

"Will do." He nodded. I wheeled Tara to the door, where Nurse Irene intercepted and pushed her out to the car; which Todd had waiting for us at the hospital entrance.

"So what's the game plan?" Tara asked, watching the nurse return the wheelchair back inside.

"Why you're staying at the hotel with us, of course." I closed the car door before she could respond.

"How you feeling now?" Todd whispered in my ear as I opened the door to the backseat. "Like I'm walking on air." I climbed in and sat next to the sleeping beauty. We were lucky enough to get a room at the Sunrise Inn, which was only a couple of blocks from the hospital. Traffic was cooperative, and the drive to our room took less than five minutes.

Todd helped Tara out of the car as I removed the baby carrier from the car seat. Filled with pride, I barely felt the ground beneath my feet as Todd escorted Tara behind me to our room. I set the carrier on the sturdy round table of our temporary home and admired Suzy's precious little features.

Tara slowly sat at the edge of the bed as Todd caringly adjusted pillows behind her to help her lie back easily. Confident that Suzy was content for the time being, I slipped into the bathroom to retire the pillow beneath my shirt. Honestly, it felt incredible to be trading in the pretend baby bump for a real breathing little life.

"It's amazing that we pulled this off." Tara was leaning back against the pile of pillows that Todd was still adjusting behind her. "It all sounded perfect in the beginning, I knew we'd pull it off. It just feels so surreal now, like we got away with something," I expressed as I walked toward the bed.

"This really is best, I am so thankful to have a sister that I can count on. You have helped me through this dilemma—it would have been a real disaster without you." Her lower lids filled with moisture as she slowly shook her head.

I joined her on the bed and lay next to her. "I've always had your back and will continue to keep it up forever if necessary." I grabbed her hand.

Todd chuckled in the background. "Until death do you part?" His wisecrack comment broke our moment of seriousness. Tara shook her head, then changed the subject. "So how long will you guys be staying?" She shifted in short movements in search of comfort. "We'll stay and help you out for as long as you want. We can wait a little while before we run home to show off the newest member of the River's family." I rolled onto my back and stared up at the glittery popcorn ceiling. "Look, it's like stars up there." I pointed to the ceiling.

"That's pretty cool. You do know that you guys can actually go at any time. My roommate knows I was going to be having surgery and will be there to help me out." Tara was now looking up at the bizarre application above us. "What kind of surgery does she think you're having?" I shifted my body to its side to face her. "She thinks I had to get a surgical correction for a hernia." She chuckled. "What?" I laughed in disbelief. "Did I mention my roommate is blonde? She's a sweetheart, but very, well let's just say she optimizes the current blond jokes."

"You are just so awesome, that's hilarious. We'll stay for a few days anyway though. I don't want to leave you just yet." I got up off the bed, to allow her to get comfortable and rest. "Sounds like a great plan. I'm not ready for you to leave just yet either." Tara rolled onto her side and admired the heavenly vision in the car seat. "She looks so peaceful, doesn't she?" I focused on the same view as my sister. Tara nodded, then closed her eyes for some rest.

I joined Todd at the table where he was silently watching television. I was feeling confident that we had made it in the clear; but I couldn't deny the possibility of a change of events either. "Can you believe we're parents?" I grabbed his hand. "I'm not putting all my eggs in that basket until we make it home with her." He mumbled with his eyes still fixed onto the television. The fact that he still carried a negative vibe planted traces of doubt deep inside of me as well; which tightened my grip on his hand.

While Tara and Suzy slept, Todd and I enjoyed the serene setting. Knowing the peace and quiet would not last long, I stared at the sleeping baby as if she was a ticking time bomb ready to explode. Determined to master Suzy's routine I watched the clock on the wall and waited for her next siren of hunger. As her bottom lip began to quiver, I jumped up to prepare a bottle. Soon the cries from the newborn pierced my ears. I rushed to finish her meal as Todd scooped her up to soothe her.

"Clara? Do you need some help?" Tara groaned as she rubbed the sleep from her eyes. "Nope, I've just about got it." I shook the bottle, then tested the temperature on my wrist. Tara adjusted herself to watch Todd as I handed him the bottle. I watched Tara as the cries came to a halt. Her eyes were glassy, her lips were pressed together, her sadness was screaming out to me. I could only imagine how she was feeling. I could generally read her like a book, but this situation tested me, and it had me thinking about how it would be in her shoes at this moment. The passionate look on her face only made the doubt Todd felt grow within me again; this time with more intensity.

I knew that the next few days were going to be challenging ones. I just had no idea that they would prove to be a true learning experience for us all. In the beginning I was overwhelmed with joy and anticipation at the mere thought of teaching and molding this tiny newcomer into a model citizen. Those feelings however, were quickly turned into an unexpected dose of doubt.

After three night of very little sleep, it became obvious to me that I was not the teacher. I was a student. Suzy was giving us a few lessons of her own and although I was eager to learn, I was afraid of failing the many tests that were sure to follow. With every scream for my attention I ran to her aid with a smile. I was already housing feelings of guilt. Every time Suzy's cry filled the room, I witnessed Tara's drooping eyes roll in frustration; telling me she could do better. The tension in the small room was thickening with each restless night. It was easy to see that the quarters were too close for this experience to be cherished by all.

My fears of failing as a parent were gradually masqueraded by fears of resentment; that may have been consuming my sister. I knew this was hard enough on her. I didn't want to make things ever more complicated by forcing her to feel as the third wheel in the caring of her child. The two hour feedings were taking their toll on me and I was growing more and more tired. I wanted to get home and find a manageable routine.

Todd's movements were sluggish as he sat next to me at the table. "She finally asleep?" He covered his mouth as he yawned. "Yeah, isn't she beautiful?" I admired the angel nestled snuggly in my arms. "Definitely." He tipped his head toward the bed to move my focus to Tara; who had a pillow over her head. "We should start thinking of getting home." He suggested as I looked back to him; despite the bags of exhaustion that were set above his cheek bones his eyes still contained an enthusiastic, yet skeptical twinkle.

"I agree. I'm worried about Tara. I thought we could help her in her recovery. But I haven't had the time to care for her at all. Suzy has required my attention more than I ever imagined." I continued to rock her, to keep her eyes from opening. "Having regrets?" Todd leaned in to whisper. "No. She's worth it. Both of them are worth it. I would do anything for Tara, and Suzy has already stolen my heart, I'm exhausted, but I enjoy every second she cries for my attention." I stood up and placed Suzy in the carrier.

With Suzy sleeping comfortably in her carrier I walked to the bed and laid down next to Tara. I removed the pillow; and revealed her tears. "What's wrong?" I sat up, surprised by what I saw. Her response was a silent shake of the head. "I thought the pillow was being used as a sound barrier." I tried to remedy the situation with some humor. I could hear Todd moving closer to us to hear Tara's response. "I'm not real sure if these are tears of frustration or relief." She wiped her eyes dry. I waited patiently for her to clarify her words. Todd handed her a tissue, then sat next to me on the bed. We waited quietly for her to collect her thoughts.

After clearing her throat she blurted her words, "I feel like the worst mom in the world. I'm actually happy that you will be taking Suzy with you when you leave; which makes me feel terrible. I'm such a horrible person, I have no connection to her at all." She blew her nose, as her eyes began to swell again with tears. "You're gonna make an amazing mom someday." Todd assured her. "That's right, you will be the best mom a child could ask for, under better circumstances. Right now you are overwhelmed with so many emotions; and when you combined that with a lack of sleep you're bound to explode with frustration." I grabbed her hand. "I know you're right Clara. But right now, I don't know that I like myself for how I'm feeling, I'm not even sure I want anyone else to either." She placed the pillow back over her face. My insides were entangled with guilt; I looked to Todd in hopes to be inspired with the right words that would help us all cope with the emotions that had hit us like a tornado of confusion.

Todd got up and walked to the other side of the bed and laid next to her "Tara, I admire you for what you are doing. Realizing that you are not ready to be a mom, does not make you a bad person. I can't imagine anyone not liking you for having Suzy's best interest at heart. I think you are a smart and remarkable person and I'm honored to call you my sister, just as I'm sure that Suzy will be honored to call you Auntie. I want to thank you, and will always love you for giving us such a beautiful daughter."

I wiped my own eyes as Tara slowly removed the pillow from her face. She looked at Todd, who gave her a wink. "Oh Todd, I can see why my sister loves you so much. And I can see that Suzy will have the best parents." Tara looked back to me with a smile. "*That,* I can promise you Sis." Todd said as he got up to tend to Suzy who was beginning to wake up. I nodded to confirm Todd's promise. "I'm not feeling the guilt of separation I thought I would. That scares me." Tara looked to the baby in Todd's arms. "There was no way to plan how we'd feel. I'll be honest, I do feel a connection to Suzy, and that is what *I* feel guilty about." I confessed.

"We are a sorry bunch aren't we?" Tara found her smile. "We'll probably feel better after some real rest. I think we really have to get home. I'm sure Mom is pacing the floor waiting to meet her granddaughter." I stood up. "I do need to get back to the dorm. Maybe I can study a bit before classes start back up." Tara slowly adjusted herself to a sitting position. "Are you going be alright if we leave? Do you still need us to stay and help you?" I held onto the cans of formula I had collected from the table. "Oh no, I'll be fine. I do still kinda feel bad handing over that annoying little thing to you. Are you sure you're okay with this?"

Without hesitation, I nodded "Oh yeah I'm fine, and so is she. We'll get her home and settled in. Once we get into a working routine, we will all be just fine." I thumbed through the number of diapers in the bag and took a mental count. "I'm holding you to that Clara." Todd yawned. I shook my head in response to his wise crack comment and placed a pink baby-tee inside the bag.

"Mom's going to be so excited to see you guys. I'm sure she's been stewing all week." Tara slowly moved herself to the edge of the bed, still wiping her face dry with the back of her hand. "I'm excited to get home and show off my lack of belly and new baby." I pulled my hair up and secured it with a hair clip. "I'm happy you mentioned the belly. I think you need to still wear the first stage of the cotton belly. As you can see, I still have a lot of flab left. People may be a little skeptical, or at the very least; jealous, of the belly vanishing so quickly."

I looked down at my flat belly. "Good point, I better slip that on now while I'm thinking of it." I dug through my bag until my fingers happened upon the plush garment. Todd helped Tara to her feet while I fastened the addition of a spare tire around my middle. "Do we have everything packed?" Tara slouched over slightly as she walked slowly toward me. "Almost. But, you can just sit and relax while we get the mess wrapped up." I pulled out a chair at the table for her to sit.

"She is beautiful when she's quiet, isn't she?" She admired the sleeping baby in the carrier on the table. "Yes she really is, you did a great job. Thank you." I leaned up against her with a soft, subtle nudge of gratitude. "I really should be thanking you." Tara replied without moving her attention away from Suzy. I kissed the top of Tara's head as she sat in a daze. "We'll call it even." I whispered.

I placed my hand on her shoulder as I reached across the table to grab the diaper bag. My fingers squeezed her shoulder briefly as I turned toward the door. I grabbed another bag on my way out of the room to help Todd pack the car with our belongings. Once everything was nestled nicely inside the car, Todd closed the trunk. "That's everything." His hands rested firmly on his hips, as he appeared to be taking a mental note of everything we brought. "Wait, I've got one more thing to do before we get Suzy." I winked, then opened the passenger door and climbed into the front seat. "Clara, what are you doing?" His voice instantly caused me to smile. "You'll see."

I opened the glove box and pulled out a brown paper bag, then crawled into the backseat. I reached into the bag to retrieve my surprise, as I admired Todd's perplexed expression through the back window. I stuck the yellow diamond shape sign to the glass, all the while waiting to see Todd's reaction. My smile grew large as Todd shook his head to the "Baby on Board" sign. I quickly joined him on the sidewalk behind the car to admire the sign for myself.

Before I could hear his response, cries poured from the open door behind us. The feeling of pride overwhelmed me as I ran to Suzy's aid. It warmed my heart to hear the sweet sound of such an innocent child so dependent on its mom; so dependent on me. I ran through the door, past my sister and scooped the helpless child up into my arms, forgetting that I wasn't the only one there to attend to her needs. I smiled proudly as her cries subsided to my touch.

Her eyes locked onto mine, melting my insides, now *I* was the helpless one. "There, there Sweetie. Mommy's got you." I rocked her gently in my arms. "Are we ready? Is she alright?" Todd's voice nudged my attention. "Yes we're fine, and definitely ready to take our baby home." I placed my bright eyed little girl back in her car seat carrier. "I'm sure happy you came in when you did, I had no idea where the off switch was located on that thing." Tara grabbed the edge of the table to help her to her feet.

I fastened her snuggly into the baby carrier and handed it over to Todd. He took hold of the handle, then wrapped his free arm around my waist. "I haven't figured out how to hush the cries either, lucky for me Clara has the magic touch. You can rest assured that Miss Suzette Jessamond Rivers is in the best hands possible." Tara hung onto Todd's every word. "I don't doubt that. Clara is going to be a terrific mother."

I slipped away from Todd's grip which allowed him to take Suzy out to the car. Tara wrapped her arms around me. "I mean it Sis. Seeing you and Suzy together, it just feels right. This is how it was meant to be. I just know it." I was truly speechless. A single tear rolled down my cheek as I held her close. "Alright we're ready!" Todd hollered from the car.

We released our grip and I helped her slowly through the door and out to the car. With the car packed full, we pulled away from the hotel parking lot. Tara played navigator as she directed the way to her dorm. She didn't live too far from where we had been staying; which brought the dreaded words of good-bye quicker than I had hoped.

We stood tearful on the sidewalk in front of her building. I opened my mouth a few times before I was able to speak. "I'm not sure what to say. This feels like such a dream." My eyes caught a slender image with long blonde hair walking toward us from the main entrance. "I'm going to miss you guys." She held me tight. "I hate that you are so far away from me. You need to come and stay with us this summer." I forced myself to release the grip. "I'm planning to come up for a week, sometime before I start my summer job." She looked toward the girl standing halfway up the walk. "That's only a couple of months away. I guess I can handle that."

"It'll be here before you know it." She assured me. "I know you're right, I do. I'll be calling you though . . ." "With every new sound Suzy makes?" Tara interrupted. I nodded. "Good, you better." She leaned in with a lowered tone. "I will. Did you want to say good-bye to her?" I pointed toward the backseat of the car.

Tara walked over to the car and peeked her head inside. Todd diverted his eyes out the driver side window; as if to give her some privacy. I couldn't hear any words but her smile was subtle as she wiggled her fingers in a hesitated wave of farewell. I waited for her to back away from the car, before stealing one final farewell.

"Misty!" My eyes shifted toward the blond Tara called out to. "Come meet my family." She motioned her toward us. "Hi, I'm Misty." She extended her jewelry covered hand for a friendly greeting. "You must be the sister. Tara-Dear said she had an identical twin sister, but I didn't realize you guys would look so much alike." I tried not to laugh as I gripped her hand. "Yes, I'm her twin; Clara. So you're the one who will be taking good care of my sister?"

Misty turned her attention to Tara "Yep. So how was the surgery?" "Went just fine, I'm just a little slow moving." Misty looped her arm through Tara's left arm, "I'm gonna take good care of you, so don't you worry 'bout a thing." Misty pulled my helpless sister closer to her. "Looks like you're in good hands. So I guess I better get the family home." I winked as Tara gave me a playful glare. "Call me when you get home." She said as I opened the car door. "I will."

I smiled as I closed the door. *Finally, I Clara Rae-Ann Rivers am officially the Mommy*! I was beaming with bliss as I looked back at Suzy who was sleeping peacefully in the back seat. I adjusted my seatbelt and watched as my sister grew more distant as we pulled away from the curb. "You okay?" Todd rubbed my thigh; the heat from his hand warmed my leg. "Yeah, I just hate to be separated from her; it's kind of hard to explain, and right now she needs me more than ever." I stared out the window at the rapidly changing scenery. Todd's words of comfort, and reassurance of the plan, simply floated past my ears in a muffled tone that I tried desperately to ignore.

The drive home seemed to go quicker than the original ride on those busy roads; even with the added stops to attend to Suzy's needs. Half way home I relocated myself to the backseat. It became apparent that it would be better if I stayed in the back, to better assist her frequent calls for attention.

Swirling in a sea of emotion I anticipated what the days ahead had in store for me. My mind was working overtime as I tried mapping out a mental agenda of a workable routine. But as Suzy demanded another feeding sooner than I had planned, I realized I wasn't the one who would be making the schedule. Suzy was in charge now. With her large, dark eyes of persuasion, I was already putty in her tiny little hands.

Chapter 11

Suzy's First Birthday

Getting our baby girl home had lifted an enormous weight from our shoulders. It seemed the most complex phase of the plan was complete. Though as the months progressed and our lives altered to accommodate our newborn, it didn't take long for us to realize that the real challenges lay ahead.

It was several months before Suzy allowed us to experience a decent night's sleep. She was nearly eight months old before she was sleeping though the night. It took practically a year to get a consistent routine. Per the request of my sister; whom I felt I owed my soul to for giving me such an amazing gift, I called regularly with Suzy updates. I tried to limit the bragging to a minimum, but Suzy had become such a huge part of me it was hard not to start every phrase with her name.

With every new hurdle she introduced us to, like the sleepless nights, ear infections, teething, and rashes, we jumped over them with both feet successfully. The endless lessons kept us on our toes. The constant adjusting of our routines took some getting used to, but even with the utter chaos at moments, our lives seemed to be more complete.

The year passed quicker than we could have ever imagined. She was now all over the place, getting into anything within reach. Suzy could now walk all over the house, as long as she had something to hang on to. The days of her running through the halls didn't seem to be that far off. It seemed unbelievable that her first birthday was already here.

"So is everything ready for the big day?" Tara said from the other end of the receiver.

"You bet, the family's all coming, and the decorations are all set." I finished tying the ribbon on a package covered in pink and purple hearts.

"I can't believe it's been a year," Tara sighed.

"It's gone by so fast, and she's grown so much since the last time you were up, you'll be blown away." I looked at a picture on the wall of Tara and Suzy at Christmas.

"I don't doubt that. Hey. Um. Can I ask a favor?" She changed the subject.

"Sure, what's up?" I brought my attention back to the gift I was wrapping.

"Well, I'm bringing someone up with me. I was hoping—I mean—could you please just not embarrass me and assure me that no slips will come out about the whole Suzy thing?"

It took me a second to comprehend what she had just asked; I was able to control the volume but not the question itself. "Are you serious? I'm *not* telling anyone anything, and what is all the panic over your new friend anyway? Wait—is it? It's a guy, isn't it? A boyfriend perhaps." I nodded as I was sure that was what she was concerned about.

There was a brief pause. "His name is Sean Johnson. We've been dating for a few months now, and I *really* like him. He's so perfect, you're going to just love him too." I could hear the infatuation in her voice.

"I assure you, everyone will be on their best behavior." I pushed the gift to the center of the table next to the others.

"Great! I'll see you tomorrow." In unison we said our good-byes. "Love you, sis, bye."

With a slight giggle and big smile, I hung up the phone. My smile faded as I pondered the favor she had asked. I was taken aback by the comment about spilling the beans regarding Suzy. I tried not to take offense to her question, but I was offended. That little girl was my life. I loved her with every fiber of my being and would never say or do anything to jeopardize that.

Looking around at the collection of decorations and already wrapped gifts, my mind was overwhelmed by how fast this day had come. It felt like only yesterday that we had brought her home for the first time. It was the oldest cliché, and I'd heard those words uttered by mothers before. Never had I imagined that one day very soon I'd find the truth in those words myself.

I finished tying the last bow upon the largest gift, just as Suzy's subtle whimper drifted down the hallway. The familiar sounds of her warning was enough to announce she was awake. I cleared the floor of a few rolls of bright pink streamers before I followed the increasing pitch of her still-sleepy whimper.

Entering her room, I announced my arrival. "Hey, sweetie." I walked toward her crib as her little hands rubbed her eyes. As I got closer to her, her chucky little arms extended up to me. Her weeping had hushed to sniffles and a relaxed smile. I scooped her up, allowing her head to take comfort upon my shoulder. I kissed her softly on her large black ringlets. "Come on, sugar bear, let's get you freshened up and ready for a snack." Her arms tightened their grasp, and as always, I was more than happy to return the gesture.

While preparing her a dish of fruit and crackers, I realized we were in need of some last-minute groceries. Suzy nibbled away at her snack as I created a list for the market. "Down." Suzy's arms raised high above her. Her eyes locked onto her cat as it inspected the mess she had made beneath her high chair. "One more bite, and we'll go bye-bye." I handed her a cracker from the scatter of food on her tray. Suzy's little fingers removed the treat from mine. Her bottom lip drooped as she took the last bite.

"Good girl." The words escaped moments before she threw the cracker on the floor; startling the cat. Her giggle made it impossible for me to correct her. "Down." Her arms rose for me to remove her from her seat. I cleaned her hands and mouth as she fought the procedures of the wet cloth. Once her mess was all cleaned up, she was removed from her high chair. "Bye-bye." Suzy's hands opened and closed in front of her face.

"Yep, we're ready to go."

With only a few cars on the road, it was evident that we had left at the perfect time; I hated to drive though the bends leading to town on thick traffic days. The drive was pleasant and we arrived to a nearly empty parking lot. As I found a parking spot close to the door, I felt like I had struck gold. I laughed to myself as I packed Suzy to the entrance; it was amazing at how some of the smallest things made me content nowadays. Suzy had brought many changes to my life. Some changes I had expected, but I was surprised by the changes in myself. Changes were subtle, yet they were there, and they were changes for the better.

With both my list and Suzy in hand, I walked into the store. The lines were short, a great indication that we'd be in and out in record time. I couldn't believe my luck. I placed Suzy in a cart and cruised down the aisle eliminating items from my list one by one.

With only a few needed items remaining, I stretched to reach the teething cookies on the top shelf. My fingers grasped the package, just as my chest knocked a box of baby cereal to the floor.

"Here, let me help you." I spun around to the familiar voice; I stood stunned at the sight before me.

"I can tell by the look on your face that you're not willing to let bygones be bygones." Brad placed the box back on the shelf. I felt my body heat up as I forced myself to bite my tongue to keep from causing a scene.

Brad pulled his eyes away from my burning glare and focused on Suzy, whose large brown eyes matched his. "And who might you be?" His hand rubbed hers.

My teeth ground together as I tried not to shout, "*Get away from my daughter.*" My cheeks felt like fire as the rage within caused my knees to tremble.

"Okay, okay." He took a couple steps back and grabbed hold of his own cart and pushed it closer to me. "But this is a supermarket and a free country. I'm allowed to shop anywhere I want. Now listen closely, sweetie, 'cause this is the part that you're gonna wanna hear.

There's not a damn thing *you* can do about it. So get used to it, I ain't going anywhere. Bet that stings a little, huh?" He grinned, visibly proud of his speech.

I stepped in front of Suzy to block her from his view then calmly looked him in the eyes. "True, but I don't have to like it, and I can assure you that if you ever step anywhere near my property or my family, I'll kill you. That is in no way a threat. That is a promise." I placed my hands firmly on my hips to hide that they were shaking tremendously.

His eyes sized me up from head to toe. "Do you have any idea how hot you are when you're mad. You're saucy and I like it." He winked then pushed his cart down the aisle without a single glance back.

I wrapped my arms around Suzy and held her close. My body trembled with anger as he disappeared around the corner. I pressed my lips against her forehead. "I love you, sweetie." Her hand reached out and grabbed my arm. "Wuv you." Her words wrapped around my heart. Not wanting to run into him again, I rushed with my cart to the checkout.

Standing in line, I stared at her beautiful olive-toned skin, dark eyes, and black hair. I couldn't help but wonder how he couldn't have noticed he was looking into a mirror image of himself. I wasn't about to take any chances. I stood close to her to block her from his view if he should appear around the corner. Luckily, I never saw him again before leaving the store.

By the time I reached the house my heart's rapid rhythm had mellowed. I played his facial expressions over and over inside my head and was relieved that he never once looked at Suzy with any moments of questionable concern. Confident that he hadn't considered Suzy as a possibility of being his, my muscles began to unclench the painful grip they had on my neck.

I tried to push the incident to the back of my mind as I grabbed the groceries to carry them inside. "Hey, babe." Todd's greeting startled me as he stepped out of the house. I readjusted the grip I had on the bags as they nearly slip from my arms. "Well, you're home early. Why don't you grab the other bags out of the car." I looked back at the car as he stepped off the porch with arms raised slightly. "Gee, I'm happy to see you too." His bottom lip hung in a pout.

I stopped next to him and kissed him on the cheek. "I'm sorry. Love you. I'm so happy to see you, sweetie. Better? Can you get the groceries now?"

I smiled with a wink and handed him the bags I had in hand. "I'd rather get the birthday girl."

He looked toward the car. "That would be great too, she could use a diaper change." He removed the bags from my grip. "Yeah, okay. I'll get the groceries."

With a chuckle, I went back to get Suzy as Todd took the groceries inside.

The question of whether or not to tell Todd about the encounter at the grocery store was nagging at me. My mind replayed Brad's words as I got Suzy changed. I carried her out of her room, still undecided about what I should say. The stress must have been written all over my face; Todd focused on me with an intense stare the moment I entered the kitchen. "What's wrong?" His eyes pierced mine; his eyebrows were raised in curiosity.

I set Suzy down onto the ground to go play. "Aw, nothing really." I shook my head and looked away.

"All right." He hopped up and took a seat on the island in the middle of the floor. "Just spill it." He crossed his arms. I slowly lifted my head to make eye contact as he motioned me toward him with his hand. I dragged my feet as I wandered across the floor and settled myself between his knees that hung over the edge of the countertop. "So what's bugging you?" His eyes grabbed mine, and I became putty in his hands.

"I ran into Brad at the store."

Todd's eyes dropped their hold on mine for a split second. "Did he see Suzy? Did he say anything?" His body shifted as he voiced his questions of concern.

"He saw her, but he didn't seem to make the connection." I shook my head. His chest grew as he took a deep breath of relief.

"That's good. It has been nearly two years now. I doubt he made the connection or did the math. I wouldn't let it bother you."

I felt tightness around my heart. "Just seeing him bothered me. Then when he talked to me, I wanted to gouge his eyes out and feed them to him."

Todd's eyes grew large. "Ouch! You've got a mean streak, don't you? I gotta say, I think I like it." He pulled me in, closer to him.

"I'm serious." I slapped his shoulder. "I can't forgive him, and I can't stand the thought of him being her biological father."

He automatically shifted his body weight upward; his eyebrows darted together. "He will never be her dad. I promise you that." His stern voice was reassuring. I looked down at Suzy, who was playing on the floor with her ponies. My entire body tightened with pain at the thought of losing her. "I hope you're right. She means everything to me." I rested my head on his chest, focusing on the sweet giggles filling the room as she played happily.

Todd's arms wrapped around me firmly. "I promise." His whisper of reassuring words allowed me to exhale and fall into his trusting net of safety.

"Thanks."

"You are very welcome." His lips pressed upon my forehead. "I love you, sweets." His voice was low and sincere.

"And I you, rebel." I smiled as he lifted my chin so his eyes could gaze into mine.

"Kicky." A sweet voice broke our trance of infatuation. "Where's Kitty?"

I looked down to the large dark eyes staring up at me. She was pulling herself to her feet, using the drawer handles for support. Once her feet were steady, she opened her hand to reveal a handful of hair. "Oh, honey, you need to be nice to Kitty." I backed out of Todd's hold and moistened a paper towel. Todd tried to contain his laughter as I removed the cat hair from her tiny fingers.

"Kicky!" Suzy beamed with a smile from ear to ear as the cat entered the room.

My smile was getting harder to control as I admired the bravest cat. Tierra was incredible with Suzy, she'd let her crawl right over the top of her, chew on her ears, and then come back for more. They were an amazing duo.

"Suzy, you are lucky Tierra has no claws or she may just scratch you someday." I took her tiny hand into mine.

"Mine." Suzy's eyes were large as she looked up from her now clean hand.

"Yes, honey. The kitty is yours, but you still need to be nice, okay?" Suzy's head lifted slightly, and her eyes focused on the scenery behind me.

"Nice Kicky."

I turned around to see Tierra looking back to Suzy. I grabbed her chubby little arm and rubbed my sleeve with the palm of her hand. "Pet the kitty like this—see, nice." Suzy giggled then dropped to the floor and crawled to the cat. I shook my head as she plopped onto the kitchen floor, using Tierra as a pillow.

"Good try, sweets, but I think it's a lost cause." Todd grabbed my arm as I stood up, pulling me back to him.

"Maybe so, but why don't you get down there and try while I get things ready for the party tomorrow?" I smiled big, exposing my pearly whites, and batted my eyelids.

"Cute, but fair enough." He pushed me back as he slid off the counter.

"Thanks." I blew him a kiss as I walked away, leaving him to tend to our baby girl.

It was a long night getting everything cleaned up, and the decorations hung, but waking up to the results was worth it. Everyone was due to arrive by noon, which gave me plenty of time to get Suzy ready for her big day. I was up bright and early, ready to start the day. Before waking up the rest of the house, I prepared a large breakfast, set Todd's plate on the dining room table, then went to wake him. The sooner I could get him up and going, the sooner he could start on the honey-do list I had created for him to tackle in the backyard.

The sun was beaming into our bedroom through a gap between the curtains. The light highlighted the big lump of covers that were piled over Todd in bed. "Rise and shine, Toddie-boy. Breakfast is on the table, and so is the list of things I need done before everyone gets here."

The covers barely moved. "What time is it?" he moaned. "It's 8:30, and I've got to get Suzy up and going too. Time to get up." I looked down at him from the bedside, blocking the sunlight.

He lifted his head. "I have plenty of time." He rolled over, pulling the blankets up to his chin.

"Todd!" I snapped my fingers.

"All right, I'm up." He crawled from the bed, wearing a pair of white boxers. His hair stood straight up on one side, and his eyes were still half closed.

I stood at the foot of the bed as he staggered across the floor. "Happy?" He mumbled while wiping the sleep from his eyes.

"Yes, very much so." I puckered my lips for a playful kiss. He reached out and ruffled my hair as he passed by me. "Lucky for you I haven't done my hair yet."

He shook his head at my words as he headed out the bedroom door. "Yeah, lucky me."

With Todd heading for the shower, I headed to Suzy's room. I slowly opened the door and peeked inside. She was already awake. She was sitting up in the crib playing with her favorite rattling teddy bear. Her eyes never lifted from the toy in her hands. "Happy birthday, angel." I entered the room as she lifted her smiling face.

"Mama." She pulled herself up to her feet; her eyes flashed brightly as she dropped the bear and extended her arms.

I lifted her up out of bed and gave her a good-morning squeeze "Love you, pumpkin, you have a big day ahead of you." Her eyes brightened as if she knew what the day had in store for her. It was amazing at how fast the past year had flown by. What was even more amazing was how much she had grown and changed from when we first brought her home. She had been an amazing teacher through this journey and had molded all of us to suit her needs. Our little family had become quite the team because of it.

I had dressed my little birthday girl in her new lavender dress. Suzy's shiny black curls were pulled up into a ponytail tied with a lavender satin ribbon, matching the satin on the upper portion of her sleeveless dress. She looked like a beautiful doll. I was alive with excitement at the opportunity to show her off to the family. Her large brown eyes, chubby cheeks, and astonishing smile made her the most adorable image I had ever seen.

"Knock! Knock!" my mom said walking in through the front door. "Where's that birthday girl?" Dad stumbled in behind her carrying two large bags full of gifts.

I shook my head at the sight of all the gifts. "You guys are spoiling her," I said, walking into the room carrying Suzy, who was unaware that the goodies coming into the house were for her.

Todd rushed to relieve Dad of one of the bags. "Babe, where do you want the gifts?" Todd looked to me to direct him. "Set them on the table in the dining room." Before my dad could get his hands on Suzy to steal her away from me, Tara arrived through the door. Her concentration was clearly locked onto our little girl.

"Oh my! She's so beautiful." Tara rubbed Suzy's chunky little arm.

"She got big, didn't she?"

"I think she doubled in size since Christmas." She grabbed her little foot and admired the lilac-colored flowers on the little white dress shoes.

"You want to hold her?" I held her out in front of her.

"Oh, I don't know. She doesn't really know me, and—"

I placed her back on my hip to give my arms a rest. "Just take her—she won't break, I promise."

My eyebrows raised in anticipation, awaiting her response. "I know she won't break." She removed Suzy from my grip and transferred her to her hip. "She's lovely, isn't she?" Tara gasped as she readjusted her hold.

"She's perfect." I looked over Tara's shoulder at her friend. "You gonna introduce me to your friend?" I watched him looking around the room.

Tara spun around so we were standing side by side. "Sean, this is my sister Clara. Clara, this is Sean." His eyes shifted back and forth between the two of us before shaking his head. "Wow, you two really are identical." I looked to Tara with a smile as I realized we were both wearing blue shirts with our hair pulled back.

"It's nice to meet you, Sean." I extended my hand with a chuckle. His hand took mine into a firm shake.

"Yes, it's a pleasure to meet you as well."

Suzy's hand reached out toward Sean; he smiled proudly then took hold of her little fingers and kissed them. "It's an honor to be here for you too."

As he released her hand, Grandma Marsh slipped in between Sean and myself. "You think I can interrupt a moment and steal my great-granddaughter?" She removed Suzy from Tara's grip without waiting for an answer.

She looked back to Sean. "Hello, young man, I'm the grandmother. It's nice to meet you."

Without hesitation, Sean smiled with confidence. "Grandma Marsh, right? I've heard so much about you. All good things, of course." He extended his hand. She took hold for a shake.

"Of course." She winked. Releasing her grip, she readjusted her hold on Suzy, then walked away singing happy birthday wishes.

I watched Grandma join the rest of the family gathered around the couch. Suzy's little cheek was pressed onto her great-grandmother's shoulder. She looked so peaceful; her eyes shined a radiance of pride. My mind swarmed with my own memories of snuggling with that wonderfully sweet woman when I was little. My eyes swelled as my heart filled with an overwhelming gratitude that Suzy would be able to experience that same relationship that I had as a child.

Tara grabbed my arm. "I can't wait for you to see what I got Suzy, Sean helped me pick it out. Hey, are you okay?" Her words pulled my attention back to her and her guest.

"Yeah, I'm fine, little more emotional than usual. So Sean helped you pick out the gift, huh?" I looked back toward Sean to change the subject.

"I have five older siblings and a handful of nieces and nephews." He nodded with a half smile. His body shook unsteadily as he spoke. I could tell he was uneasy, only assuring me that he was totally into my lovely sister.

An uncontrollable smile accompanied my tingling insides as I could feel his admiration for her. I pulled Tara close. "I'm just happy you're here."

She gave me a tight squeeze. "I wouldn't have missed it." Her soft words only confirmed what I already knew.

"Hey, babe, you want to come here a minute?" Todd hollered from across the room. I smiled as my shaky legs carried me across the floor. "You ready?" he asked as I stood next to him. I nodded then took hold of his hand. We stood at the end of the dining room table. I looked out at the guests sitting in the living room who were now focused on us.

This had seemed the perfect time to break the news we had, but looking out at my sister's face, I was hesitant.

"All right, everyone!" Todd began the speech we had rehearsed. "We've been waiting to get you all together to deliver some news." I watched the faces before me brighten in anticipation for the words they knew would come next. My smile widened brightly as Tara winked. Their suspicions were confirmed as I nodded. "I'm pregnant."

The room filled with cheers of approval, causing my eyes to instantly flood with tears of joy.

"How long have you known?" Mom piped out through the crowd.

"I've known for six weeks. I'm about three months along." I stared out at the blank stares that expressed an array of mixed emotions. Tara broke the abrupt silence. "Congratulations on the news and for keeping the secret."

Chapter 12

Time to Reminisce

The party was a success. Suzy's room was full of new toys for her to play with, and our ears were overflowing with family stories, both new and old. With evening approaching, people were expressing their birthday wishes and farewells. As the house cleared, Tara and I started picking up the mountains of colorful gift wrap that had taken ownership of my living room.

"Hey, Gram! Did you forget something?" I asked as Grandma Marsh walked back inside.

"No. I sent your grandfather on home without me. Thought I'd help with the clean up." She fluffed a pillow on the couch.

"That's not necessary, Gram, we've got it." I cleaned the cake from Suzy's face.

"Oh, that's quite all right. I haven't seen much of you two in a while. I'd like to talk, much like we did when you were younger."

Tara put her arm around Grandma Marsh. "I'd like that."

I nodded in agreement with Tara. "Let me get Suzy down to bed, and I'll join you in the kitchen."

Putting my exhausted child down to bed was easy. She was so worn out from her busy day;she curled up with her blanket and closed her eyes without a single fuss. Her head never left her pillow as I escaped silently out her door.

Happy to have some help with the aftermath of the party, I entered the kitchen, ready to tackle the dishes piled in the sink. "I'll do these if you guys want to just pick up the rest of the wrapping paper off the floor." I turned on the water to fill the sink. "Or you could just come and sit for a minute. We'll get things cleaned up. But first, come here. Sit down and relax." Grandma pulled a chair out at the dining table then sat in the one next to it.

"We better do as she says." Tara took a seat at the table across from grandma.

"Yes, listen to this old, wise woman. Now come and take a seat." She smiled as she patted the table softly in front of the vacant chair at the head of the table.

I surrendered to the convincing invite, turned off the water, and took a seat in the chair that had been pulled out for me. My eyes wandered over the paper and toys that now covered the floor throughout my house. "Where did the guys go?" Grandma asked, pulling my attention away from the mess and back to her.

"Todd had to go get some things set up for the tournament in the morning at his dojo. Sean went with him." I scooted my chair closer to the table.

"Great, then we have time to talk." Feelings of concern invaded my body as her voice took a more serious tone.

"What's on your mind? I'm not in trouble for not calling, am I?" Tara chuckled.

"Well, that is a topic we will discuss at a later date. Today, I want to talk about the babies."

"I'm sorry, I've been meaning to come over with Suzy, I've just been busy and very tired. Very, very tired," I quickly apologized.

"I understand all of that, but that is not what I mean. I want to know how this arrangement you've set up is working."

Her words grabbed a hold of my attention and my heart and squeezed them firmly. We had never told her about the switch; my mind scrambled to recover any loose ends I may have left. My eyes took to Tara as I prayed Grandma was referring to something unrelated. I was shifting nervously in my seat. I could feel my face tingle as I was sure the color was leaving rapidly to match the pale white coloring of Tara's. I felt like a scared little girl about to face her worst fear.

"W-what arrangement?" Tara stuttered.

"By the looks on your faces, I'm sure you know what I'm referring to. Don't worry, I haven't told anyone else. I'm not here to judge. I simply want to know how it's been working and if you still think your plan was the right thing for Suzy?"

My voice was trapped behind a knot that had formed in my throat. My body froze, as the faces before me became hazy.

"You know?" Tara's voice entered my ears in a muffled tone. "But who told you?" Tara spoke the question that was playing loudly in my mind. I could feel my eyebrows move closer together as I pulled myself together in anticipation for an answer.

"No one told me. I figured it out all on my own. I know you girls better than you know yourselves. I could read it on Tara's face from the beginning. I don't know the details, and I don't need to. I just need to know that there are no regrets."

Color was returning to my face, and I felt I could swallow again. I looked to Tara, curious to hear her response. "No regrets, Grandma. Clara has been able to provide Suzy with far more than I ever could have. And now she'll have a little brother or sister to play with." She paused as her eyes filled with tears. "I couldn't be happier." I reached over and took her by the hand.

"Can I assume those are tears of joy?" Grandma's face was serious and contained no smile.

Tara nodded. "Yes. Ninety-five percent of these tears are of joy. Only a small portion of them are dedicated to the sadness that I couldn't have been the one to do this for her. Not a day goes by that I don't wonder how things could have been under different circumstances. But I stand by my decision with no regrets." She wiped her eyes dry with a lavender-colored napkin.

"How about you, Clara? Now that you are having a child of your own, how do you feel about the whole thing?" Grandma was concentrating on me.

"My only regret is that I didn't get to experience the pregnancy with Suzy. Now I get to see what I missed out on. I love Suzy with all my heart; I have had an attachment to her since the first time I strapped on that fake foam belly. Nothing could ever change that. Not a moment goes by that I don't look at her and think about how lucky I am to have and love her as my own. No regrets—I never could have handled it if she were given up for adoption. I just can't imagine someone else raising her. She belongs in our family. No one could love her like we do."

I could feel the warmth of color returning back to my cheeks, and I felt I could swallow again. Grandma Marsh hung onto my every word, and as I spoke my final word, she instantly jumped in with her concern. "I understand. I just wanted to check in with you and make sure everything was still all right."

I paused briefly before asking my own question. "Why didn't you tell us from the beginning that you knew?"

The corners of her mouth rose and she nodded her head briefly as if she were waiting for the question. "I wanted to see if you'd come to me. I knew if you wanted my help, you would ask. When I realized that you guys were able to take care of it yourself, I decided to stay close and catch you if you fell."

Unable to find words to reply, I paused. Tara sat up tall in her seat and proudly answered, "But it worked. I mean we were actually able to get out of a situation without having to run to you. This is the first time we didn't need you to pick up the pieces of our dilemma, and it felt great." I nodded in agreement.

"True. You did it all on your own. Though I honestly don't know that I can say I approve of the plan you worked out. But I do understand why you did it. I love you girls, and I don't have to approve of what you did or what you are doing in order to support you. I have your backs no matter what. Now with that being said, my next question is about Suzy. You ever plan on telling her?"

That question had overwhelmed my thoughts many times, and as Tara answered with a simply response, I chuckled silently as I had uttered those same words. "We will cross that bridge when we get to it."

I nodded and then finished her sentence, "I think she has the right to know, but we'll wait until she's older."

Tara got up from her seat. "Yes, much older," she said before going to the kitchen. Grandma Marsh watched Tara grab a soda from the fridge. "I wanted to tell you many times, Gram. I hate to keep secrets from you. It just seemed best to not tell anyone." I grabbed her hand.

She looked back to me with a smile. "I feel much better. It sounds like all is well. I wish we could have had this talk in the beginning. But what's done is done, and I will stand by your side in support. I just want you both to know you can always come to me about anything. I love you and shall not judge."

I knew her words were genuine, and it reminded me of the inspiring talks we'd had when Tara and I were little girls.

"Gram, you're the best. I really miss these talks."

She rested her other hand on top of mine. "Me too, sweetie. But you know I'm always just a phone call away. Now what do you say we get this place cleaned up?"

I pulled my hand out from between hers. "I will definitely take you up on that offer, and I will make a point to call more often." I stood up, opening my arms to seal the deal.

With the extra hands there to assist, the mess was cleaned up in no time at all. We were picking up the last of the wrapping paper on the floor when Todd and Sean returned. "Looks like I timed that just right." Todd closed the door as Sean entered.

"Yes, I should say that was perfect timing." I handed him the black garbage bag I had just tied.

Todd's smile reversed to a frown as he grabbed the bag. "Oh, here let me get that for you, dear." Todd's movements showed less enthusiasm than his comment suggested. His shoulders shrugged low as he carried the bag toward the back door. Grandma smiled as she watched Todd leave the room in nearly a pout.

"So, Tara, where did you and Sean meet?" Grandma asked as she took a seat on the couch near Sean. Tara stood before her by my side with pink-colored cheeks. "School," Tara answered bluntly.

Grandma waited to hear the remainder of the story, but when nothing more was said, she pried a little deeper. "I assumed that much. I want to hear the story."

I laughed as Tara squirmed a little to the request.

"What are *you* laughing at?" Tara smiled uncomfortably.

"Aren't you gonna answer the question? No sense in being rude." I contained my laughter while avoiding her piercing stare.

"There really isn't much to tell. We take a few classes together, end of story." Her eyes never left mine in an attempt to get me to change the subject. A look I've seen many times, although this time I wasn't about to help her out.

"The truth is"—Sean came to her rescue—"I was a thorn in Tara's side. I've been pestering her since the first time I saw her in my English lit class. She avoided me like the plague, shooting down my every attempt to take her out. Luckily I'm a persistent guy, and I was able to wear her down."

Our attention shifted back to Tara, who was turning a deeper shade of red. "So he wore you down, did he?" I chuckled.

Tara shook her head as Sean continued with his story. "The first date was a pity date." He stood up and walked to Tara. "Wait, she won't let me call them dates, they were get-togethers. Either way, they were a good start. She only said yes to get me to stop bugging her." I looked to my sister to see her nodding in agreement.

"Well, since he's here with you today meeting your family, my guess would be that it must have been a pretty good date—or I mean get-together." Grandma looked to Tara with a smile.

"Something like that. I discovered we had a lot in common, and he just kinda grew on me."

Sean's eyes widened and he crossed his arms. "Oh, is that what happened?"

Tara nodded. "Yeah. Pretty much. He's my best friend. That's why he's here." Sean grabbed her hand.

The glimmer in her eyes warmed my heart. I could see there was so much more there between them than an amazing friendship, and I was truly happy for them both. "All I can say is, you better treat her well or there will be hell to pay." I winked at Tara as I delivered my message to Sean.

"That is one thing about twins, son, you're getting a package deal." Grandma was pointing at me.

Sean laughed. "I know. I've been warned. And I completely understand."

Tara wrapped her arm around him. "He has a twin sister." My head tilted as I waited to hear about his sister. "Her name is Dawn. She's my best friend." With those words, I felt the connection that Tara must feel. I was confident he was perfect for her, and I gave her a wink of approval.

As we shared our secret moment, the sounds of Suzy's cries swirled down the hallway and settled between our gaze. Her alarm pulled me away to answer the call. Tara followed me to get Suzy up. I pushed open the door, and the cries stopped instantly. "I like him, he seems nice." I approached the crib to remove Suzy.

"He really is." She looked back toward the door. "Think I should have left him alone out there with Todd and Grandma?"

I lifted Suzy from her bed. "He'll be fine."

I looked into Suzy's droopy eyes then kissed her softly on the forehead. "Sweetie, you're warm. Tara, can you grab the ear thermometer out of that top drawer, please?" I pointed to the dresser by the door.

"Clara, is she all right?" Tara's voice was shaky.

"She's fine, just get the thermometer." I laid her on the changing table and removed her shirt to help cool her down.

"Here." Tara handed over the thermometer.

As the unit beeped, indicating it was done, I read the temperature aloud. "One hundred and one." The face of the nervous auntie flushed its color. Her eyes pierced mine with a sense of helplessness. "She'll be fine, can you go get a washcloth and wet it with cold water?" I barely finished my request and she was running from the room to assist.

Suzy's skin was warm, her face pale, and her eyelids were heavy. She lifted her body slowly to a seating position on the changer, her bottom lip drooping in a heart-jerking pout. "We'll get you better, honey, come on." She wrapped her arms around my neck as I scooped her up. Her hot cheek pressed up against mine as I carried her down the hall. "Here, I'm gonna get her some medicine." I handed her over to Tara, who was stepping out of the bathroom with the wet rag.

"Take her? But I don't know what to do." Tara took hold of Suzy.

"Just sit with her on the couch, rub her forehead and cheeks with the rag. I'll only be a minute. You'll be fine."

When I returned to Suzy with the fever reducer, her little fingers were wrapped around Tara's finger with the cold washcloth soothing her. Using the eyedropper, I gave her a dose of the cherry-flavored medicine.

"Now what?" Tara continued to rub the sad face with the cool rag.

"We wait and see if the fever drops. She's working on getting some molars, the fever is probably just from that."

After an hour, I took her temperature again. We were all relieved to see that the temperature had dropped a few degrees.

"Good job, Clara. Thanks." Tara stared at the double digits that now read on the screen of the thermometer.

"Thanks?" Sean chuckled.

"Yeah. I, uh, I was thanking her for settling this auntie's poor heart. I was a bit worried." Tara tripped over her words to cover herself quickly.

"You'd have done the same. You will make a great mom someday, I'm sure." Sean grabbed her hand.

"You bet she will," I agreed with Sean as Tara laughed a shaky, nervous laugh.

Todd returned from taking Grandma home. "How's the patient?" Todd closed the door.

"She's fine. Fever is down, and the spirit is returning to her eyes." I sat Suzy up on Tara's lap.

"Da-da!" Suzy's arms extended toward Todd as he neared the couch. "Sounds like she's fine." He answered her call and picked her up.

"Won't be long and there will be two little ones asking for your attention," Tara said as we watched Todd snuggle his little princess with his large arms, making Suzy look so tiny.

"I'm ready. Maybe this time we'll get a boy. And we'll have one of each." He looked at me with a smile.

"We'll be happy with whatever we are blessed with. Whether it's a boy, a girl, or a baby elephant." My eyes pierced his as I pressed my opinion.

Todd looked at me with a smile. "Actually a baby elephant would be kinda cool, let's go for that."

Chapter 13

Make Room for One More

The weekend came to an end far too quickly, and I found myself saying good-bye to my sister yet again. The farewell was bittersweet. I hated to see her go, yet it was nice to get back to a routine. As excited as I was to open my home to everyone to celebrate with Suzy, I was even more excited to have the event come to an end.

I was getting more sleepy than usual and looked forward to some quiet time. The house was cleared of all guests, and life was back to normal. Or rather, the new normal of morning sickness and the occasional power nap. It was a nice relief to have the news delivered; it was getting harder and harder to keep it a secret. Now that the family knew about the baby, it was time to let everyone at work know as well. A task I planned to do first thing tomorrow morning. But for now, my eyes were begging for a rest. Suzy was down for a nap, and Todd was washing the car. So I surrendered to the couch that was calling my name.

When my eyes finally opened, they were focused on Todd and Suzy playing with her new ponies on the living room floor. "Why didn't you wake me?" I rubbed the sleep from my eyes.

"I figured you needed the rest." His eyes widened as Suzy handed him a small pink brush for his pony. Seeing them together tugged at my emotions, emotions of contentment. He'd been a remarkable father to Suzy, and I knew the new addition to the family was only going to make our home even more complete.

Although it was nice to see Tara was finding a relationship in her newfound friend. I was feeling guilty about having the perfect family. Things were going just as planned for her, and she seemed satisfied, yet I felt like I was robbing her of true happiness.

"You okay?" My attention was redirected to the caring eyes of Todd.

"Perfect." I smiled.

Todd dropped onto his hands and knees and crawled over to me at the couch and laid his head on the cushion near my belly. "I'll agree. You are perfect."

I puckered my lips and prepared for a kiss.

"Mmm, an invitation I can't pass up." His lips met mine. "Will you be telling everyone at work tomorrow?" His fingers ran through my hair.

"Yes. I'm ready to scream it out to the world now." I nodded.

He placed his hands on either side of my face in a soft caress. "I don't think you'll have to scream." His voice was hushed.

The phone rang, and Todd jumped to answer it. "Hello? Yeah, she's right here." He handed me the phone with a quirky smile that told me I may want to avoid this call.

"Hello," I answered.

"Clara, it's Belle. Sorry we missed your little party. Just wanted to call and let you know we got Suzette a savings bond for two hundred dollars, we will be sending it in the mail." Her voice was as stern as usual.

"That's great, I'll be sure to watch for it. I'm sorry you missed the party too. You missed an announcement that Todd and I made." I sat up to get comfortable.

"Really? What? Are you pregnant?"

"Yes. I'm about three months." I bit my lip.

"Boy, you guys don't waste any time, do you?" Her voice held a hint of irritation.

"My due date is October 15. We're very excited to be expanding our family." I looked to Todd, who was trying to hear what she was saying.

"That's just great. Two is plenty though, don't you think?"

"Two of each is our plan. I'd like a house full of kids, at least four." I smiled as Todd's mouth dropped.

"That's absurd. That's just not at all wise in this day and age. I'm not at all interested in carrying on with this conversation."

"Thanks, Grandma, I'll be sure to call and let you know when the bond arrives." I turned off the phone as there was already silence on the other end.

"What was that all about?" Todd took the phone and hung it up.

"Oh, just Belle being Belle, and me giving her a taste of her own medicine." I rubbed my belly as the nausea started in.

"I knew something had to be up when you called her Grandma." He sat next to me.

"Yeah, I think she hung up on me." I smiled with pride.

"You bitch, you," Todd laughed.

"I know and it felt great." I grabbed a cracker from the table.

"You're looking pale, you okay?" Todd's face studied mine.

"Not sure." I sat still, waiting for my body to tell me if I needed to run for the bathroom or not. It wasn't long, and it became obvious that I needed to jump to my feet and make a sprint for the toilet.

My body was in a whirlwind of changes, some more manageable than others. Each day presented me with something new that would send me running to my *Expecting Bible* to help me determine if my newfound symptom was part of a normal pregnancy or not. My body was trying out every possible symptom, from fatigue to nausea and everything in between. The "morning" sickness made its visit at all times of the day, and I never knew what would bring on the next round of it. I have to admit though, the episodes of sickness were certainly making it difficult to keep my eyes on the prize.

The next morning, I arrived at work and made my announcement with no need for screaming.

"We know," Sonya replied in response for the whole crew.

"How did you know?" I was thrown off by their reaction.

"Seriously? You've had the stomach flu for the last two months. You're dragging your feet at the end of the day. And you've been eating chili cheese corn chips with macaroni and cheese for lunch every day for the last month. We knew. We've just been waiting for you to confirm," Sonya explained as everyone behind her nodded their heads in agreement. The room full of smiles was reassuring that the news would not be bringing the same ill effect that my last announcement had created.

"Congratulations, Clara. Now let's get back to work, guys!" Kathy's words sent the crew scrambling back to their desks, including myself. I was surprised and somewhat disappointed that everyone already knew. Nonetheless, the effect was still comforting. Knowing that the cat was out of the bag lifted the heavy cloud from my shoulders.

In the weeks to follow, I found it necessary to keep soda crackers on hand to curb the nausea and hunger that I was constantly battling throughout the day. Fortunately the atmosphere in the workplace was a more pleasant experience than in the months during the pregnancy of Suzy. Of course with Patsy officially gone, being at work was more enjoyable for everyone.

By the time the date arrived for my twentieth week ultrasound, I was on edge. "So what time is your doctor's appointment today?" Trevor helped himself to a pile of papers on the corner of the desk.

"It's at noon—why, are you in on the baby pool?" I logged into the computer to check my e-mails.

"Yeah, I've got my money on it being a boy. You'll find out today, right?" Trevor sat down at Patsy's old desk, where he'd been assigned to work after Patsy was let go.

"As long as baby is positioned right, I should know around noon today what's been bouncing on the bladder all this time." I opened my drawer to pull out my soda crackers.

"You gotta call and let us all know as soon as you find out," he insisted. I nodded, knowing that I would be anxious to share with the world the news the moment I got the word.

I tried desperately to get some work done. As I looked through the day's agenda, my eyes migrated toward the clock on the wall. It seemed as if time was set on slow motion as I anticipated the upcoming appointment. I barely made a mark on my daily list by the time the hands on the clock lined up where I wanted them.

I left my office with a smile and a bounce in my step. I barely said a word to anyone as I kept my eye on clocking out and meeting up with Todd. I rushed out the door and in to my car. Barely recalling the drive to the doctor's office, my mind was jumbled with pictures of my life with the new baby.

Todd was waiting for me at the front door of the clinic. "You ready, sweets?" He placed his arm around me.

"That's a silly question." I laughed as I pushed open the door. The plush furniture in the waiting room was occupied by a handful of expectant mothers. After checking in, I took a seat with Todd at one of the vacant blue sofas that sat back to back in the middle of the floor. I handed him a *Men's Health* magazine and then admired the massive belly on the otherwise small-framed body sitting across from me.

"I'm two weeks over my due date." The lady rubbed the pink shirt that covered tightly over her belly then sighed. "How far along are you?" she asked as she looked at my green sweater that showed the small mound beneath it.

"Five months." I pulled my sweater tight to show the baby bump.

"Wow. You're large for five months, you must be having a very healthy baby."

"We hope so," Todd said as he put his magazine down and exchanged it for a new one.

A nurse entered the waiting room wearing scrubs decorated with Mickey Mouse and carrying a bright purple clipboard. "Kathy Warren." The overdue lady sighed once again as she struggled to her feet. "That's me." She waddled across the floor with her hands supporting her back with each step. We continued to sit and wait as more women walked in and others were called back.

After waiting over an hour, our time finally arrived. "Clara Rivers." I grabbed Todd's hand and pulled him along to follow the nurse to the exam room. "Go ahead and step up on the scale." She pointed to where she needed me. Handing over my purse to Todd, I stepped up onto the platform to be weighed. "Looks like you've gained ten pounds since your last visit." She extended her hand to help me from the scale.

"Is that normal?" I sat at the end of the paper-covered table. "When it comes to pregnancies and babies, the norm hits in a wide range. But yes, you're doing well."

Todd sat in a chair up against the wall. He placed my purse on the floor under his seat while the nurse took my blood pressure. "All right, go ahead and get comfortable, and the doctor will be in shortly." As I watched the nurse close the door behind her, Todd stared at the charts of breast growth during pregnancy that decorated the wall. After a few minutes, Dr. Morgan entered the room. She was a tall, slender middle-aged lady wearing a long white doctor's coat. Her hair was as yellow as straw and worn in a braid that extended down to the middle of her back.

"Hello, Clara, how have you been feeling?" Dr. Morgan thumbed through the medical chart then looked up to make eye contact.

"I'm still nauseous in the morning but feeling better than I did in the beginning," I answered as she made her notes in my chart.

"The nausea should start to subside even more from here on. Go ahead and lie back, and we'll see what the little one is up to."

I did as instructed, and Todd joined me, standing by my side. As my fingers interlocked with his, Dr. Morgan prepared the ultrasound unit. "All right, let's see that belly. We'll get some measurements, and then we'll take a look at Baby." Without hesitation, I helped to pull up my shirt, exposing my belly. A cloth measuring tape was placed at the top of my abdomen and stretched across my belly button. Once the doctor had the number she was seeking, she wrote it down. "You're growing nicely and well above average. So now let's see how Baby looks." She grabbed a bottle of lube from the warmer and smeared some onto my belly.

The doctor glided her hand wand over the designated area she had created on my skin with the slippery gel. Within moments, a vision appeared on the screen and an unusual series of heartbeats were heard. "Oh my, that is a surprise." Dr. Morgan smiled. I stared at the screen to discover her findings.

"Twins?" Todd asked before I could respond to the vision of two beating hearts before me.

"Yep, identical twins. I can tell you what you're having if you're still interested?" She smiled.

"Yes." I squeezed Todd's hand.

"You're having two little boys."

"Yes!" Todd stuck his hand out for a high five.

"I'm happy you're happy. There's no turning back now." Dr. Morgan connected her hand to his. Still watching my boys on the screen, I pondered the reality of twins. We had spoken of the possibility on numerous occasions, but to see it as a reality stirred emotions of excitement and overwhelming fear.

"You're all right with there being two of them?"

I looked to Todd. "You bet, now I'm no longer outnumbered by the girls in the house."

The goop was cleaned from my belly, and I was allowed to sit back up.

"There are risks associated with having twins, and so I will want to see you more often. Other than that, everything looks pretty good. Keep up on the vitamins I gave you, and get plenty of rest. Do you have any questions for me?" She sat back and waited for my response.

"If I did, I forgot them the moment you said 'two of them'. I'm sure once I leave here, I'll think of a whole list. But right now, I have nothing." I shrugged.

"That's all right. If you come up with anything, just write it down and bring them with you next time. I want to see you in two weeks, make an appointment with the receptionist out front before you leave." She stood up.

"I will, thanks." I slid off the table.

"Congratulations on the twins, and see you in two weeks." She opened the door and left the room.

Todd left the clinic and headed back to the studio as I sat in my car in the parking lot debating whether I should go back to work or go home. I pulled my cellphone from my purse and dialed.

"So spill it," Sonya answered.

"You want to know what I'm having?" I laughed.

"Well, yeah!" She said before yelling to the others in the background that she had me on the phone.

"I'm having boys."

"It's a boy! Wait, did you say *boys*?" Her tone dropped from the first initial scream. "Yes. I'm having twin boys, and I think I'm gonna take the remainder of the day off and get some rest." I started the car.

"I'm sure that will be fine. I'll see you in the morning."

I put the phone back in my purse and headed for the house. My mind was rushing with the list of items I needed for the babies' room—times two. Earlier in the day, I had felt confident that I was prepared for our new addition. But now I was overwhelmed with the mental list I had created. I rushed home and called my comforter.

"Hey, sis." I plopped onto the couch, kicking my feet up onto the coffee table.

"Hello. Did you have your appointment?" Her voice rose with excitement from the other end of the receiver.

"I just got home." I said with a yawn as my body begged for a nap.

"What did you find out!" she asked.

"I'm having twin boys." I rubbed my belly as I waited for her reaction.

"Cool, have you thought about any names yet?" she responded without hesitation.

"Haven't gotten that far yet. I've been stressing about all the extra stuff I'll need for two babies. I hadn't really planned on their being two in there." I stared toward the guest room that I'd planned on turning into the nursery.

"Don't stress, you'll be fine. Everything will work out. Besides, that's what baby showers are for."

I nodded but couldn't find words to respond. I knew she was right; she always was. My mind and body were just too overtired to comprehend the reality of it just yet.

"Karson, with a *K*," she said as my mind wandered.

"What?" My attention was brought back to the conversation.

"For a boy name, I think one of my nephews should be named Karson."

"I do like that. I'll have to see if I can find another *K* name." I melted into the cushions of the couch.

"I've gotta go, sis. I'll call you later this week." Tara brought the conversation to an end.

As I hung up the phone, my eyelids grew too heavy to keep them open any longer. I cuddled up on the couch and continued with the nap that I desperately needed. My body was no longer in my control; the two little lives within me were now calculating my movements and schedule. They were making it obvious that I was in need of more sleep.

My eyes opened when Suzy climbed up onto the couch next to me. I wrapped my arm around her and looked up at my mom, who was standing over me. "I'm sorry, I was gonna come over after I got my nap." I sat up, forcing my body to follow the lead of my waking eyes.

"No problem, honey. I called your work to see what you found out, and they said you were home." She sat down on the couch.

"Did they tell you anything?" I asked as I set Suzy down on the ground.

"No, I asked, but they thought you should be the one to tell me. So what did you find out?"

I watched Suzy play with some toys she found under the coffee table then looked back to Mom with my answer. "It appears that Suzy will have a little brother to play with. In fact, she's going to have two."

I watched her facial expression; her smile of anticipation vanished as her mouth dropped in shock. "Twins." She grabbed my hand. "I remember when I found out I was pregnant with you and your sister. I was terrified and excited. I didn't really know how to feel. But I can tell you now that it is very rewarding and an amazing experience. And however cliché this sounds, it's true. Everything will work out."

A tear rolled down my cheek as she summed up everything I was feeling perfectly. She understood me so well; I was so proud to call her Mom. Her wink tugged at my heart as I was overwhelmed with respect for her. "You always know exactly what to say. I love you." I squeezed her hand, hoping that I could be at least half the mom she was to me for my own kids.

"Well, I'm going to need some extra clothes for Suzy, I want to keep her overnight. You can just get her tomorrow after work." She stood up.

"Oh, you don't have to keep her. Todd will be home soon. I feel better after that little nap." I said with a yawn.

"That's not why I want her, I know you're fine. I invited Cyra and Mindy over tonight for some cheesecake. I'm sure Mitch and Ken will be drinking beer with your dad out on the patio. Thought it would be fun to have the little princess there. Show her off a little," she explained as she walked down the hall toward Suzy's room.

I followed close behind her. "That will be fine, just make sure she gets down at a decent time. If she goes down too tired, she won't sleep well, and she'll have you up all night." I grabbed the diaper bag from the closet.

"I've done this before, dear. We'll be fine." She opened the top drawer and removed a lavender pair of pajamas.

"I know. I can't help it, the mothering just comes involuntarily." I smiled as I stuffed the bag with extra clothes and diapers.

"Yes, I've raised you well."

There was truth to those words for sure. She had raised me to know right from wrong and how to stand up for what I believed in. Only it was I who had to decipher what to do when those two paths decided to become one. No doubt she disagreed with the decision in the beginning, but to see her eager to show off my prize for humoring a "wrong" while standing up for what I believed in brought joy to my heart as it displayed her approval now.

Chapter 14

A Christmas to Remember

The tree was decorated with silver and various shades of blues. Lights covered the spruce sprigs that decorated the doorways. Beautifully wrapped presents lined the tree's snowflake-covered skirt. The women were setting the table with Christmas dinner and Mom's finest dishes as the men watched the television, a normal holiday tradition that Mom looked forward to from one festive event to the next. Belle and Grandfather Matthews spent the winter in their home in the Bahamas, making Thanksgiving and Christmas among Mom's favorite holidays for family get-togethers.

This would be the first Christmas for the newest family members. The parents' house filled fast with relatives eager to see the twins.

"They are adorable, Clara, what are their names again?" my cousin, Anna asked as she pulled down the blanket to see the quietly sleeping duo.

"Karson and Kolton." I felt like a recording as I announced their names for the twentieth time that day.

"Your sister is sure a great aunt. She's doing a great job entertaining your other little one." Anna pointed toward the two of them sitting on the floor staring at the gifts from a distance. Suzy and Tara had a great relationship, and it made me proud to have been able to provide that opportunity.

"They look like a great pair. What do you want to bet they are guessing what's inside those boxes?" Sean said as he sat next to me on the couch.

"Aw, you know my sister well." I chuckled.

"I'd like to think so. I'd also like to devote the rest of my years to learning everything about her." He focused on Tara with a glow that screamed out his deep feelings for her.

"So does that mean what I think it means?" I slowly rocked the bassinet to hush the subtle fuse of Karson as he began to wake from his nap.

"That would depend on whether or not you give me your blessing." He turned his attention to me.

"*My* blessing? Don't you generally seek the blessing of the father?" I scooped Karson up as he began to increase his volume.

"Yes, but being a twin, I know that she would only say yes if she had your approval. So before I lay my heart out on the table for her, I want to know that I'm not risking it getting squashed. If you don't approve of me, let me know now. I'm a big boy, and I cherish your honest opinion." His hands shook as they grasped his leg.

"I value your understanding about the close relationship I have with my sister. I'm honored that you came to me for a blessing. And I'll be honest—I have never seen my sister so happy. I can tell by the way you two look at each other that you guys have feelings that run deep. I would never step in between true love. I give you my approval, my blessing, and I'd be honored to have you as my brother. I'd welcome you into the family with open arms." I rocked Karson in my arms; soon he reduced his squeals and began to admire the twinkling lights behind me.

"That means a lot to me, sis."

"Did you need me to prepare a bottle for Little Man?" Todd looked over my shoulder to see the rare view of the open eyes of his son.

I looked at my watch. "Might as well, get two ready. Kolton will be waking in about fifteen minutes wanting to eat." I admired Karson's big blue eyes as he stared in a daze at the view behind me.

"Yeah, and he has no patience when it comes to his food." Todd kissed the top of my head before walking away to prepare the bottles.

"All right, dinner's on the table!" Mom yelled from the dining room. The guys wasted no time rushing to their seats surrounding the food. As everyone joined around the table, Kolton filled the house with his own demand for dinner; which signaled Karson to sound his alarm as well. I quickly tried to soothe both screaming babies as I waited for Todd to return with their bottles. As I rocked the bassinet with my foot and bounced Karson in my arms, Sean arrived back by my side. He scooped Kolton out of the bassinet and proceeded to walk around the room with him. My mind wondered if he was playing the "wonderful uncle" role or if he was practicing to be a wonderful dad.

As the cries reached an intense volume of ear-piercing heights, Todd arrived with the bottles. "Thanks, man, I'll take him from here." He relieved Sean of the whimpering child.

"No problem." Sean walked back to the dining room table. Todd joined me on the couch. I coaxed the bottle into Kolton's mouth and rested my head on Todd's shoulder.

"Love you," Todd said as he pressed his cheek against my head.

"I love us."

By the time the boys were fed, burped, changed, and resting soundly in their bassinet again, almost everyone had finished eating. They were sharing stores of past holidays as we took our seats at the table. I wasted no time and loaded my plate with samples of everything before me. Just as I prepared to taste the ham I had on my fork, Sean pushed his seat away from the table and stood up. I sat back and waited to hear his proposal.

Sean cleared his throat, bringing all eyes in his direction. "I'd like to take this time to say thanks. I realize that is more of a Thanksgiving request than a Christmas Eve tradition, but nonetheless my words of thanks are in order. I'd like to start by saying thank you, Ms. Matthews, for inviting me to your wonderful home for a great holiday dinner. Clara, thank you for our earlier talk and your words of honesty, and Tara,"—he looked down at her and took her hand—"thank you for everything. You are my inspiration. You are the reason I get up in the morning. I love you, I'm thankful to have you by my side. I vow to devote the rest of my life making you as happy as I am, if you would do me the honor of becoming my wife." He reached into his pocket and pulled out a little black ring box. As he opened it, she looked to me with wide eyes that were desperate for approval. With a smile, I nodded.

Tara leaped from her seat and into his arms. "Yes!" With the happy couple hanging on tight to each other, family members jumped up with cheers and words of congratulations. I sat back and let them enjoy the moment. I took a bite of my ham and refocused my attention to the living room as the commotion woke the boys. I pushed my seat away from the table.

"No, no, dear, I got this." Grandma Marsh patted me on the shoulder.

"Are you sure?" I watched her nod and walk away toward the increasing squalls of my boys.

As she rocked them in the bassinet, she sang them a lullaby. Soon the cries were replaced with the subtle softness of Grandma's song. While the little ones were being tended to, I quickly shoveled in the delicious food from my plate.

"Slow down, Dear." Mom stood over me. "They are in good hands, just eat and relax. You have plenty of family here that are eager to help." She placed her hand on my shoulder.

"I know." I continued to eat dinner. "Just makes me feel guilty."

"Don't be silly. Look at your sister. Doesn't she look happy?" We watched Sean place the ring on her finger.

"They are perfect. I'm happy for them both." I loaded my fork with mashed potatoes.

"They are perfect. I just hope Sean doesn't disappoint me," Mom said as she stared at Sean with stern eyes.

"I think he'll be fine. But if he turns out to be a bad apple, I've got your back. I'll help you set him straight." I placed my hand in hers.

Mom laughed. "I don't doubt that."

The room grew quiet again as Grandma's soothing song put the boys back to sleep. "See, the babies are fine." Mom squeezed my shoulder before walking to the living room to join the rest of the family that were admiring the rock on Tara's finger. Todd and I took the opportunity to finish eating. "That was nice of him to mention you in his speech of proposal. He sure knows how to earn the brownie points, doesn't he?"

Todd pushed his plate aside. "Yeah, he knows how to play the game, huh? That's all right, though, I like him. I think they are ideal for each other."

I rested my hand on my stomach as I began to wonder if I had eaten too much. "Yeah, he's all right. He definitely has a lot of respect for your sister. She's all he ever talks about." He looked down to see Suzy trying to climb up into his lap.

Suzy joined us at the table. Tara gradually broke herself away from the crowd, making her way toward us. I pushed my chair away from the table. "All right, my turn. Let me see it." I extended my hand out to take hers, to admire her ring.

"It's beautiful, isn't it? He did a great job." Tara's hand shook inside mine as she beamed with excitement. I barely noticed the sparkling rock on her finger; I was too busy admiring the sparkle in her eyes.

I stood up and wrapped my arms around her in a congratulatory embrace. "I'm so happy for you."

She pushed me out in front of her. "You'll be my maid of honor and help me plan the wedding, right?"

"Of course, that goes without saying." I pulled her in for another hug.

"All right, why don't you share your sister with the rest of the family?" Dad's presence stood over us. His forehead crinkled with a look of concern, yet his smile appeared to be sincere.

His face was covered with a multitude of emotions. His sad puppy eyes begged for some attention from his little girls who had grown and left him behind. We pulled him into our huddle. "I love you, Dad," Tara comforted him.

"I love you, guys. I'm proud of the women you have become." His eyes swelled and he quickly released his hold to break away from the ocean of feelings that were about to crest over him.

"He's handling it better than I thought he would," I laughed, watching him mope off toward the kitchen.

"I think I'll go talk to him." Tara squeezed my arm as she past by me to catch up to Dad. The couch was surrounded by family admiring the sleeping duo. Suzy and Sean were sitting on the floor playing with building blocks. Mom was sitting at the dining room table looking out at the same scene I was.

"This is what the holidays are all about." I took the seat next to Mom.

"This is my most favorite Christmas Eve feast yet. Thank you guys for such a great day." She grabbed my hand.

"Thank you for putting together such a great meal. You did a great job. I just wish I could have helped out more."

"Don't be silly, you have plenty to do with your busy family. Look at that." She pointed toward Sean and Suzy playing on the floor. "You thinking what I am?" she asked.

"I'm sure I am. I wonder if she'll ever tell him." My muscles knotted at the thought.

"Only time will tell, honey."

She was definitely right. I just wasn't sure if I wanted to fast-forward time to get it over with or pause it to assure that day would never come. Either way it was out of my control, and as Mom said, "Only time would tell."

"Clara, did you want to help assist in the diaper changes?" Todd's hands warmed my body as he rested them on my shoulders.

"Not really, but I would love a shoulder massage." I dropped my head forward in hopes he'd respond to my request.

Unfortunately he only squeezed them a couple of times then released his grip. "That's it, huh?" I looked back at him.

"Yes, for now that's all you get." He smiled as he pulled my chair out, a gesture to direct me toward the messy diapers, I was sure.

"I'll help with the cleanup after I tend to the dirty deeds of motherhood," I said as I followed Todd's lead.

My intentions were sincere when I said I would help with cleanup. I had every intention of making it to the kitchen to lend my assistance to the dishes or whatever job Grandma Marsh would find for me. But after tending to the boys' diapers and getting them back to sleep, Suzy insisted on having some mommy time.

I was more than happy to take advantage of the houseful of people to watch over the boys while Suzy and I had some time together. "What would you like to do, sweetie?" I adjusted her hair ribbons as she sat on my lap.

"Outside, Mommy." She climbed down from my lap and pointed to the window.

"We better get our coats." I watched her face brighten with delight. I barely finished my sentence and she was running for her shoes by the door.

I bundled her up in her furry pink coat and escorted her out to the front yard. With her tiny little hand in mine, we entered the cold breeze that was swirling gently around us. She pulled me down the path and sat at the end of the sidewalk. "Mommy, sit." A request I wouldn't deny—I sat on the edge of the walk next to the cutest little two-year-old I knew.

"So what do you think, Suzy?" I watched her play with a couple leaves from the driveway.

"Here, Mommy." She handed me one of her leaves.

"Thanks, sweetie, what are we playing?" I wrapped the long narrow leaf around my finger like a ring.

"Fower for you." She gathered a few more from under her feet to create a bouquet.

"Want me to tie them together for you?" I picked a blade of grass.

"Here, fix." She handed over her collection of green. I wrapped the grass around the leaves and tied it into a knot.

"Here you go, sweetie." I handed over our bouquet of weeds.

"For you. Keep." She scooted herself closer to me. "For buthers too." I wrapped my arm around her and pulled her close to me.

"Thank you, sweetie. What do you think of your brothers?" I rubbed her arm to help keep her warm in the winter air.

"Like. Cry lot." She looked up at me with her glowing red chunky cheeks.

"So you think we should keep them?"

She bit on her bottom lip as she thought about my question. "Yeah. Like the toys."

Laughing over her response, I scooped her up to take her back inside where it was warmer.

"Walk over?" She laid her forehead on my shoulder pressing her frozen cheeks against mine.

"I think it's time to warm up and check on the boys." I carried my cold, sleepy little girl back to the house. Opening the door, the lack of chatter and laughter hit me like a tons of a bricks. The silence was unsettling. I closed the door behind me and set Suzy on an empty spot on the couch. "Lie down for a little bit, okay?" She curled up without protest.

I looked to my cousin Beth, whose eyes were large with fear as she watched me. "What's going on? Where is everyone?" I looked around the room to see only a few people, all of which were sitting in awkward silence.

"It's Grandma Marsh. She's having chest pains. Ambulance is on its way." Before I could run to her aid, I could hear the ambulance coming up the drive. I rushed outside. "She's in here!" I waved my arms, letting them know they were in the right place.

They ran up the sidewalk and into the house. Tara met them in the living room and led them back to the kitchen. I followed close behind, but before I could get to where I could see Grandma, Tara came back out and led me back to the living room. "We should stay out of the way." She stood in front of me to block me from going into the kitchen.

"I gotta see her. Is she okay?" I looked around her to see if I could catch a glimpse of what was going on.

"We need to let them do their jobs. We'll know more once they check her out."

I found a seat and joined the awkward silence of the rest of the family. Slowly, one by one, family members started to fill the living room, but no one had anything to say. Soon Todd joined by my side. "They're gonna take her to the hospital. It was a heart attack." I tried to think positive, but I was shaking frantically with doubt on the inside. In a desperate plea for comfort, I buried my face in Todd's chest. "I'll take the kids back to the house. Why don't you go ahead and ride with your parents to the hospital?"

Sean approached us carrying the diaper bag. "I'll go back with you and help with the kids. Tara is gonna follow the ambulance to the hospital, she wants Clara to ride with her." As we began to make our plans, Grandma was carried through the living room on a stretcher. She looked so helpless; my eyes filled with tears.

I wanted to rush to her side, but she was hurried through the house and loaded into the ambulance. "All right, if you've got the kids covered, I'm going with Tara to the hospital." I grabbed Todd's arm.

"Go. They'll be fine." Todd nodded.

Tara grabbed my sleeve and led me out the door. "Mom, we'll meet you up there!" Tara yelled as we flew past them and jumped in the car.

Even though Grandma had made it to the hospital before we did, we were directed to the waiting room upon arrival. Tara tried to stop medical staff that would pass by, but no one could give us the answers we desired. "Can't you at least tell me when we can see her?" Tara yelled at a nurse who was walking by.

"Come on and sit down. They promised to let us know as soon they heard something." I guided her toward some nearby chairs.

"I know, I just feel I should be doing something."

"Have we heard anything?" Mom asked, entering the waiting area with Dad.

"No, not yet. I can't get them to tell me anything." Tara pulled away from my grip and rushed to Mom's side. "They said they would come to us, as soon as they had some news." I sat down in a chair; desperately trying to remain calm.

"I'm sure they will." Mom took a seat next to me.

"Since when are *you* my rational one?" She grabbed my hand.

"I think when I had the kids, a new brain was implanted. Parenthood apparently comes with its own programming that is installed when you become a mom. I see a lot of things differently now." I squeezed her fingers.

"I've noticed. You've really grown up into a nice young lady that I'm very proud of."

Looks of concern instantly covered Mom's face as a short male doctor of Indian descent entered the room. "Marsh?" he asked looking in our direction.

"Yes, that's my mother, how is she?" Mom stood up.

"She is resting. She will need a triple bypass, and we don't feel we should wait. We will be scheduling surgery for the morning. You are welcome to go and see her now if you'd like," the doctor explained as we all focused intensely on his words.

Mom nodded, unable to find words to respond.

"Check in at the nurses' station, and they will direct you in the right direction," the doctor instructed.

"Thanks, we appreciate all you have done for my grandma," I said as my sister dragged me past him, her hand gripping tightly around my arm. She pulled me along as she rushed us to the nurses' station. I was pleased to have gotten more cooperation with the nursing staff, in comparison to the response we got with our first attempt in locating Grandma. Tara released her grip as they willingly provided us with the information we needed.

Once we had the information of where her room was, we quickly followed the hall that led the way to the last room on the left. We arrived to the slightly ajar door, and I slowly pushed it open. I was not prepared for the view. Grandma laid helplessly in the sterile white room, hooked up to an IV. Her eyes were open but sagging with exhaustion. Her smile welcomed us, even though her pale complexion told me we should leave her to rest.

"Come on in." Grandma's voice was hushed. I stepped inside, leading the rest of the crew in with me. "I see you brought the whole family." She used her remote to adjust her bed, lifting her upper body to a sitting position.

"You can't escape the family that easily," Mom said as we took a seat in one of the chairs that sat next to her bed.

"I actually had a different escape in mind, but this definitely made for a speedy getaway. Sorry if I ruined the party." Grandma smiled.

Hearing her joke around made me feel a lot better. She sounded weak, but her spirit was still strong. My nerves were still on edge for her upcoming surgery, but I kept telling myself that the surgery was routine and she would be fine. Her smirk told me that she was strong and not worried. So I tried not to worry either.

"Clara, dear, your mind is not with us. I hope you are not pre-occupied by me." Grandma raised her voice to get my attention.

Everyone was focused on me. Mom's eyes were piercing mine, begging me not to mention the surgery. "I was thinking about the boys, they are home with Todd and Sean." I tried to cover my distraction with my kids.

"I'm sure they're fine, but you should go home. I'm really tired and have a big day tomorrow. No sense in worrying about me, I'll be just fine." She winked.

"I know you will, Gram, and we should probably let you get some rest." I stood up and walked to her bedside. "I love you." I leaned down and kissed her cheek.

"I am so proud of you. You are a terrific sister, mother, and young lady." Grandma squeezed my hand.

"You're the best grandmother a girl could ask for. I love you." I backed away to keep from feeling we were doing a good-bye speech.

"We will be back in the morning," Tara said as she grabbed my shoulders.

"That won't be necessary, dear. No sense in you guys sitting around while they do their thing. I'm sure you all have better things to do on Christmas than sit around waiting for me."

Mom grabbed Grandma's hand on the other side of the bed. "You are far more important than anything else right now. We will be here first thing in the morning to see you go into surgery, and we will be here waiting for you when you come out. We love you. Get some rest, and we *will* see you in the morning."

Chapter 15

In Need of a Christmas Miracle

The night was long due of the anticipation of Grandma's surgery, which weighed heavily on us all. I tossed and turned most of the night, and now that the sun was shining through the window, I was forced to start the day uncharged.

"Mama! Mama!" Suzy's excitement filled our bedroom as she ran down the hall yelling my name.

"Someone must have found their gifts from Santa." Todd sat up in bed and waited for Suzy to enter the room.

"Come look, come look." Suzy's eyes were wide as she pushed open the door.

"What's up, sweetie?" I sat up, trying not to laugh as she ran to the end of the bed.

"See!" She climbed up on the bed and pulled on Todd's hand.

"I think we better get up." Todd pulled the blankets back and got out of bed, Suzy still hanging onto his hand.

"Yes! Up!" Suzy jumped into Todd's arms. "Mama, up!"

"Suzy, did you get Auntie up?" I got out of bed and grabbed my blue bathrobe.

"Come look!" Todd said with Suzy's enthusiasm as he carried her back down the hall to the living room. I tied my robe while I dragged my feet down the hall to get the boys. I pushed open their door, only to see they were gone. At first my heart fell down into my gut, but then, as I remembered that Sean and Tara had stayed the night, I prayed to find my missing babies with them.

I tried not to panic as I rushed down the hall. The subtle fuss of Karson waiting for his food found my ears, and I relaxed my step. "Someone must be hungry." I entered the kitchen where Tara was preparing the bottles while Sean juggled a baby in each arm.

"I just hope I am doing this right." Tara shook the bottles to mix up the formula.

"Just test the warmth on your wrist." I demonstrated with a pretend bottle in hand.

"Mommy, look!" Suzy grabbed my arm and pulled me toward the living room.

"Oh yes, let's go have a look."

By the time we entered the living room, her eyes locked on the big plush pony that rested beneath the Christmas tree. She released her grip from me, ran to the horse, and wrapped her little arms around its neck. "Mine!" she screeched as she hung on tight.

"Yes, I believe it is. It must be a gift from Santa." I winked at Todd, forgetting for a brief moment about the dreaded agenda that the rest of the day held for me.

"Looks like Santa did good." Tara walked in feeding Karson, with Sean close behind her, feeding Kolton.

"Do you want me to take one of them?" I reached out to Tara.

"No, we're fine. Enjoy your Christmas." Tara sat on the couch. Todd started to pull out the rest of the gifts from under the tree.

I couldn't help but smile as I watched Suzy's eyes widen with each gift that Todd set in front of her. Her hands soon followed her stare as her little fingers tore at the paper, sending colorful pieces flying in all directions. She barely scanned its contents before grabbing another.

"Well, you know one way to keep her occupied." Tara said with a smile, her eyes full of as much excitement as Suzy.

"I should have wrapped empty boxes, she tends to like the packaging better than the gifts."

Todd wrapped his arms around me as I snapped a few pictures. "Merry Christmas, sweets." He pulled me into his chest.

"Merry Christmas." I leaned back, absorbing myself in his embrace. His lips pressed against the back of my head before releasing me to answer Suzy's call for more gifts. I took a quick picture of him handing her another package wrapped in red.

"I think I'll go get ready to head to the hospital." Tara set the empty baby bottle on the coffee table.

"I'll take him." Todd put his coffee cup next to the bottle and relieved Tara of the tiny bundle. "Why don't you go ahead and get ready too? Sean and I can handle the kiddos. We made a great team last night," Todd said as Sean laughed in agreement from the couch. I snapped a few more photos of the guys holding the boys and followed his advice.

Leaving Suzy to play with her new toys, I left the living room, unnoticed by my preoccupied little girl, and took a quick shower. I threw on a pair of jeans and a T-shirt—not quite the outfit I had planned for Christmas day.

"Knock-knock." Tara walked into the bedroom as I pulled my hair back into a ponytail. "You about ready?" She plopped herself on the edge of my bed.

"Yep. Just give me a minute to add a little color on my face." I sat at my vanity and started to apply some foundation.

"I sure enjoy seeing you and your family." Tara lay down on her belly and watched as I applied my blush.

"I enjoy having you. I hate that you live so far away. I'm hoping after school that you'll get a job closer to home so I can see more of you."

I watched her smile grow in the reflection of my mirror. "I'm proud of you, sis. I'm happy with the life you have provided for Suzy."

My body warmed with gratitude. "Thanks." I finished my makeup with a little gloss on the lips. "Well, that's as good as it gets." I adjusted my bangs in the mirror. "Shall we go?" I spun around in my chair to face Tara.

"Yeah, we better." She climbed off the bed and stretched.

"Merry Christmas, sis. I love you."

"Ditto," she whispered with a wink then pulled me from the room, grasping my hand.

I found Kolton and Karson sleeping soundly in the bassinet in the living room, while Suzy rolled around on the pile of shredded paper she had created in the middle of the floor. "We'll open our gifts later today." Todd took a picture of Suzy giggling on her mountain of gift wrap.

"This wasn't how I imagined the boys' first Christmas. I feel guilty for leaving, but I know I should be there." I stared at the sleeping pair.

"It's Christmas all day. You go and be there for your family, we'll be here for *you* when you get home." Todd took hold of my fingertips.

"I love you." I pulled myself to him and kissed him softly on the lips.

"I love you too. Don't worry about us, Sean and I have it covered."

Leaving my family on Christmas day was difficult; feelings of guilt rushed through my veins as I neared the front door. I hesitated briefly as I turned the knob and prepared to leave with my sister. Once I stepped outside, my mind focused more on Grandma Marsh. Her surgery weighed heavily on my heart, body, and soul, rapidly making this holiday just another day.

The car ride over was a quiet one; neither of us knew what to say to the other. Moments of awkward silence encumbered our surroundings. My mind scrambled for things to say—anything that would take our minds off of what we may find when we arrived at the hospital. I was literally numb, and words of comfort appeared to be extinct.

We arrived to find Mom and Dad already in the waiting room. "Hey, dear." Dad stood up to greet us as we entered.

"Do we know anything?" Tara took a seat next to Dad.

"Nothing yet, just playing the waiting game." Mom answered from her chair, her arms crossed like a scared child looking for comfort. I sat in the chair next to her and grabbed her hand. My voice was still on mute, as my mind seemed to be at a loss for words.

We sat patiently as the time crept along. I stared at the couple across from us; they appeared to be in their midthirties. The man had an attractive lumberjack quality. He was tall, slender, and rugged with a needed shave, crinkled jeans, and flannel shirt. I watched him pace the floor with his broad shoulders slumped forward, as if heavy with concern. The lady—his wife, I presumed—sat motionless in her chair. She had a simple look with little to no makeup. She was of a medium build with coal-black hair, which she wore in a tress that draped over her right shoulder. Her bright-yellow shawl served as a blanket as she tried to get some rest in the chair. From the looks of them, I could only assume that they had been here all night.

"They are here for their son." Dad leaned in front of Mom and spoke softly. I nodded, as I had wondered if they were waiting for word on a child. "He was in a car accident with his grandparents—her parents, I believe they said. The grandparents are in stable condition and doing well, but the boy was in critical and needed to undergo an emergency surgery. He is only three years old." My chest tightened as he explained their story, a tragic story that was in need of a Christmas miracle. I thought of my own children at home and was sickened by the thought of having to be in this young couple's shoes.

Within moments of Dad having told me their story, a lady in a long white coat approached them with a shake of the head. I could not hear anything the doctor told them, but as the mom dropped to her knees screaming, I knew what that simple shake meant. My stomach turned, and my heart ached for the couple. I wanted to provide them with the comfort they needed. The truth was I didn't know how to provide words of comfort to my own family; I didn't know what I could do for them either. I felt helpless.

"Matthews?" A doctor wearing green scrubs approached the waiting area. I studied his face as he neared us; it contained neither a smile nor looks of concern. I stood up as the room grew hazy, much like a dream. My nerves itched as I waited for his words to present themselves. "She is in recovery right now. Everything went as planned. We'll monitor her over the next couple of days. But I feel comfortable saying the surgery was a success."

My body calmed with relief, allowing me to finally locate my voice. "Can we see her?"

The doctor placed his hands in his pockets. "We'll want to get her set up in her room first. Now may be a good time to get a bite to eat in our cafeteria. I hear they are serving hot turkey sandwiches for the Christmas lunch special today." He pointed toward the sign on the wall that directed the way to the food.

"Thanks, Doctor, for everything." Mom lifted her hand and met his for a shake of appreciation.

"She should be ready for visitors in about an hour. I'm sure she's looking forward to seeing some familiar faces," he said with a smile, before leaving the waiting area to tend to other patients.

I closed my eyes for a brief moment and inhaled the refreshing news. My heart unclenched the weight of concern, allowing my airway to flow more freely. I was relieved that Grandma Marsh was going to be okay, even though streams of guilt were beginning to control my emotions. Guilt of my gain over the grieving couple's loss. The loss of their child on a day focused on miracles didn't seem fair.

"At least I feel like I can breathe now." Tara grabbed my arm. I opened my eyes and placed my hand on top of hers.

"If we have an hour, I'm gonna call home and check on the kids. I'll meet you in the cafeteria." I released myself from Tara's hold and dug for my cell phone in my purse.

"I'll go with you." Tara grabbed her jacket off the chair.

Mom gave a subtle nod and walked alongside Dad toward the cafeteria sign.

Walking in the opposite direction, we went outside. The bitter cold breeze snipped at my cheeks and stung my nose. I barely noticed the tall stone statues located at the corners of the covered entry. Standing at the top of the steps, I dialed home. The call was brief as Todd quickly assured me that everyone was doing fine and that he had everything under control. "I just wanted to give you the update. We don't know a lot, but the surgery seems to have been a success. I'll call you after I've seen her for myself, which should be in about an hour. Give the kids big hugs for me. I love you all so much."

Once we said our good-byes, I put my phone away and studied the intense look on Tara's face. Her pressed lips and down-drawn brows told me she was deep in thought. "What's on your mind, sis?" I buttoned my coat back up to keep the cold wind from hitting my chest like a sledgehammer.

"All of this just puts things into perspective for me." She opened the door.

"How do you mean?" I walked inside, rubbing my hands together in attempt to find them some warmth.

"Oh, it's nothing really, just the usual epiphany. Shedding some light on what is really important. Like having a family who loves you, feeling lucky for what you have, and knowing what you want next."

"You saying you didn't realize we loved you before all this?" I walked next to her as she continued to follow the hall toward the cafeteria.

"No, not that. I just realized how much I want to start my own family. I want Grandma Marsh to have the chance to meet *all* her grandchildren before she passes." She stopped before entering the dining area.

"Having a family is amazing. I'm excited for you to start that chapter in your life as well, but follow the appropriate steps first. Finish school, get married, get settled down in a cute little house, then have kids."

She nodded as she seemed to take my words into consideration. "That's what I meant. I hadn't planned on kids until much later in the equation." She walked off and joined the parents at a nearby table. I was a little uneasy about the conversation, though I wasn't sure why. There was just something in my gut telling me she had other motives. I'd always been able to read her like a book. Today was no different; she had something planned, and I was determined to figure it out.

I joined everyone else at the table. "The special is very good, you should get a plate," Dad said before taking a bite.

"I'm not that hungry." I looked to Tara. "I think I'll have a salad," we said in unison. Giggling, we stood up and went to the salad bar. "I think I know what you're thinking of doing." I grabbed a plate.

"What do you mean?" Tara grabbed a plate as well.

"You know what I mean. Look at me." I waited for her eyes to meet mine. "Grandma will be around for a while. Don't do it."

Her green stare dropped from mine. "I don't know what you're talking about." She dished up her plate.

"Just tell me you'll wait until you've finished school." I added a scoop of tomatoes to the mound of lettuce on my plate.

She paused before gradually lifting her chin. "You don't understand, you already have your family. I want what you have." Her eyes filled with tears.

"I do understand. But I also understand that we have done everything we have so that you could finish school and make something of yourself. I can't allow you to throw away your future now. Finish school first. Okay?" My eyebrows rose, asking for agreement.

"I know you're right. One day I'm going to finish school, I'm gonna move closer to home. Have a nice job, nice house, and an even nicer family. Two boys and two girls." She topped her creation with some ranch dressing.

"Don't forget the cat and dog." I laughed.

We allowed Tara to talk about school and her job to entertain us for our hour of waiting. "I think I'm going to look into transferring closer to home after the semester," she added after all her bragging of her job.

"What do you think Sean will think of that?" Mom sat back and waited for Tara to answer.

"I don't know. He does have family this way too. But he's got a year to graduation." She took her last bite of salad.

"So wait a year, then see where you guys are—it'll all work out. We want you home, but you've got a fiancé now. All decisions will need to be made with the other in mind as well. You will have to make sacrifices, and so will he. Talk to him about how you feel and what your plans are." Mom winked as she gave her motherly words of advice.

I wrapped my arm around Tara. "I love ya, sis, but you know Mom's right. Things will work out, they always do."

"I know I'm doing the right thing with school, and I love my life with Sean, I really do. It's just that it's hard enough to leave after seeing you guys, but having this ordeal with Grandma—that just makes me feel like I belong right here with my family. I don't want to wait a year to move closer to home. I'm debating whether I want to go back at all. I should be right here." Tears flooded her vision .

"It's definitely nice to have you home, and I hate to see you leave. I would set you back up in your room in a heartbeat. But then what kind of a dad would I be if I allowed you to throw away your life like that?" Dad's stern look pierced hers; his shadow seemed to grow and blanket over us.

"Daddy, I know."

Mom looked at her watch. "Tara, we are all allowed moments of weakness. Especially in times like these. You're strong, smart, and we are all very proud of you. We know you love us, whether you're here or miles away doing what you have worked so hard to achieve. Your grandma would tell you the same thing, she would not want you to give up your schooling and your happiness with Sean to be here. Let's go see her, maybe that will make you feel better."

I was concerned about Tara as we made our way back to Grandma's room. She was obviously overwhelmed with everything that was going on. I wondered if part of her emotional overload was due to the commitment she had promised to Sean. I squeezed her hand as we entered the room. Grandma looked tired, but her smile was energizing. Her coloring was close to her normal glow, and her eyes twinkled as we all invaded her small room once again. "Good to see you guys. You look better than the last time I saw you." She smirked.

"Funny, I was gonna say the same about you," Mom responded as she went in for a hug.

I sat in the same spot I had the day prior. Only now the vision was less bleak. "It's very nice that you all have come to spend Christmas here with me. I appreciate it deeply, but I think you should go home and spend the rest of the holiday with your families." Grandma's voice was stern.

"She's right, ya know. You should be home with the little ones. They are what Christmas is all about." Grandpa Marsh helped to argue Grandma's words.

"We'll go home shortly. We just want to stare at Grandma for a little longer. She scared us a great deal, and I'm not ready to leave just yet," Tara explained, with eyes fixed onto the patient in question.

"Aw shucks, all this attention for little ol' me?" Grandma batted her eyes.

"Gram, I'm sure you could use some rest. We won't bother you for too much longer, we're just happy to see you doing so much better." I grinned as her presence alone made me feel secure and invincible, much like she did when I was a little kid.

"I don't want to chase you all off, but some rest would be nice." She winked.

"Yes, Grams, I understand." My body carried me across the sterile white-and-gray flooring and into her arms, as if I were in her trance. "You're the best, but you know that. Love you." I held her tight.

Chapter 16

A Plea for Help

Grandma Marsh had made it home by the beginning of the New Year, a relief to us all. Her incident had affected every one of us as a real eye-opener. I was overwhelmed with the reality that my grandparents would not be around forever. My kids needed to know them, and I was bound to make sure there would be memories for them to cherish forever.

It was evident that my sister took it hard as well. I could see that her fears were focused on the fact that the grandparents may not see her succeed. Her actions proved her determination, which only grew stronger in the years to follow. She pushed herself extra hard at school. She took on extra curriculums and studied long into the night. The extra work was putting a damper on her relationship with Sean.

Things seemed to get a little better after the wedding. They married soon after he graduated. It was a beautiful fall ceremony done in autumn colors—scarlet, tangerine, and amber, accented with white chiffon—colors I would have never thought of but so happy she did. The ceremony was elegant yet fun. Suzy was a stunning flower girl; her dress of satin sported the three colors. The bodice was amber, which faded to the tangerine color, which gradually turned crimson at the hem.

They moved closer to home when he got a job at a law firm three towns away from my work. We were only two hours from each other; I was ecstatic. Tara transferred to the university up the road from their new house. Everything seemed to be going as she had planned. Yet her spirit hadn't returned. She wasn't herself; she became more distant and distracted than ever.

"Mom, I want my hair in a pony today. We have PE!" Suzy yelled down the hall as she got ready for kindergarten.

"All right, bring me a comb and a hair tie. I'm trying to get the boys ready for Grandma Cece." I slipped a shirt over Karson's head as he struggled to reach a toy train on the floor. "Karson, hold still for just a moment, then you can play." I pulled his arm through the sleeve of the shirt.

"This fine, Mom. All done." My stubborn three-year-old continued to reach for the train as I held him close to get the other arm through the sleeve.

"Need some help?" Todd entered the boy's room with Kolton giggling from under his arm as he packed him into the room like a sack of potatoes.

"Can you get him dressed for me? Karson is bit of a busybody this morning." I loosened my grip on him to grab the pair of pants I had laying on the bed.

"Just this morning? Karson!" Todd yelled as his son wiggled away from me and started to run out of the room.

"What, Daddy?" He stopped in his tracks and starred at his father with wide eyes of green.

"Get dressed, then you can play." Todd helped Kolton into his shirt.

Karson sulked as he moved toward me, with his sister following close behind. "All right, mom, I'm ready." Suzy entered the train-decorated room holding a comb and red ribbon in her hand.

"Just one moment." I slipped the sweats on Karson then set him free to run. Suzy, wearing a red sweater and blue jeans, stood patiently in the doorway until I motioned her toward me. I pulled her long black ringlets into a ponytail and tied it with the red ribbon. She had grown into such a pretty little girl so fast; I hardly remembered the chubby little legs that had been replaced with long skinny ones. Luckily for me she still had the round cheeks that helped support her large brown eyes that I loved so much.

"I'll take Suzy to school." Todd let Kolton loose to play with his puzzles.

"That would help out a lot. Thanks." I watched Kolton play quietly in the corner of the room. His bright-red hair was a mess of curls that we kept trimmed short. He had freckles that covered most of his face, a mirror image of his brother. Only much like Tara and I, they were complete opposites. Kolton was a lot like my sister,—quiet and well mannered. His mind was constantly moving to make sense of everything. Karson was more like I was as a child—curious and full of energy. He was always in motion, yet if you could get his feet to stop moving, he'd turn into a genuine snuggle bug.

With Suzy now ready for school, Todd grabbed the purple-and-white zebra-print backpack near the door and left me to chase after Karson. "See ya, sweets, have a nice day!" he yelled as they walked out the door.

"You too, love ya!" I gathered the boys' jackets and got ready to take them to my parents. "All right, guys, let's get going, Mommy needs to get to work." I collected their shoes and sat on the couch. Kolton took a seat next to me and lifted his foot. He knew the routine and was happiest when everything went as scheduled.

"Karson, come on, you're next." I watched the hall for him to answer my call. He darted from the room, carrying a toy train.

"Take this?" His hands held the bright yellow train tightly as he ran across the living room.

"Remember, Grandma has lots of toys over there for you to play with, including a whole new train set. This one can stay here." I picked him up and plopped him onto the couch. His bottom lip pushed out in a pout as it usually did when we'd have this same conversation every other morning. He was my persistent one and more likely to try to break away from the routine at any given chance.

"All right, coats on. Then we are out of here." I helped Karson with his, as Kolton carefully lined his arms up with the sleeves on his own. Once the boys were bundled for the rain, they led me out the door. I quickly grabbed Karson by the hand as I closed the door behind me, in an attempt to keep him from puddle jumping. Kolton went straight for the car, as I escorted his brother down the path behind him. Reaching the driveway, I was relieved to have made it there without anyone finding the mud that lined the walkway to the car. "Froggie go jump!" Karson yelled before stomping his foot into a puddle of water behind us, bringing my sense of relief to a sense of disappointment.

I opened the door to the car and let Kolton climb in. I then looked down at my pants that were now decorated in a splatter of wet, muddy dots. "Why did you do that?" I sighed in an effect to control the scream of anger that was desperate to escape.

"I love you, Mommy. No be mad, it was the froggie." His smile was sincere and his eyes large with innocence.

"I love you too, honey." I buckled him into place.

I turned up the heat in hopes to dry the mess on my leg. After a ride filled with giggles and train noises, we arrived at my parents'. "Put your hoods on." I stepped out into the downpour. As I opened up the backdoor, Mom ran down the sidewalk with her large rainbow-colored umbrella. "Come on, hurry in." She grabbed Kolton by the hand.

"I stay out and play. I froggie!" Karson stomped in every puddle on the way up to the house.

"Just so happens we are having a froggie picnic today. The main course is going to be ants on a log. You'll have to play outside another day." Mom turned to little frog boy for a response.

"Really? Ants? Cool!" He ran from my grip to the front door. I laughed to myself as I remember eating the treat of raisins with peanut butter on celery as a child myself. "Thanks, Mom, you're the best." I held onto the hood of my coat to help guard my face from the pellets of rain beating down on me.

"Yes, I know. Now get onto work before you drown." With a wave of the hand, I did as I was told.

Growing up, I had always known I had a great mom. Though many of my memories were linked to different kinds of punishment she dealt me. Even then I knew she was doing her job and I deserved every reprimand she gave me. I didn't like it, but I understood it. Leaving my kids with her during the day gave me great pride. I knew they were in good hands, even better hands then when I was little. She was a great mom but an even better grandma. We did fun things growing up but nothing like what she did for my kids. It reminded me of the relationship I had with my Grandma Marsh.

By the time I arrived at work, the rain had let up to a light sprinkle. I ran across the parking lot to the door and shook off like a wet dog before entering. "Did you find the rain okay?" Sonya laughed as I brushed off some of the mud on my pant legs.

"Funny," I smirked, removing my coat. "What's the day look like, am I gonna have to go out in this?" I hung up my coat.

"I don't think so. I heard the intern is going to the school to do the pictures on the remodel. Trevor's ranting about some photos that were messed up. He said you guys would be busy for the next couple of days." Sonya handed me my time card.

"Nice, wonder what he's talking about." I pushed the card into the time clock and placed it back under my name on the wall.

"I'm sure you're about to find out. Ready to start the day?" She pushed the door open.

"Yeah, why not." I followed her into the room of loud, busy keyboards.

"See ya for lunch?" Sonya turned toward her desk.

"Definitely, call me when you're ready." I continued past the collection of desks to my office at the back of the room. Trevor was already at his chair. He stopped looking at the sheets of proofs when I entered the room.

"So what's on for today?" I inhaled, preparing myself for whatever the big dilemma was about.

"You look like a drowned rat," he laughed.

"Thanks. You know I think I liked you better before you would talk to me." I sat at my desk with a smile.

"Oh now, don't be like that. I'm just playing." He sat back and kicked his feet up, placing his hands behind his head full of messy sandy-brown hair.

I ignored the stare of his mysterious dark eyes and logged on to my computer.

"Yes, the silent treatment always a delight, and as much as I enjoy my job without your mouth yapping in the background, we have an issue." He sat back up in his chair and pulled himself up to his desk. I raised one eye. "So do I have your undivided attention?" His arms crossed in front of him.

"Just spill it. I'm not interested in your games today, Trevor."

"All right, so here it is. We have some serious editing to do with the Cookie Bake-Off. There are no decent shots to use for the article." He waved the proofs at me then tossed them back down before him. "Aw, relax. I'm sure there is something we can use." I pulled a large brown hair clip from the top drawer and used it to hold back my wet hair. "Let me check my messages, and then we can tackle that one together, okay?" I picked up the phone.

"That'll work. I'll be at my table when you're ready." He grabbed the proofs and left the room.

I listened to the messages on my voice mail and wrote down the two messages that I needed to respond to. One was from Grandma Marsh, asking about Suzy's sixth birthday party, and the other was from Sean, asking me to call him back. The urgency in his voice begged me to call him first.

"Hello, Grubber and Associates, how may I direct your call?" a lady answered who sounded like she was talking through her nose.

"Sean Johnson, please." I tried not to snicker at the way she spoke.

"Just one moment, I'll transfer you. Please hold."

I scrolled through my e-mails as I waited to hear Sean's voice on the other end.

"Hello. Sean Johnson speaking." The familiar voice brought my attention off the messages on the computer screen.

"Well, don't you sound all professional? It's Clara, I'm returning your call." I sat back in my seat and spun myself to face the door and away from the work on my desk.

"Yeah, I could really use your help, advice, assistance, or something. I'm really at a loss and not sure what else to do." His voice was quiet with sadness.

"I'd love to help, is this about Tara's depressive funk?" I played with a spiral that escaped from my hair clip.

"You noticed?"

"I think everyone has noticed. She took Grandma Marsh's heart attack very hard. Her depression just hasn't seemed to get any better. I'd love to help, though I find it only fair to warn you that I have tried talking to her before, without success." I continued to stare at the wall, eager to help, but much like him, I felt helpless.

"I'm coming down near your work today. Can we meet somewhere?"

I spun to face my desk and grabbed my schedule book. "Why don't we meet at the Lemon Tree around noon. Can you get here by then?" I penciled him in.

"Yeah, I can do that. I appreciate this, really." The desperation subsided in his voice.

"No problem. I'll see you there." After hanging up the phone, I called Grandma Marsh to let her know the party was at the bowling alley in three weeks.

With messages answered, I started toward Trevor's dungeon, where he still preferred to sort his pictures. I stopped by Sonya's desk on the way. "I'll have to do lunch with you tomorrow. My brother-in-law is having a crisis and needs my help with my sister." I shrugged my shoulders.

"Sounds complicated, but I understand. I should have known. You're always cancelling on me. But I forgive you." She winked.

Ready to start work, I left Sonya's desk and turned the corner to the hall leading to Trevor. I walked by the day care, where my kids had played on days when Mom was unavailable.

"Sure miss those kids, Clara. You need to bring them by, I got some new trains that Karson would love!" Cassie yelled out at me. I stopped at the half door and looked in at the room full of kids. Cassie was barely twenty; she was tall, slender, and pale-skinned. She wore very little makeup and bright-blue in her hair; which she wore back in a ponytail. She was quirky, and the kids loved her.

Cassie was especially fond of my wild child; they had an amazing connection. "I will have to do that. I'm considering separating them on occasion, bringing in one of them while Mom takes the other. I think it'll help them when they start school." I nodded, as if agreeing with myself.

"That sounds like a great idea. I also got some new puzzles and picture-find books that Kolton will enjoy." She pointed to the back shelf.

"You're amazing, and I'll be sure to get them in soon." I waved to the group of children playing with the blocks as I walked away.

"It's 'bout time." Trevor looked up as I entered the room.

"Sorry to keep you." I stood over the display of proofs on the table. "Where are the pictures of the winner of the contest? I took a few pictures of her with the check. Did they not turn out?" I shuffled through the lineup.

"That's the problem. She doesn't want her last name or photo used in the article. We have to find something else. I have removed all pictures that had her in them, and this is what we have left." The frustration in his voice echoed off the dark walls of the small room.

"All right then, let's see what we've got." I took the seat on the side of the table next to him and looked over all the photos before us. By lunch, we had sorted through them and narrowed it down to a handful that were considered as possibilities. We broke away for lunch at noon, and I walked across the street to the Lemon Tree Café to meet Sean.

I arrived before he did and grabbed a table close to the door. I was placing my order for a Caesar salad when he walked in. "That's what your sister always orders here too." He sat in the chair across from me at the table.

"Can I get you anything, sir?" The young waitress held her tablet with pen ready.

"I'll have an iced tea and the roasted beef sandwich with horseradish on sourdough, and the soup will be fine. Put this all on one tab, I'll get hers as well." He placed his order then looked to me.

"That's not necessary really." I shook my hand in protest.

"I insist and will not take no for an answer. This is my way of thanking you for having met with me." He watched as the waitress walked away to place the order. "Looks like I win." He smiled.

"So like I said on the phone, I would like to help you. I have been trying to pry it out of her for a while. I just haven't gotten anywhere with her." I grabbed a breadstick from the basket in the middle of the table.

"You're right, things did go south for her after that crazy Christmas, but I thought she would turn around after Grandma came home. Things seemed okay for a while, but lately, she's impossible. The truth is I love her dearly, I want to make this work. But lately, I honestly dread going home—she doesn't talk, and when she does, she's yelling at me for every little thing she can think of. I'm not sure how much more I can take of this." His face was pale.

The waitress set our drinks down in front of us. I took a drink. "I'm gonna talk to Tara. I'll see if I can't get through to her. Maybe I can get away during the weekend and take her to the spa. Let me talk to Todd about leaving him the kids and having some time with my sister." I took another drink of soda.

"I'll pay for it, anything to save my marriage. Save your sister really. I just want her to be happy again, back to the same ol' Tara I met back in college, I miss her." He sat back as our food arrived.

"Me too. She has changed, and it frustrates me that she can't share it with me. We have so many secrets between us, we have always told each other everything. I just don't understand why she can't talk to me now." I took a bite of my salad.

Sean was quiet for a moment while he ate his sandwich, giving me an opportunity to eat my lunch before having to go back to work. "There is one more thing. You have to promise not to tell her I told you, though." The crease across his forehead told me he was serious.

"I promise." I leaned forward to hear his hushed words. "We've been trying to get pregnant since we got married. The last doctor told her that because of her endometriosis, we may never be able to have kids. She seemed all right at first, even through all the different doctors. But at the last appointment, they mentioned adoption, and she freaked out. I'd never seen anything like it. That was a couple of months ago. She said she couldn't talk to you about it. I don't understand, and I didn't know where else to turn."

I finally understood and knew exactly why she was in a deep depression. I knew I couldn't explain it to him, but an escape with my sister was a must. "I'll talk to her and promise not to tell her we met today." The pain in my abdomen was unbearable; I swallowed hard as my lunch tried to make a comeback.

"I appreciate it. More than you know." He slid a hundred-dollar bill across the yellow tablecloth.

"Don't worry about it, I'll pay for the getaway with my sister." I stood up. "I'll call her tonight after I talk to Todd. Thanks for giving me some insight on what's been going on." I walked away as a tear rolled down my cheek.

I walked straight to my car and locked myself in it for my own personal breakdown. I wanted to run to Tara and let her cry on my shoulder, for I could only imagine what she was going through. Getting her away for a day of relaxation and a much-needed release of the burden she was keeping from me was inevitable. Now to figure out how to get her to tell me what I already knew.

Chapter 17

Much-Needed Sister Time

With only a couple of minutes left of my lunch break, I wiped my tears and rushed inside to clock in. I avoided making eye contact with Sonya as I darted for the bathroom. In hopes of hiding any evidence of its disturbance, I touched up my makeup. The smudges cleaned up easily, but the redness was still present. "That'll just have to do." I looked in the mirror and took a deep breath.

As I turned for the door, Sonya walked in. "What's wrong?" She locked the door behind her.

"My sister has been real depressed lately. Sean wants me to talk to her. He just told me part of the problem is they found out they may not have kids. They have been trying for a while and was told her infertility may be caused by her endometriosis. I feel helpless, I'm not sure how I can help. I didn't even know she had an issue. I feel I don't even know my own twin anymore."

I leaned up against the wall, near the door. "Just let her know you are there for her. Has she looked into surgery?" She stepped away from the door; as if no longer blocking me in.

"I don't know. Is there really a surgery to cure it?" I waited patiently for her to reply.

"My sister had surgery, it's supposed to increase your odds of having kids by, like, twenty or thirty percent. I don't remember by which exactly, but it worked for her."

My mind was taking note of that possibility. I would definitely mention it to Tara, if she ever told me about the problem herself. "I'll have to ask her. Hey, I don't suppose you still have your connections to the Passion Studio Spa Resort?" I brought my hands together in a begging plea.

"Just let me know when, and I'll set it up." She fluffed her hair in the mirror.

"Thanks, I owe you one." I unlocked the door.

"It's my pleasure. You could use some relaxation too," Sonya proclaimed what I already knew.

I met up with Trevor, who was already in the back room collecting the pictures we had chosen. "Maybe we should look into getting you a watch that works." He looked up from the collection on the table.

"There's nothing wrong with a girl being fashionably late." I sat in the chair next to him. "I can't wait to see how this photo turns out, I think it'll be perfect." I pointed to the image on the sheet of proofs as I imagined the finished product.

I lost my focus when a disturbing chill ran down my neck and back. Trevor had brushed my cheek with his hand as he moved a spiral of my hair behind my ear. I jerked away in a state of shock.

"Mindy, you've been crying. What's wrong?" He stared at me with eyes of concern.

"I'm fine. Who's Mindy?" I turned in my chair to face him.

"Mindy?" He stood up, shaking his head as if confused.

"You called me Mindy." My voice was hesitant.

"Sorry about that. Sorry for everything. I just noticed you'd been crying and wanted to help." He leisurely moved toward the door.

"Come back here and sit down." I pointed to his chair, like I was speaking to one of my own kids.

"I crossed a line. I need to go." His head dropped to study the floor. "Sit. I don't feel you crossed anything. I feel you need to talk about this Mindy girl—come and sit." I pushed the chair toward him with my foot.

"You probably won't leave me alone until I do, huh?" His feet slowly moved him toward the chair.

"See, you know me so well. Since we have to work so close together on a daily basis, its time I knew you just as well. Now sit." I smiled, crossed my arms, and sat back in my chair; prepared to hear his story.

"Well actually, Mindy was my wife, and the truth is you remind me of her. You have since the first day I met you. See, Mindy and I dated through high school, and shortly after graduation, we discovered we were going to be parents. So we did the right thing and got married." He paused.

"You have a kid?" My head tilted in bewilderment.

"A boy. Gage. He was only eight months old when he and Mindy were on their way home from the store. They were hit by a drunk driver." He turned his head to look toward the door. The lack of color in his face told me the remainder of the story.

"I'm so sorry, Trevor." All of a sudden, my problems seemed so minor.

"It was seven years ago." He got up and stood behind his chair. "Their memory will always stay alive in my heart. Some days you just seem so much like her. I almost forget she's even gone. I owe *you* an apology." His knuckles showed white as he gripped the back of the chair.

"No apologies are necessary, nothing happened, nothing's going to happen. It's all good, so let's get back to work." I stood up and gathered the scatter of proofs.

"Wait. You're not getting off the hook that easy. Why were you crying?" He loosened his grip on the chair, allowing color to rush back into his fingers.

"My story doesn't compare to yours. I'm having a breakdown over my sister's dilemma." I handed him a handful of the papers.

"Well, I can tell it's a big deal to you, so I hope things work out." His smile was genuine.

"Me too." I walked past him and out the door.

I led the way back to the office where I placed everything on his desk before sitting at my own. "So we're cool?" Trevor sat down.

"Paranoid much? Relax, it's all good." I laughed it off as I turned on my computer, trying to focus on the bake-off project. I was concerned there would be an awkward vibe between the two of us, but as he finally relaxed and got back to work, things were just as they were before.

I cropped, enhanced, and played with the colors until I was satisfied with the final product. "All right, I just sent it to you. See what you think." I watched as he checked his computer.

"I think you're a genius and a lifesaver. It's perfect. Prepare it for publishing." He gave his usual thumbs-up of approval.

Leaving a job well done at work, I felt good about the day's accomplishment. I also felt good about being done and on my way to get the kids. After weaving through a lineup of traffic, I arrived at my parents', exhausted. I dragged my feet, kicking up water from the occasional rain puddle that decorated the sidewalk. "Mommy, Mommy!" Kolton met me at the door, a sound that amplified my smile even more. His enthusiasm always did wonders to my own energy level.

"Hey, sweetie." I scooped him up into my arms, finding my second wind.

"Come see fort!" He squirmed to be put down.

I stepped inside the door and set him back on his feet. His tiny hand wrapped tightly around mine as he pulled me into the dining room. "Come on! Hurry! See!" The chairs were lined in front of the table with a large blue-and-white checkered blanket which was draped over the grouping, creating a large fort. He let go of my hand and rushed under the blanket, where I could hear the giggling from all three of my children. "They've been playing under there all day." Mom entered from the kitchen.

I enjoyed the sound of their laughter. I couldn't imagine life without children. I felt a burden of guilt for having an amazing family when Tara may not be able to have one herself. Knowing that I held her first and, possibly, her only child made me sick. I was the one to always make things right; I always felt that was my job.

Growing up, I was by no means the responsible one, but I was always my sister's protector. I was frustrated that I felt as if my hands were tied on this one. "What's on your mind?" Mom's hand rested on my shoulder. With a smile, I pointed toward the couch.

"I talked to Sean today." I sat down, talking in a hushed voice.

"What about?' Mom sat next to me, keeping the same whispered tone.

"Tara. I know why she's been such a bear lately." I debated saying anything since it was supposed to be a secret.

"What's going on?" She looked back to the kids to see that they were still playing and out of earshot.

"Well, I need to talk to her more. I'm hoping to get a day booked at the Passion Studio Spa and get her to tell me herself. I just need to talk to Todd about keeping the kids for a full day." I fell back into the cushions of the couch.

"Is it anything I should be concerned about?" Mom's voice rose.

"I don't think so. She just needs a day of pampering." I almost felt bad for not telling her everything, but it didn't seem right telling her just yet.

"Well, if Todd can't watch the kids, I'll take them. Just book the day for whenever and rest assured you'll be covered. You could use some pampering yourself."

"Mom! You want to come in and see our fort!" Suzy peeked out from under the blanket.

"Maybe next time, honey, we need to start getting ready to go." I looked at my watch.

"I think I'll leave the fort up for them to play under tomorrow. Karson has been content in there all day with his trains." Mom's smile showed relief.

"Whatever works for you works for me." My ears echoed with their cheerful laughter.

"I'm thinking of doing some separation with the boys. I may only bring you one of them in the morning." I stood up as Kolton brought me his shoes.

"Then just keep Karson here, and get him after work tomorrow." She set Kolton on the couch.

"Are you sure?" I kneeled down and adjusted his sock before putting on his shoe.

"We'll be fine." She looked down at me. "Karson, come here a minute." I kneeled down on the floor to his level.

He peeked out from his hideout with a shiny blue train in hand.

"We leave?" His bottom lip pushed out.

"I want to talk to you about that, come here." I opened my arms for him. He ran across the floor to rest his head on my shoulder with his hand still gripping the train. I wrapped my arms around him and whispered in his ear, "Do you want to stay the night here? Just you?" I paused in wait for his response.

"Koko stay too." He reached for his brother's foot.

"Nope, just you with Gram and Pa." I pushed him out in front of me so I could watch his facial expressions. He bit at his lower lip, then nodded. "K."

"Okay, if you're staying, give me love." He held me tight for a brief second before running back under the grandma-made fort. "Suzy, you ready?" I made my way back to my feet.

"Bye, Grandma." She waved as she ran to her backpack by the door.

"Call me if there's a problem." I followed Kolton to his jacket.

"We'll be fine. Don't worry." She sat back on the couch.

"Ut oh! Kars." Kolton stopped on the top step of the porch and looked back inside.

"Karson is gonna stay here tonight. You get to come to work with me tomorrow." I closed the door.

"K." He continued down the steps.

A sigh of relief escaped my lungs as I mumbled, "That went easier than I thought it would."

I held my breath the whole way home in preparation for the breakdown I expected. I finally let my guard down when we arrived home, and he curled up on the couch to watch some television. "That was too easy. I hope the rest of the night goes as smooth." I seasoned some steak as Todd peeled the potatoes.

"I wouldn't count on it. I think the test will be at bedtime." He rinsed the spuds off in the sink.

"I'm afraid you're right. I'm also afraid my sister may be reaching her breaking point." I placed the meat in the frying pan.

"Did you see her today?" He grabbed a knife.

"No, I saw Sean. He's concerned for their marriage, he wants me to talk to her." I looked out the doorway to assure Suzy was still in her room.

"You've talked to her before. It hasn't helped her mood at all." He continued to cut the potatoes for hash browns.

"There's a bit more to the story now. They've discovered they may not be able to have kids at all. He doesn't understand why she says she can't talk to me about it, and he doesn't understand why she's opposed to adoption." I continued to watch the doorway for uninvited ears.

"The plot thickens." Todd grabbed another frying pan.

"Mom!" Suzy yelled down the hall. "Can you come play dolls with me?" Her voice carried through the house as if it were an urgent request.

"After dinner! I can't right now!" I replied then paused to recollect where I was in the conversation with Todd. "So I think I need to have some one-on-one with Tara. I know she needs me. The tricky thing is getting her to talk to me without me telling her I know what's going on. A getaway, like a spa day." I waited for his response.

"I think that's a great idea. When were you planning on doing this?" He adjusted the heat on the stove.

Kolton entered the kitchen. "Eat!" He grabbed my leg.

"I'm fixing dinner right now, just hang in there, honey." I ruffled his little curls then looked back up at Todd. "Sonya is going to set it up for me as soon I give her the okay. Mom said she'd help watch the kids if you needed her." I flipped the steaks in the pan.

"Actually, I may just plan on taking the kids to the zoo that day, maybe I'll have Sean go along to help with the boys." He opened the fridge and retrieved the salad.

"You've got to be too good to be true. I love you so much." I blew him a kiss with my little boy wrapped around my leg. Dragging Kolton along with me, I grabbed my cell phone and sent a text message to Sonya: 'Make a Res 4 the 1st Sat avail.'

After finishing dinner, I kept my date with Suzy and her doll-house. We were getting ready to send her dolls to a movie when my cell phone buzzed, indicating a response from Sonya. I deserted my little girl at the puzzle box movie theater as I read the message on my phone. "Sorry, sweetie, Mommy's gotta make a phone call." I used her bed as leverage to get to my feet. Suzy hardly moved as I darted from the room to find the house phone.

I grabbed the phone and sat next to Todd. His legs draped across my lap as he sprawled himself out on the couch. "Feel free to rub my feet," he whispered as I dialed my sister's number.

"eHeye skdjsklfj Hey." She answered my call after only a couple of rings.

"Hey yourself, how are you doing these days? I haven't heard from you in a while." I rubbed Todd's legs as he wiggled his toes.

"Just been busy with school. I've been meaning to call, but you know how it is." Her voice was mellow.

"What are you doing next Saturday?" I helped Kolton as he climbed onto the couch, where he perched himself on his dad's legs.

"Nothing that I know of, I'll probably just stay home and relax though."

I climbed out from under Todd's legs as he and Kolton began to play. "I've got the perfect relaxation treat for you, and I set it up for next Saturday." I sat at the dining room table to move away from the loud giggling coming from the living room.

"What kind of treat?" Her tone sounded nearly normal.

"You, me, and the Passion Studio Spa Resort—oh yeah, it's happening, and it's gonna be awesome." I could feel my body shiver with excitement.

"I don't know, I'll have to talk to Sean, make sure he doesn't have any plans." Her voiced dropped again.

I ran to the kitchen and retrieved Todd's cell phone off the counter. "Todd's taking the kids to the zoo, he's gonna call Sean and invite him to go." I tossed Todd his phone. He calmed Kolton down and dialed Sean's cell number while I continued to talk to Tara. "It's a well-deserved escape for us both. We are going with the VIP treatment. Not many people get in without being on the waiting list for a month first. This is a perfect time for us to relax and have some much-needed sister time. I miss you." I watched Todd give the thumbs-up and waited for Tara to respond.

"Well, Sean's talking to Todd now. I guess it's set. Next Saturday, the boys will play with the kids, and we will play in mud," Tara sighed.

"Awesome. I can't wait. I wonder if we really will get to have a mud bath with cucumber slices on our eyes. This is gonna be great." My feet begged to jump for joy as I felt like a child about to go to Disneyland.

"I guess we'll find out in a couple of weeks. How's Suzy?' She changed the subject.

"Suzy and the boys are growing like bad weeds. Mom's got Karson tonight, we're trying a little separation therapy. So far, so good." I watched Kolton wander the living room like a lost puppy.

"Is Suzy doing well in school?" She brought her focus back on Suzy.

"She is doing very well. Reading is her favorite, and she's at the top of her class. It is only kindergarten, but we are very proud. She's going to be in her first karate tournament the weekend after her birthday party. Todd is pretty excited for that. You'll have to come and watch her."

"Is that Auntie?" Suzy ran down the hall. I nodded. "I want to tell her." She reached for the phone. "Auntie, I've got my second yellow belt now. You have to come watch me beat up some boys. It's gonna be so fun. You have to be there." Suzy's excitement rambled her words out rapidly. "Mom, she said she'll be there." She handed the phone back to me.

"Well, she sounds very excited," Tara said with more enthusiasm than I had heard in her voice in a long time.

"She is, and I hope you are just as excited about our spa day, I know I am," I smirked.

"I'm getting there. I really do need this time with you." Her words were music to my ears and a definite step in the right direction.

Chapter 18

Spa Day

After long two weeks, the day finally arrived for my date with my sister. I wasn't sure if I was more excited for the day with Tara, a day away from the kids, the fact that we were going to the most raved-about spa in the state, or the combination of the three, but whatever the reason, I was as energized as a birthday girl getting the gift of her dreams.

I was pacing the floor, watching out the window as I waited for Tara and Sean to pull into the driveway.

"They'll be here soon." Todd wrapped his arms around me as I stood in front of the couch gazing at the outdoors.

"I know, I'm just so anxious to get going." I clapped my hands together.

"Really? I couldn't tell," Todd laughed.

"Are you laughing at me?" I turned to face him.

"No. I love that you are so happy. I enjoy seeing you like this, and I think you and Tara should plan these trips every year."

The sound of a car door pulled me from Todd's hold. "They're here! And you're right." I ran outside. "Tara! You ready?" I held up my keys for her to see.

"Well, I'm here." Tara walked up the sidewalk with Sean following behind her. "This is going to be so much fun, you'll see."

I watched Todd shrug his shoulders as she ignored my response. I refused to let her harsh my buzz about the day of fun before us.

I started the car. "Mommy!" Karson screamed from the top step. I let the car warm up as I returned to the porch to say my good-byes. "Come see lion." Karson grabbed my hand.

I kneeled down. "Next time, sweetie. You have fun, and tell me all about it. Okay?" He nodded and then ran back inside.

Suzy looked out at Tara from the doorway. "Auntie!" Suzy ran past me and grabbed Tara's legs. Tara rubbed her back.

"Hey, Suzy. Have fun at the zoo with Uncle Sean."

"I will." Suzy broke away and ran back into the house.

"Hey! Where's my loves?" I yelled into the house.

"Oh yeah, sorry, Mom, have fun." She ran back out and squeezed me tight.

"You too." I kissed the top of her head.

"One more." Todd carried Kolton out to me. I grabbed his little cheeks and kissed him on the forehead. "Have fun seeing all the animals. I'll be home tonight. Be good." I then kissed Todd on the lips.

"Be careful. Love ya," Todd said as he set Kolton down.

"Will do, you too. Love ya more!" I said as I hurried down the steps to the car. "Let's go, sis." I gave her the thumbs-up. "At least we no longer have to fight over who's driving," I laughed as I climbed in. Tara had no response.

For most of the car ride, Tara said very little. I quit making small talk after her one-word answers became meaningless. In desperation for a break of the uncomfortable silence inside my cage on wheels, I proposed a stop. "There is a little park just up the road here. I think you'll love it. Mind if we stop for a stretch of the legs?" I looked to her for a nod.

"That's fine." She continued to watch the view on her side of the car.

We pulled onto the gravel road lined with dogwoods that were starting to bloom a magnificent shade of pink. The trees were planted close together, creating a wall that blocked out the view of anything else.

"I've been meaning to bring the kids here. I think Suzy would love this." I continued down the road that carried us further into the trees until we reached an archway of roses. The arch was large enough to stretch over the road and was covered in blooms of red, pink, and burgundy. The white sign next to the arch read "Spring Park."

"This really is beautiful." Tara smiled as she admired the roses. My body warmed with delight to see her smile. I parked the car under one of the large maple trees that lined the parking lot. "You ready to see more?" I reached into the backseat for my camera.

"More?" She whipped her head around to see nothing, except the frame of maple trees.

"Yes, more. There's a trail." I opened my door.

"How did you find this place?" Tara got out and took a deep breath.

"Took photos here for a story we did. Amazing, huh?" I put my jacket on. "Come on." I walked toward a path at the end of the circular lot. The trail was lined with stones and sheltered by branches of green above us. The songs of chirping birds rode along the subtle breeze that played aimlessly along the tunnel of trees. "Almost there." I fixed my eyes on the opening of blue ahead. I stopped just before reaching the end of the trees. "Come up here, you'll want to see this." I stepped aside, allowing Tara to be the first to walk out into the opening. The pathway was surrounded with blooming flowers and led to a large white gazebo.

I watched her head move as she examined the brilliant view. She strolled down the path and up into the gazebo. Her arms crossed and rested on the railing looking out at the view of the lake on the other side. "So what do you think?" I sat on the bench seat across from her and took her picture.

"This is great." She turned around to face me.

"I've done a lot of thinking here." I looked past her, out at the green pines that formed the background of the lake.

"Really? You come here often?" She walked over and sat next to me on the bench.

"Sounds like a pick-up line." I laughed. Watching Tara shake her head and grin, I felt like I was with the old Tara, the sister I knew and loved. "It's been a while. I think the last time I came out here was after I had the boys. In fact, it was the spring after that crazy Christmas. I was juggling a lot, with work, three kids, and this girl that was calling Todd on a regular basis. That turned out to be a crush on her part, but I was overwhelmed. So I drove out here, did some thinking, some crying—I think I may have screamed a little. But this place just makes a great 'bad day' remedy." I took a picture of the scenery as I continued to talk to the lake.

"You should have called *me*." Tara grabbed my leg.

I shook my head. "You were dealing with things yourself. I didn't want to bother you." I placed my hand on hers, still avoiding her face.

"I had no idea you and Todd ever had problems, you seem to just always have had it all figured out. You've always known what you wanted. Your plans have always worked out on their own. I have always worked so hard to get what I wanted. Yet as I reach my goal, I wonder if it was worth all the hard work."

I spun to face her. "Is that what you think?" I raised my voice as I continued my rebuttal. "I have worked hard for everything I have. You've got the better job, bigger house, and an amazing man who cherishes you. Your life *is* amazing—yes, you've worked harder than I have, but you have so much more to show for it. I am proud of your accomplishments, and you should be too."

Tara stood up and walked to the other side of the gazebo. "Sometimes it's not the material things that matter. You know that." She walked down the steps and back onto the path to the car. I followed her down the trail with mixed emotions. I was happy that those were the most words I had gotten out of her in a long time; it seemed like a great breakthrough. Yet I was also concerned that I may have upset her, causing her to close up even more.

I placed my camera and jacket in the backseat. "We're still making pretty good time, we ought to make it to the spa with time to spare." I looked at my watch before starting the car. I made sure not to elaborate on the conversation we just had by the lake as we continued our drive to our original destination. "Getting excited to get all pampered?" I turned off the gravel and back onto the main road.

"I've got to tell you. I'm not sure I'm the pampering type."

I turned down the music, thrilled to have her contributing to a real conversation. "You'd be surprised. Todd's mom took me in for a facial and massage when I was pregnant with the boys. I didn't think I'd enjoy it much either, but it was so relaxing. I can't wait to see what more they do at the Passion Studio. But really, I'm more excited to be sharing this day with you." I started studying the road signs to see where we were.

"I do miss doing things together too. That's why I'm here."

I was relieved that I was able to ditch the awkward silence back at Spring Park. That park had proven yet again it was a magical place; I only prayed it had worked some of its wonderment on Tara. She did appear to be more talkative and closer to her old self, but I knew she still had to open up to me about her baby situation before she could be placed on the right path of healing.

My enthusiasm took on its own life as we approached the large gold letters on a white stone sign telling us we had reached the resort. We followed the long winding driveway that led uphill to a large fountain. "That's pretty cool." Tara pointed out the water feature in the middle of the parking lot. My car looked like a lump of coal next to the gleaming gem of vehicles that surrounded it, but I was too eager to care.

"Wow!" I pointed out the white stone building that was built within the hillside. The doors were glass with gold trim. The gold letters *PSSR* decorated the front of the stone on the right side of the door; the openings of the *P* and *R* were windows. I took photos of the entrance focusing on the roof of grass. The hillside looked as though it was a large blanket covering the top and sides of the building. I was anxious to see the inside. "Do you take that thing with you everywhere?" Tara stood next to me.

"Yes, I do. But I'm supposed to be taking pictures for an advertising story that we're going to be doing." I snapped a quick photo of the fountain.

"Let's see the inside." Tara walked toward the glass doors.

"Look who's excited now," I laughed.

"I'm more curious to see what the inside looks like." She looked down at the sparkling sidewalk that led to the entrance. "This place is amazing." I took another picture of the letters on the front of the stone wall.

As soon as we entered, a petite redhead greeted us. "Hello, and welcome to Passion Studio Spa Resort." She wore a dark-blue suit with her hair pulled back in a bun; she reminded me of a stewardess. The lobby was sparkling white with smooth tiling on the floors and walls. The light fixtures that hung down from the stone ceiling were decorated in colorful mosaic glass, adding that perfect splash of color. "Hello, my name is Clara Rivers." I approached the counter.

"Aw yes, Clara, and your sister, Tara. We've been expecting you. Please. Follow me."

Our steps echoed through the spotless lobby as we followed the lady in blue. She stopped at the wall and pushed a button, which opened a hidden door. The movement of the wall revealed a new world: the room was small with a little bench; the walls and floors were covered with cedar planks, like a rustic cabin. "All right, you will find robes in the closet." She pointed straight ahead to a tall narrow door. "And you can change inside that bathroom, there are baskets under the sink for your belongings with your names on them." She pointed to the door next to the closet. "When you are ready, you may sit on the bench, and someone will be right with you."

She stepped aside and allowed us to step up into the little room. "Do we remove all our clothing? And how will they know we are ready?" Tara looked around the room.

"You may leave on some undergarments if that makes you feel more comfortable—though not necessary—and the bench." She closed the door. I went straight for the closet and grabbed a robe and threw it at Tara, then grabbed one for myself. "And the bench." Tara mocked the answer she received.

I opened the door to the bathroom and snapped a photo of the cabin-inspired walls. The sink was a granite bowl that sat on top of polished stones, which were arranged inside an opening of the large wooden countertop. The mirrors were framed with knotted boards, which matched the flooring. I changed into my robe listening to the waterfall sounds that filled the small area. "That running water is gonna make me have to pee." Tara looked up at the speakers in the corners of the room.

"That's why they play it in the bathroom," I laughed as I opened the doors under the sink in search for the baskets with our names on them.

"T. Johnson! Hey that's me." Tara pointed to the empty white basket next to mine under the counter.

"S. Miklun. You don't suppose that's Sami Miklun the model and actress, do you?" I dropped my items in my basket and pushed it back in place.

"Maybe, you think we'll see her?" Tara's eyes started to look alive again.

"I don't know. Maybe." I shrugged my shoulders then quickly took a picture of the lineup of baskets under the sink.

"Shall we sit on the bench?" Tara used her fingers to make quotation marks when she said *the bench*. I quickly sat down and looked to the side of us to watch the wall where we had entered. Shortly after Tara sat down, the wall facing the bench opened. We shifted our focus to the sound. A slender blonde in loose-fitting white pants and a matching tank top stood before us. "Clara and Tara, I'm sorry the camera will have to stay here with your stuff." She pointed toward the bathroom. I jumped up and put it away as instructed.

"Okay, come with me." She turned and started to walk away. We followed her down the hall, which was decorated in the same white tiling and mosaic lights as the lobby. "So I understand you will be reviewing your visit with us today for your paper." She continued to lead us down the hall without turning around.

"Yes, that's correct." I studied the walls for secret openings.

"What do you think so far?" She stopped at the end of the hall.

"Pretty impressive." I watched her open the wall with a push of a button.

The door opened to a cave. The walls were rigid rocks of gray and black. The ground was covered in ivory-colored pebbles. A rope of dim lighting outlined the room as a thin baseboard. From the door it appeared there were two wooden-framed beds up against the back wall. Our guide reached in and flipped a switch that turned on the lights around the two beds and the sound of rain.

"Go ahead and disrobe, climb in, and I'll return in just a moment." She motioned us inside before closing the door and disappearing. Upon closer examination of the softly lit room, I could see the beds were, in fact, tubs of mud. "Look, we have our own waterfall." I pointed to the back wall that had water running down its many ridges. I removed my robe and used the steps on the side to climb inside. The mud was warm, and it gushed between my limbs as I eased in. "Ew, this feels so wrong and so good all at the same time. Tara, get in." I sank into the brown mess covering everything but my head.

Tara laughed as she stood on the step looking down into the mud pit.

"Come on. I did it, now it's your turn, and you better hurry before she returns and sees you standing there naked," I laughed.

"Ahhh, I can't believe I'm doing this." She placed one leg into the goop. "Ew!" She then allowed the rest of her body to follow. "I guess it's not as bad once you're in, but the thought is overwhelming." Tara sank her shoulders into the warmth, resting her head on the railing.

The door opened, and our guide returned with a guy dressed in matching attire to hers. "How is everything?" His deep tone was as relaxing as the ambiance.

"Fine." I admired his blond hair, which was slicked back into a little ponytail. His eyes were bright blue, and his smile was hypnotizing. They walked to the far end of the room.

"Very fine," I mumbled to Tara.

"Stop." Tara smirked.

Candles were lit, and soon the room smelled of lavender. "Hello, I'm Dane, and you are?" He stood over me.

"Clara." I looked up at him, with feelings of guilt for enjoying the view.

"I'm going to help you relax. First, I'll have you lift your head." He showed me a rolled-up white towel. I did as he instructed. He ran his fingers through my hair to lift it from the mud and placed the towel behind my neck. "Okay, you can lean back now." He sprayed the ends of my hair with a bottle and wiped the muck from the red strands.

A mixture of mud and herbs were rubbed gently into my face. He then placed a warm towel to my forehead. By the time my new handsome friend left us, I felt like a limp noodle, left to simmer in nature's brew. "My face feels like it could crack." I spoke through my teeth.

"Yeah, mine too. Hey, don't you think you're enjoying your guy a little too much?" Tara muttered.

"Nothing wrong with looking. I'm happily married, but God gave me eyes to enjoy all the views that present themselves. It would be rude not to admire a magnificent work of art like that." I tried not to giggle, in fear of breaking my mask. Tara simply shook her head.

I closed my eyes and enjoyed the pleasant smells of lavender and the sounds of raindrops. I felt like I was wrapped inside a warm blanket, and I melted into the moment. Forgetting I was there with my sister, forgetting about the stress of life, and having a moment of complete relaxation. A smile forced itself through its restrictive layer of soothing herbs.

When I finally opened my eyes, the towel was being removed from my forehead, and the pasty mess was being washed off my face. "All right, there are showers around the wall. Get cleaned off, and we'll return for you when you are ready." The petite gal with long blond curls said as they walked out of the room.

"We just step out, and get mud everywhere?" Tara stood up.

"I guess." I stepped out and hurried to the counter of candles, where I could see there was a dark entry that led to a black door.

Behind the door was a shower room. The brightness upon entry was harsh on the eyes. I blinked a few times to adjust to the decor of white tiling matching the lobby and hallways. The room contained no mirrors or sinks. There was a toilet, which was enclosed by a glass-block wall in the far corner and large shower heads that lined the closest wall.

I turned on one of the showers and watched the mud dilute in a puddle of brown water around my feet.

"At least it's not in the hair, it should rinse off easily." Tara turned on the shower next to me.

"This reminds me of gym class. It's like standing in one huge shower." I looked around at the stark white walls, thinking it could use more color than the mosaic light fixtures and mud that now covered the floor.

"The trick will be not walking in the mud on our way out." Tara wiped the mud from her arms.

"I was thinking the same thing."

Once all traces of the pasty earth was removed from our bodies, we dried off with some towels we found hanging on the wall. We carefully walked back to the mud room and put on our robes. "So what do you think so far?" I looked to Tara, who was waiting patiently by the door, as if ready to escape.

"It was interesting." Her comment brought me back to the task at hand. Her wall of defense seemed to go up as soon as she'd realize it was dropping.

The door opened, and Dane was the only one standing there. "Follow me." He walked down the long bright hall, stopping at the next room. He pushed the button, and the door opened. The room was much like the one we were just in with stone walls; only the lighting was brighter and the floor was wooden like the changing room. There were candles lit on every surface and two massage tables in the middle of the floor. This room had subtle sounds of birds singing overhead. "You're gonna love this, I promise." I stepped inside the room, eager to get started.

"Disrobe, cover yourself with one of those towels, and lie on your stomach on the table. Someone will be with you shortly." He then turned and walked out the door.

"Have you noticed how brief, and to the point they are? It's like they're programmed." Tara removed her robe.

"I like it, less talk and more action. Bring on the masseuse." I lay face down on the table.

As soon as we were both in position on the table, the door opened. I watched the feet approach us through the hole in the table where I was resting my cheeks. They went right in to action without speaking a word. The fingers that worked out all the knots in my neck and back were delightful. Hot rocks were placed on our backs while they rubbed oils into our legs and feet. I couldn't see Tara's face, but her moans told me she was enjoying it more than she thought.

The massage was incredible, and my body was more relaxed than it had been in years. "We will leave you for a moment to put your robes on," a friendly voice informed before leaving the room.

"So?" I smiled as I grabbed my robe.

"You were right. That, I could do again. The mud, not so much." Tara tied the belt to her robe.

Next we were whisked away to another bright room with what looked like salon chairs. I was relieved to hear actual music, versus the nature sounds from the other quarters. We sat in the chairs, where our feet were placed in miniature hot tubs to soak in the jets of bubbling water, while being served a glass of chardonnay. "None for me, thanks." Tara lifted her hand in protest.

"I'm the one driving, the wine will be nice to help you relax." I took a sip of mine.

"All right, guess it couldn't hurt." She grabbed the glass.

Our chairs were reclined, and the ladies proceeded with our facials. A face and scalp massage that made even Tara smile with delight. The day was more than worth it, even if I didn't really get a chance to talk to Tara. I was so relaxed and enjoying myself; I almost hated the thought of bringing up anything that would welcome back the tension they had worked so hard to relieve.

By the time the ladies had finished with our feet, we had finished my glasses of wine. "How do you feel now?" I looked to Tara, who was smiling.

"Great. I'm happy we did this." Tara relaxed back into her seat.

"All right, we'll dry off your feet and walk you back to the dressing room." They wrapped our feet inside the towels, massaging them to soak up the water. I was tempted to step back into the pool of water so she would have to do it again, but I controlled myself.

As we were escorted from the room, I glanced behind me as I heard other footsteps. My mouth dropped, and my hand squeezed Tara's arm, as our earlier suspicion was confirmed. Sami Miklun was being led into the massage room where we had been prior. I wanted to squeal out to her, say something, do something, but my volume was stuck in the form of a knot in my throat, and then she was gone. "Did you see?" I whispered to Tara as we arrived at the door of the dressing room.

"Yes, and thanks for the best day of my life."

Chapter 19

The Truth

Driving back home, I was full of enthusiasm to get back and share my day with everyone. "I can't believe we saw Sami, I'm so happy you were there as a witness." I pulled out onto the road to take us home.

"That was pretty amazing." Tara continued to smile; her spirit was back in her eyes, and I was thrilled to be sharing the ride with my sister. The sister I had grown up with.

We talked and joked for most of the ride back, but as we got closer to home, she began to shut back down. "What's going on, Tara? You've been in a depressing funk for a long time. We had such a great day today, and now I can see you clamming up again. I don't like it, and I want to know what I can do to help. Help me, help you." I took my eyes off the road briefly to see if she was listening. Her focus never left the road ahead of us, making it impossible for me to see if my words had any impact at all.

"There are just some things going on that are out of your control." Tara continued to stare at the road.

"You can at least talk to me about it, so you don't have to work through them alone." I turned down the radio.

"I'm not alone. I have Sean." The sarcasm in her voice told me her words were meant as a dagger.

"So perhaps it's time to tell him *everything*." I was surprised that I didn't want to retract the words as they slipped out. I honestly felt it was time to inform him of her secret sacrifice.

"Pull over." Tara pointed to the pull off up the road.

"You're not getting out." I shook my head.

"No. I want to talk. But I want your undivided attention." She pointed back to the pull off. I was thrilled to finally have her initiating the talk that would help her, yet nervous about what she wanted to say. I slowed down and eased into the opening on the side of the road. Upon parking the car, she got out and walked to the guardrail.

I stepped out with jacket in hand and joined her on the railing. I watched the cars speeding by as I waited for her to start her story. "You know things got difficult after Grandma's ordeal, and against our conversation at the hospital, I quit taking my birth control. I hoped to get pregnant. I prayed for it every month. As months went by with no success, I became frustrated. I saw doctors, telling Sean it was to get to the bottom of the terrible monthly cramps I was having, not a complete lie by the way." She stood up and leaned on the car, facing me before starting with the remainder of the story.

"I found out I had endometriosis. My fallopian tubes were completely covered. We were told that if we wanted kids, I would have to undergo surgery. They could remove the tissue, and we'd have a six-month window. So after the wedding, we decided to do it. I had the surgery, and six months later, we still weren't pregnant. So the second time I went in, they removed the tissue and put me on fertility medicine. Six months later, still nothing. I now have too much scar tissue and have been labeled as infertile. I will never have any kids of my own—ever. Yet you and I know that's not exactly true. You tell me how I am supposed to explain *that* to Sean." Tears spilled over her lower lashes.

"I don't have all the answers, and I wish I could have been a shoulder for you throughout all of this. I do understand and know why you blocked me out. I also know you need to tell him. Sit him down and explain everything to him, from the beginning." I choked back all emotions to help express my thoughts.

"You have any idea what that could do to my marriage?" She wiped away the tears.

"You have any idea what it could do to your marriage if you don't? It's eating away at you, and you are becoming unbearable to be around. We need to get you to a better place emotionally. And I feel the truth is the only way to do it."

"I feel better having talked to you about everything and knowing where you stand on the idea of telling Sean. But I don't know if I can do that yet. That's a choice I'll have to make later." She stepped away from the car and looked to the door.

I quickly stood and grabbed her arms. "I wish you could have told me sooner. We're supposed to tell each other everything." I gripped her tight and pulled her close to wrap my arms around her.

"You're the last person I wanted to disappoint. I succeed at everything, that's who I am. But to fail at having kids, that's not something I wanted anyone to know. I didn't want you to feel guilty about Suzy." She sobbed into my ear.

I pushed her out in front of me. "No one will see you as a failure, I promise. I do have feelings of guilt about Suzy, but what's done is done, and there is no turning back now. I will help you through this—we are a team and that's what we do—but before we focus on the baby thing, let's focus on Tara, okay?" I opened her door.

"Okay. Have I really been unbearable?" She climbed into the passenger seat.

"Understandably so." I nodded.

The remainder of the ride was fairly quiet; I no longer felt I didn't know the person sitting next to me. I knew her more than ever and understood her dilemma. I presented my advice on how I thought it needed to be handled, but she was right; it would have to be up to her about how to deal with it in the end. I would stand behind her 100 percent on whatever choice she made, whether I agreed with it or not.

We arrived back at the house as it was getting dark. The guys were already back home, and I could see through the front window that play day continued. "Looks like Karson found a new train." I pointed to Sean who had Karson on his shoulders.

"You mean horsey?" Tara stared at the same image I was.

"No, we're talking about Karson. Everything is train-related." I reached into the backseat and grabbed my camera.

"Hey, so how did the separation therapy go for the boys?" Tara said as I opened my door.

I paused momentarily and shook my head. "They survived the night apart, barely. But Mom ended up with both of them the next morning." I stepped out of the car.

"It's a start. Baby steps." Tara got out and closed her door.

I stopped halfway up the walkway and altered the adjustments on my camera then zoomed in on the window of the house. "That won't turn out." Tara's voice went in one ear and out the other. As Sean and Karson were centered in the window, I snapped the shot of their silhouettes as they both were laughing. "I'll be sure to send you a copy." I continued to the house.

"It won't turn out, all you'll see is the glare of the window from the flash." Tara followed close behind.

"Did you forget what I do for a living?" I laughed as I reached the porch.

"Hey." Tara grabbed my arm before I could reach for the door. "Thanks for today." She smiled. "Thanks for going with me. I had fun." I opened the door.

"Mommy, we saw lion and bear and—"

"Kolton, let your mom get in the door first." Todd held him by his shoulders. Kolton looked up at his dad with wide eyes. "But, Daddy, she in," Kolton argued as Tara scooped him up and carried him to the couch.

"Well?" Todd whispered his question.

"I think we're good," I whispered back with a nod.

"How was your day, dear?" Sean asked as he set Karson on the ground.

"Choo, choo!" Karson lifted his arms up for another ride.

"Honey, come tell Mommy about your day." I sat on the ground. He ran to my lap and started telling me every detail of their day at the zoo. I heard most of his story, but my focus was on Tara, who ran into Sean's arms.

"I love you. I don't think I tell you that often enough. I really am lucky to have someone who loves me the way you do. Thanks." Tara clung onto him tightly as Sean gave me a thumbs-up.

"I do love you. Sounds like you had a great day."

Tara and I started laughing in unison as we thought about who we had seen there.

"What's so funny?" Todd looked down at me.

"You guys missed out on a great mud bath. That was Tara's favorite, by the way. And we saw someone there, that you would have been interested in seeing in a little white robe." I laughed as Tara cringed at the mention of the mud.

"Did you see someone famous?" Sean's eyes widened as we obviously peaked his interest.

"A model." I winked.

"You met someone famous?" Suzy ran down the hall wearing her pink pajamas and furry white slippers.

"Yep, we saw the blonde girl from your movie *Summer Beach*," I explained as she ran to her Auntie.

"You saw Sami Miklun? Was she wearing the pink bikini?" Todd's voice rose with excitement.

"You pig!" I laughed.

"No, Mommy, no pigs at zoo. We seen bear and monkey and gaffs and hipnose. No pigs," Kolton corrected me.

"Yeah, dear, no pigs. But it sounds like you had a great time and should go every year. Who knows who you'll see next time?" Todd extended his arm out to help me up off the floor.

"I would love to make it an annual trip. How about you?" I looked to Tara.

"If we can skip the mud, I'm game."

"I wanna play game in mud. I go, I go!" Karson started jumping with enthusiasm. Sean dropped to the ground and rolled over to the excited little boy.

"That's because you're a mud monster!" Sean set Karson to the ground and tickled him, causing him to giggle loudly. "Why don't you guys stay here tonight, and we'll order a pizza." Todd watched as Kolton jumped in the middle of the wrestling match.

"We can do that," Sean agreed in between the boys jumping on him like a trampoline.

The family slumber party was fun and exhausting. The kids enjoyed their auntie and uncle as they stayed up playing games and roughhousing well past bedtime. I enjoyed having Tara smiling again as we stayed up watching movies, eating pizza, and sipping on hot chocolate while the guys enjoyed the movies and beer.

As I prepared breakfast the next morning, I watched Tara with crossed fingers. Her expression of content contained a glimmer of hope that the transformation wasn't short-lived. Her mood had drastically changed for the better. I was concerned about how long the "upbeat Tara" could carry on without being weighed down by the secret that begged to be released.

"Can I help you with the pancakes?" Tara grabbed the milk from the fridge.

"Sure. Extra hands are always nice. My attention is always pulled into one direction or another before I can get too involved in anything around here," I laughed.

"Yes, I've noticed." Tara opened a drawer.

"Measuring cup is in the next drawer down. Don't get me wrong—I'm not complaining. I love my family, but yesterday was so nice and much needed. I hope we can do a trip like that every year." I placed some bacon in the pan.

"We will. Every April, our own little spring break."

"Mom! Can you tie this?" Suzy yelled down the hall. I looked to Tara with raised eyebrows, as if to put emphasis on my earlier comment. "I've got this. You go help Suzy." Tara took my spot at the stove. I thanked her before rushing to assist my damsel in distress. "Mom, this bow won't stay tied." She tugged at a lilac satin sash laced through the belt loops on her purple skirt.

"No problem. Watch Mommy closely." I dropped to my knees and tied the sash slowly.

"That's what I did!" Tears swelled in Suzy's eyes.

"It takes a lot of practice, but you'll get it. I promise." I stood up.

"Karson! Get out!" Suzy yelled as her little brother ran into the room.

"Come on, Karson, let's go find your brother." I took him by the hand.

"Mom. Can we do something? Without the boys. Just you and me." Suzy sat on her bed.

"What did you have in mind?" I stood by the door, still grasping Karson's hand.

"I don't know. Something special, just for us." Her eyes were large.

"I think I can arrange a mommy–daughter date. Is that what you were thinking?" I watched her nod, and the smile return to her face.

"Can we do the spa place like you and Auntie?" Her smile grew.

"Probably not, but I will think of something." I blew her a kiss as Karson pulled me from the room.

"Find Koko, come on." He pulled my hand. I followed his lead down the hall.

"See, Kolton's watching TV with your dad and Uncle Sean." I pointed into the living room.

"I no wanna." He shook his head.

"Okay, why don't you get your train track set up in your room, and I'll play after we eat." I lowered down to his level.

"K!" He spun back down the hall to his room. I rushed back to the kitchen to finish breakfast.

"I'm back." I breathed a sigh of exhaustion.

"You are a busy mom. Worth it?" Tara searched the cupboards until she found the plates.

"It's hard work. Some days, I feel challenged to the point of screaming for sanity. But no matter how bad my day, I can always look at them and say 'Yeah, it's totally worth it.'" I dished up the kids' plates.

"You're not overwhelmed with three kids?" Tara grabbed the small plates garnished with miniature pancakes and bacon.

"My family is the perfect size. Three seems to be the ideal balance for us, it works." I smiled as Karson ran up to me and wrapped himself around my legs. "Eat!" His grin bared his mouthful of sparkling whites.

"I've got your plate here, buddy, come on." Tara coaxed him out of the room.

While I dished up the rest of the plates, Tara got the kids set up at the table. As she came back into the kitchen, I handed her two plates with forks to take to the guys in the living room. I set our plates on the island in the middle of the kitchen and pulled a couple stools out from under its edge. "I take it we're eating in here." Tara took a seat in front of one of the plates as I filled a couple of glasses with orange juice.

"Yesterday was nice. You know Suzy asked me to take her to the spa? She wants a mommy–daughter day." I placed the glasses of juice in front of the plates.

"Are you gonna take her?" She took a drink.

"No. Not to the spa. I'm thinking more along the lines of Spring Park, a picnic and a camera." I sat down on the vacant stool.

"Don't you *always* have your camera?" Tara snickered.

"Yes. But I picked up a little digital camera. I got it for her birthday. So I think I'll plan our picnic for the Sunday after her party." I sampled a bite of the bacon.

"That would be a nice place for a mom and daughter to have some nice bonding time. She'll love it." She stared at the food on her plate in an obvious attempt to avoid making eye contact.

"You think you'll tell him?" I asked as she whipped her head toward the doorway as if to assure no one was within hearing distance.

"I haven't decided. I'm still teetering on the idea." She took a bite of her breakfast. I watched her as she continued to shovel food into her mouth. I could tell she was avoiding the conversation; I decided to leave it alone and ate my meal as well.

"Okay, Mom. I done. Play train. Come." Karson entered the kitchen with train in hand.

"Wait until Mommy is done eating, okay? Then I will be right there. I promise." I quickly took another bite.

"You say 'I promise' a lot. You know that can get you into a lot of trouble." Tara took a drink of her juice.

"I only say it if I mean it. I always make an extra attempt to keep my word. You should know that." I took the last bite on my plate.

"You've never let me down." She took my plate along with hers and put them in the sink.

"That's right. I will always have your back."

"Until death do us part," Tara uttered Todd's words, causing us both to laugh out in hysterics.

Chapter 20

Tara's Choice

A week had passed since the great sister escape to the spa, and Tara's positive mood had still remained. My relaxation had only lasted until I got back home that day, and with the planning of Suzy's party, I felt I was being run thin.

"Clara, its Belle!" Todd yelled out to me as I pushed Karson on the swing in the backyard. I ran to the house and grabbed the phone from Todd at the doorway.

"Clara?" Belle's voice was uncertain.

"Hello, Belle."

"You sound awful, you really need to take better care and get more sleep." Her comment made me stand straight and check my reflection in the window, as if she could see me.

"Been really busy with work, the kids, and planning Suzy's party. Will you make it this year?" I stepped inside and sat at one of the kitchen bar stools.

"I think we might. You're grandfather would like to see the kids. They are past that drooly stage, right?"

I debated lying to her, but I was too exhausted to come up with anything clever. "Yes, the boys are three now. No more drooling."

I admired the view through the window; Todd was chasing the giggling boys around the swing set. "That will be fine. We will try to make it then. You may want to get a nanny to help out a little. Three kids are too much for you, I can hear the defeat in your voice. But that could be because you started your family so young—you should have waited like your sister."

"Yes, I love you too, Grandma, and I'll see you tomorrow." I hung up the phone.

Now that I knew she may be at the party, my stress level doubled. I was really in no mood to defend my every move. I paused for a moment as I recalled the tension my mom would display when she knew Belle was going to come to any of her planned events. A smile developed as I felt a genuine connection to my mom.

My face fell into my hands as I took a break from reality. "So did she not play nice?" Todd's hand rested on my shoulder.

"She was Belle. That's all I can say. They plan on being there tomorrow." My hands found their way back to my lap. Todd spun me on the stool to face away from him and massaged my shoulders. "It will be nice for them to see the kids." I dropped my head and allowed the tension to be soothed by Todd's hands.

"Have they even seen the boys since they started walking?" Todd's hands stopped as he asked.

"I don't think they have. Karson ought to be a real nice treat for her," I laughed.

"That's just evil." He kissed the top of my head.

"He's just like I was. And she thought I was out of control, probably still does. She'll say the same about him, I'll bet money on it." I spun back around to face him.

"Don't let her bother you. I think you and the kids are perfect. That's all that really matters, right?" He grabbed my hands.

"Yes, honey, you are all that really matters," I chuckled.

"Knock, knock!" Tara's voice sang as she entered the house.

"Did you know she was coming over?" I asked Todd. He shook his head. "We're in here!" I yelled toward the door.

"Hey, sis." Tara entered the kitchen.

"Well, hello, this is a nice surprise." I stood up.

"I have a huge favor to ask." She grabbed an apple from the large blue bowl on the counter.

"Name it." I crossed my arms, uncertain I would be able to assist.

"Can I stay here a couple of days? I'll explain everything, but I just need to know if I can stay." She took a bite of the apple.

"Of course." I nodded as I looked to Todd.

"You can stay as long as you want." He added.

"It'll just be a couple days, just until I can figure some things out." Tara took another bite of her apple. I nudged Todd's leg to push him from the kitchen. At first he just looked to his leg to see what I was doing, but he finally got the hint.

"All right, I'll go check on the boys." He walked outside.

"Where's Suzy?" Tara looked out the window to the boys playing outside.

"Mom took her so I could finish wrapping her gifts and get things ready for tomorrow." I sat back down. "So what's going on?" I positioned my chin on my hands, as I rested my elbows on the counter of the island.

"I've been doing a lot of thinking, and I've realized something. My depression wasn't just about not being able to have a baby or not feeling I could share that with you. I've taken care of that, and yet I still feel miserable. Last night, while Sean and I were having an amazing date night, it hit me. You were right." She sat up on the counter behind her.

I sat back a little in preparation to hear the outcome of her night. "I love Sean. I want to be honest with him. I think keeping this from him is what's causing the pain I have in my heart. I'm going to tell him. I'm ready." She bit into the apple again.

"So if you haven't told him but you plan to, why are you staying here? I mean it's fine, I'm just curious about your plan." I was confused and relieved about her decision.

"Oh, I'm not gonna be there when I tell him. I decided I couldn't handle seeing the look on his face. I'll just call him and explain everything, give him a chance to absorb it all before he has to look at me."

"Are you sure you don't want to be there to tell him face-to-face?" I tried to hint that I felt it was the best way.

"No, I'm sure. I'm chicken, I know, but if I see his eyes, I may not do it. This is the only way. I've made my choice." Tara jumped down from the counter and looked at her watch.

"So when will you be calling him?" I watched her steady hands and felt confident that she would carry through with it.

"In about fifteen minutes. He'll be back from the gym and relaxing on the couch then."

For a brief moment the idea of him wanting Tara to fight for custody and take Suzy from me had entered my mind. A flash of Tara using my name to give birth reassured me that would be difficult for them. I started to have concerns about how he would respond, but living the lie had been an emotional challenge on all of us. I knew the time would come when Suzy too would have to know the truth. Having Sean in the loop before that happened would be beneficial.

"You okay with this?" Tara's words entered the thoughts in my active mind.

"Yes, of course." I snapped my attention back to her. "It'll be fine. Suzy is fine. I promise." Tara's stare grabbed me, and I knew she meant it.

"I know, and I knew this day would come. Just curious how he'll respond." I shrugged my shoulders.

"I'm about to find out." She pulled the phone from her pocket and left the room.

My heart instantly fell with a thud into my gut. I grabbed my chest with anticipation as she left my view. "So what's going on?" Todd entered from outside.

"She's calling Sean right now to tell him about Suzy." I bit my bottom lip.

"She's telling him over the phone?" He sat on the stool next to me.

"She said it would be easier." I studied his face in search of concern.

"So does she think he'll be mad and kick her out, and that's why she's staying here?" Todd's head tilted with confusion.

"I don't know. She thinks he'll need time to absorb it. She doesn't want to see the look on his face. Whatever the reason, she's here, and he's gonna know everything. "

We sat in silence as we waited for her to return with her report. I soon found myself pacing the floor while the eagerness imprisoned my every nerve. My jittery bones eventually took control of my movements and carried me down the hall. "What are you doing?" Todd asked as I left him to watch the boys. "Shhhh." I placed my finger on my lips and continued to wander down the hall. I stopped outside the closed door, listening closely for my sister's voice.

When my attempt to eavesdrop failed, I sulked back to Todd with my head dropped with disappointment. "I couldn't hear anything." I shook my head. His shook as well, but his was accompanied with eyes wide with a pity-for-me stare. "What?" I laughed, ready to hear a comment aimed toward my impatience. His answer came in the form of a gentle pat on the seat of the stool next to him. I obeyed his gesture and sat down.

"I can't just sit here. It's driving me crazy." I bit at the nail on my left thumb. Don't do that. Come on." He removed my hand away from my mouth and pulled me to my feet. I followed him as he led me outside. "The boys will entertain us. She'll find us when she's ready." He rubbed my back.

"Mommy!" Karson ran circles around us. "Push!" He continued to surround us with his giggles. "I can do that." I raced him to the swing, letting him win, of course.

I was pushing Karson on the swing while Todd and Kolton played kickball, when I noticed Tara enter the kitchen. "Go play ball with Kolton." I brought the swing to a stop. Once he was able to get off the stabilized seat, I ran toward the house. As I darted past Todd, I slapped him on the shoulder and pointed toward the door.

We entered the house side by side. Tara was sitting on a stool; her eyes were closed, her face pale. I sat next to her and waited for her to speak the first word. The silence lasted for only a moment before her eyes opened. "I did it. I told him everything." I waited for her to finish with his response, but the room grew silent.

"What did he say?" I leaned toward her, unable to control the question.

"Not much." She looked in the opposite direction.

Todd's hand rested on my shoulder. I grabbed it and looked within for words to break the silence. "He's probably trying to absorb it all." Todd finally discovered words to soothe the awkward moment.

"I expected him to respond differently. His silence was more disturbing than anything else I could have imagined." She wiped away the puddles of sadness filling in her eyes.

"Did he say anything at all when you told him Suzy was yours?" I held my breath.

"He said, 'I see.' I told him I understood it was a lot to take in, that I would give him some space until he was ready to discuss what we needed to do next. He didn't say anything, he just hung up the phone."

I pondered on the statement about what to do next. "Do next?" Todd asked the question that I was thinking.

"Yeah, with our relationship, if he'd stay or go." Tara shifted on her stool to face me.

"He loves you. He's not going anywhere." I grabbed her hand. "Let him sleep on it and he'll probably call you tomorrow with questions." Todd grabbed a glass from the cupboard.

"Maybe." Tara shrugged.

"He will. Remember when I was told about the plan? I know where he's at right now. He'll sleep on it and be ready to talk around lunch tomorrow." He smiled as he filled the glass with water.

"Let's do something to take our minds off everything." I looked to Todd for ideas.

"Bowling and pizza?" Todd placed the glass in front of Tara.

"That might be fun. What about the boys?" Tara looked out at the two playing in the yard.

"We go once a month with friends from work; they have a supervised playroom there. They love it." My smile grew at the thought of a fun night out.

"Sounds great. I just hope you guys are right. Sean hates nothing more than lying. I hope he can forgive me and understand." Tara took a drink from the glass.

"But he's a lawyer," Todd laughed.

"Yes, a lawyer who prides himself on searching for the truth." Tara defended Sean with a stern voice.

"You did the right thing by telling him. I really didn't think I would ever say those words. But I'm happy he knows because it's going to be better for you. No matter what he decides, I stand behind you and your choice to tell him. Now, with that being said, let's take the night off and go roll some balls." I stood to stretch my arms.

I gathered up the little ones and cleaned them up before piling them into the car. "Are you guys ready?" I went back in to the house.

"I think so. I haven't done this since high school, so no laughing." Tara passed me to join the boys in the back of the car.

"Got your keys?" I yelled down the hall.

"Yep!" Todd yelled from the bedroom.

He stepped out into the hall wearing his two-tone blue bowling shirt with the Rivers Karate Dojo logo on the back with our team name Deadly Strike below it. "It's just the three of us, it's not necessary to wear the shirt," I laughed.

"Oh, it's necessary to dress the part. This is my good luck striking shirt." He pulled on the bottom of his shirt as if to show it off.

"I'm not wearing mine, and I will still outbowl you." My hands landed on my hips as I proposed the challenge.

"Yeah, we'll see about that." He grinned as he approached me.

I pushed him out the door, then followed his lead to the car. Karson was telling his Aunt Tara about his newest train at Grandma's when we climbed into the front seat.

"Nice shirt," Tara commented as Todd started the car.

"Thanks, I'm happy to see *someone* appreciates it." He averted his eyes from mine as he pulled away from the curb. Karson filled our ears with stories about the track and schedule of his favorite blue choo-choo all the way to the bowling alley.

As Todd parked the car, I inspected the cars that occupied the spaces around us. "Oh, Tara, you'll never guess who's working tonight."

I unbuckled. "Who?" She unfastened Kolton from his booster seat.

"Cindy." I opened my door and climbed out.

"Our Cindy?" Tara helped Kolton out of the car while Todd got Karson.

"Yep. After a couple years of school, she came back and landed the manager position. She loves it." I grabbed Kolton's other hand.

The boys knew exactly where to go once we entered the bowling alley. Kolton dragged me down the side hall while Todd carried Karson to the room at the end, where we signed them in. "They'll be fine in here?" Tara looked around at the other kids playing on the climbing wall in the corner.

"Oh yeah, they'll be fine." I threw my arm around her and walked her back down the hall. The lanes were glowing in a multitude of colors as a disco light above them seemed to flash in the rhythm of the music.

We approached the counter and waited for the usual teenage boy to assist us. "Hey! T. M., how are you?" Cindy appeared from the back room.

"Fine. I didn't know you were back here." Tara's smile was contagious.

"I hear you're in the neighborhood too." Cindy nodded to me, indicating I had kept her informed.

"How did you get stuck watching the front counter?" I pointed to the shoes I wanted.

"Justin called in sick, so I'm covering for him." She grabbed two in that size from the shelf. "How about you Todd, what size?" She looked over me.

"Eleven."

"If I get a quiet spell, I'll come down and visit a little, it's great to see you." Cindy handed the shoes to Todd while talking to Tara.

"That would be great." Tara waved as we led her to an empty lane.

"Tara, you want me to get you a beer? Clara is driving home. I'm gonna have one." Todd placed a ball on the return.

"No, I don't drink." Tara looked over the collection of brightly colored bowling balls on the rack against the wall.

"After your day, a drink might be nice to help you relax." Todd started up the stairs.

"Go ahead and get her one," I volunteered her answer.

I was bowling fairly decently, staying close to Todd the whole game. Tara had finished a few beers and ordered another from the waitress when she made her rounds. "Good girl. Have some fun and enjoy your night away." Todd threw up a high five, connecting with hers as she giggled. Her rosy cheeks and enthusiastic energy indicated the alcohol was doing its job.

"Your sister is a kick." Todd pointed her out as she danced her way to deliver her ball down the lane. I couldn't help but giggle a little too as I watched her holler with delight even though her ball hit the gutter. Watching her plop herself down onto the floor to wait for her ball to return, I couldn't help but find amusement over the effect the three beers were having on her.

"How is everyone bowling?" Cindy sat next to me.

"I'm not having my best game, but the entertainment makes it worth it." I pointed to Tara sitting on the floor in the middle of a giggle fit.

"She doesn't hold her liquor well, does she?" Cindy laughed.

Tara threw another gutter ball and ran over and jumped on to Cindy's lap. "I have missed you so much. I'm so happy for you." Tara played with Cindy's blond curls. "I'm happy you're doing well too." Cindy adjusted her legs to better support my sister. "Is there a man in your life? Or are you waiting for Mr. Right?" Tara scooted across Cindy's legs, and onto the seat next to her.

"No real boyfriend. I'm having a good time with Bradley. But nothing too serious."

I watched Tara's face turn pale; before I could intervene, she jumped to her feet. "No! You can't date that rapist." Tara was face-to-face with Cindy.

"What?" Cindy's eyes were wide. "Tara, it's Bradly Cole, I don't think you know him."

I grabbed her by the arm and pulled her back.

"Oh. I don't believe I do." Tara calmed her words.

"Who were *you* talking about?" Cindy adjusted her seating.

"Nobody important." Tara motioned to the waitress then rushed up the step to collect her drink.

Cindy's creased forehead told me that the wheels were spinning inside her mind. "Lucky for us she doesn't drink very often." I sat next to her.

"Who was she speaking of?" She leaned in, ready to hear some interesting gossip.

"Hard telling, but she is working for a defense attorney. I'm sure it must be a case they are working on," I explained, in hopes to veer her away from figuring out the truth.

"You're probably right. I have to say, though, it's weird to see her like this. That would usually be you. It's like you've switched places. You guys were always good at that." She smirked.

"Aw yes, the good ol' days. I don't really miss them, nor do I regret them." I shrugged.

"I hope to have what you have someday. But honestly I don't feel I'm ready just yet." Cindy looked over her shoulder to Tara, who was sucking down another can of beer. "I hope you're driving." Cindy shook her head.

"I am. In fact as soon as this game is over, I'll take them home." I looked at the scoreboard overhead to see we only had a couple of frames to go.

"Looks like you're up." Cindy pointed to the lane.

"Awesome, send me some positive vibes." I rushed to the ball return.

"You're up, sweets, show me your best gutter ball!" Todd encouraged as he stared at the score showing me only three pins behind his score.

"Whoo hoo, sis. Knock 'em all down!" Tara hollered as she plopped in the seat next to Cindy. I gave her a thumbs-up, found my spot, focused on the center pin, and made my approach. I released my grip, sending the ball rolling down the lane. As it made its con-nection off to the right of the head pin, it sent them all flying out of the way, except two. I was left with a seven–ten split.

"Nice one!" Todd laughed in the background. I shook my head as I felt my defeat.

"You can do it!" Tara cheered. Knowing I'd never get them both, I grabbed my ball and focused on the seven pin. I hung my head in shame as the seven pin fell, leaving his partner still standing.

"Good try, Clara, you'll get him next time." Cindy clapped.

"I do hate it when that happens." I sat beside Tara.

"See. It's the shirt." Todd tugged at the base of his shirt.

"Yeah, yeah. Just bowl." I pointed back to the lanes.

"I will, just be sure to watch my score, baby." He approached the lane with ball in hand. He lined himself up, and without delay, he released the ball, sending it down the lane with great speed. The pins exploded on impact, resulting in a strike. Todd did his happy dance, waved his hands in the air and wiggled his hips. "Great, now do it again!" I yelled, happy to see him doing well, though disappointed that he was beating me.

Todd's ego was boosted as he bowled a turkey and left my score in the dust of his. Tara was in her own little world by the time we were ready to go. "I feel I've been freed and want to yell out to the world!" Tara raised her arms up high and made her announcement from the top of the steps for all to hear her.

"Come on, sis, let's get home." I wrapped my arm around her and pulled her down the aisle toward the door.

"I'll get the boys, if you want to get her out to the car before she says something she'll regret," Todd said as he changed his shoes.

"Don't be silly, it's not like I'm gonna tell everyone that you're my baby's daddy," she laughed.

"You would have to come up with something more believable than that, Tara." Cindy laughed as I swallowed my sister's comment. I laughed it off as I continued to escort her out to the car.

"Remind me not to allow you to drink in public." I helped her into the car.

"What? Why?" Tara climbed in.

"You nearly told everyone everything." I closed her door and got into the driver's seat.

"I wouldn't have said anything. You're overexaggerating the whole thing. Quit being a manby-panby." She buckled her seatbelt.

"I'm just cautious and thought you would be too." I started the car so it could warm up while waiting for the guys.

"I thought you wanted people to know now. You surely wanted Sean to know." Her arms crossed.

"What? Tara, I'm not having this conversation while you're in this condition. There really is no point." I focused on the familiar faces approaching the car.

"Maybe it would be better if everyone knew. That could fix a lot of problems," Tara mumbled.

I ignored the babblings of my intoxicated sister the rest of the trip home. I was hoping she would be more bearable once she was able to sleep off the alcohol. If not, the birthday party tomorrow was going to be a memorable one. My nerves cried out in a chuckle as I spotted Sean's car in front of the house. "This should be interesting." Todd looked back at Tara to see if she had noticed yet. "Oh boy, here we go." I pulled into my parking spot.

"Why is he here?" Tara leaned forward, only to be restricted by her seatbelt.

While Tara fought with her buckle, Todd jumped out to warn Sean of her condition. I got out and waved shyly to Sean then opened the back door to assist Kolton out of his seat. "Tara, can you unbuckle his?" I pointed toward Karson.

"Shit, girl. I can't get out of my own. This damn thing is broken." She fumbled with the clasp.

"All right, hang on a minute." I pulled Kolton from his seat then climbed in and reached over to undo Karson's, then Tara's.

The boys ran from the car to see Sean. I grabbed Tara's hand to help her from the car. "Move, I'm fine!" She pushed my hand away. I held the door as she stepped out. She took two steps past me and fell face-first onto the lawn, where she lay in laughter. "I got this, you go in." Sean ran to my aid. "Are you sure?" I stared at Tara, afraid to make eye contact with Sean.

"Yeah, go in. I'll take care of her and bring her in." Sean stopped in front of me.

"You may want to wait before you have any serious talks with her." I looked at him for a brief moment then looked back at Tara.

"I've got this."

I watched him help Tara to her feet, before I rushed to my family inside. I looked out the window to watch them. "Come on, they need some privacy right now." Todd pulled me away to help get the boys into bed. "What did he say to you?" I followed him down the hall.

"Just that he's still in shock and not sure how to respond right now. But loves your sister and the family and isn't gonna just throw that away."

My feelings toward him swelled with gratitude and admiration. I was overjoyed that my sister had found a guy to love her through thick and thin. He had proven once again to be a perfect addition to the family. Now we just needed to wait to see how he'd feel once the news truly sank in and the shock had worn off, and hoped that he'd feel the same way.

Chapter 21

Suzy's Six

The next morning, I was hesitant to run into my house guests. With it being the day of the party, I crossed my fingers and hoped that the tension I expected would not exist. I entered the living room where Tara was still crashed on the couch. "Let her sleep for a little longer. I imagine she'll have a headache when she awakes." Sean startled me with his request.

"Whoa. I didn't see you there." I grabbed my chest.

"I started the coffee pot. I can get breakfast started too if you want." He pointed toward the kitchen.

His focus was all over the place, as he too was leery about making eye contact. I knew mentally we were in the same place. I wanted to talk to him about the situation but wasn't sure where to start or what to say.

"For the record, I do understand." Sean's eyes found mine for a second to deliver his message.

"You don't resent me for the decision we made?" My insides shook as I waited for his approval.

"No. Though I can't promise I won't look at Suzy differently." He shook his head.

"As long as you don't look at my sister differently, I don't care." I looked at Tara as she started stretching, proving she was still alive.

"I could never do that. I love her. I'll stand by her side, no matter what."

"Hey." Tara announced her presence as she sat up on the couch.

"How you feeling?" I joined her on the couch.

"I've felt better." She rubbed her head.

"I don't doubt that. You think you'll be all right for the party today? Or you want to hang out here and avoid the family thing?"

"I won't miss Suzy's party, I'll be there." She leaned back.

I patted her leg with affection before getting up from the couch. Sean took my place next to her as I left to wake up the rest of the house. I almost felt sorry for her—not the hangover part but, rather, the facing Belle part. Tara had never had to experience the negative blows that Belle was famous for delivering, and if I could help it, I would protect her from those as well.

I woke up Todd and the boys. "Get up, guys, today is party day." I opened the bedroom doors as I passed them in the hall heading for the bathroom. I grabbed the pain reliever from the medicine cabinet and rushed down the hall back to Tara. "Here, take three of these. It'll help." I handed her the bottle.

"I'll make you some toast first." Sean got up and walked toward the kitchen.

"Looks like things will be fine between you and Sean," I whispered as I watched him disappear into the kitchen.

"I think so. We can only move forward from here." She nodded slowly.

"Auntie!" Karson screamed as he ran into her arms. Tara's eyes squeezed shut as she grabbed her head. "Shhh, Auntie's head hurts." I pulled him off her lap. "Auntie owie?" Karson pointed toward her head, which was still being cradled by her hands.

"Yep, let's leave her alone for a little bit and get you some toast and a banana." I carried him on my hip out of the room.

"Peanut butter!" he hollered entering the kitchen.

"Well, of course," Sean answered with a chuckle.

"You still have a banana and peanut butter every morning?" Sean took him from my hip.

"Yup!" Karson nodded enthusiastically.

PETRALIA J. L. FISK

"I want too!" Kolton entered the room, dragging a bright-green blanket behind him.

"Go sit at the table, and I'll get you guys breakfast." I pointed to the dining room. Sean set Karson down and watched the boys run from the room. I placed some bread in the toaster and grabbed the bananas. "Here, take Tara a banana, she could use it."

"Mmmm, toast and bananas." Todd wrapped his arms around me. "Breakfast of champions," I chuckled.

"I can finish here if you want to take a shower." Todd spun me around to face him.

"That would be wonderful." I pulled myself closer to him and kissed his cheek.

"Hungry!" Karson yelled from the dining room.

"You're up, sweetie." I released my grip and left him to tend to the boys while I tended to myself.

After my shower, I threw on a pair of jeans and the new red sweater I had bought just for the occasion. I was digging through my jewelry box for a pair of earrings when the collage of frames on my dresser caught my eye. It was amazing to think that it had been six years already since I had first held Suzy in my arms. I looked at the photos of the kids and picked up the one of my little princess at her first birthday, her lavender dress and chunky cheeks. I wondered where my baby girl had gone.

To see the picture next to it of her riding her bike seemed impossible. Her baby face had sculpted itself into a beautiful little girl. I set the photo back in place with the others. "I will miss those cute little baby cheeks," I said to myself, as I imagined the additional photos I would be adding to the collection, such as graduations, weddings, and someday, even grandchildren. Time seemed to be set on fast-forward; I was almost afraid to blink and miss an important milestone.

"Mommy!" Karson ran into the room and climbed up on the bed. "What are you doing?" I grabbed the earrings I was searching for from the box. "Daddy said dress me." Karson jumped on the bed.

"He did, did he? Well, I imagine I can do that." I scooped him up once he fell on his toosh on the bed.

"Hey! I not done bounce." Karson wiggled in my grip.

"Yes, you are. We have to get ready for sissy's party. We're going back to the bowling alley, and this time you get to bowl. Won't that be fun?" I carried him down the hall to his room.

"Yes! Fun! We go now?" He tried to run from my grip toward the front door.

"No, we have to get you dressed." I set him on his bed.

"Oh yeah. I wear train shirt," he announced as he began to jump on his bed.

I found one of his shirts with a train on it and a pair of pants. "Nope, I want blue one!" Karson continued to jump.

"Not today you don't. You're wearing this red one." I wrapped my arm around his middle and plopped him to his feet on the floor. "Arms up." I set his clothes on the bed.

"But."

"I said up." My arms crossed as I interrupted his rebuttal. His bottom lip hung low as his arms raised up high.

"Need help?" Tara leaned against the door jam.

I pulled off his pajama shirt and slipped on his new shirt. "I'm gonna change it." He pouted.

"No you're not, now change into these." I handed him his pants. He snatched them from my grip and did as he was told.

"You must be feeling better. You're standing anyway, that's a plus." I walked by her, motioning her out into the hall.

"I'm gonna live, I think." She turned her back toward the room. I peeked inside to see Karson was still following orders.

"So is everyone getting ready to go?" I looked around to see if I could spot Kolton. "Todd has already dressed Kolton, he just went in to take a shower. Sean is dressed and cleaning up in the kitchen. I am slowly making my way to Suzy's room to get ready to jump in the shower next." Tara pointed down the hall. "Great, where is Kolton?" I looked in at Karson again, who was nearly dressed.

"He's with Sean."

Satisfied with the status report, I left Tara to move slowly to her things stored in Suzy's room. I grabbed the bag of presents I had stored in the closet and proceeded to load the car with the party goods. Todd arrived to help as I placed the last bag of decorations in the back. "Good timing." I slapped his arm with a giggle. "Yeah, I was watching from the window." He held back his smile for only a second.

"I wouldn't doubt it." I shook my head.

"Just kidding." He grabbed my arm and pulled me in for a kiss on the cheek. "Tara almost ready?" The question barely rolled off my tongue with hesitation.

"She's in the shower."

I took a deep breath and prepared myself mentally for the encounter of family saga that I was sure to endure through the day. "Tara and Sean can come up when they are ready, get the kids I'm ready to go." I pointed toward the house before breaking away from his embrace to start the car. Todd was quick to round up the boys and I helped him buckle them in.

"I talked to Sean. They'll meet up with us once Tara is ready." He took over the driver's seat.

"Did you tell him to lock up when he left?" I watched the house move further from view as he pulled away from my parking spot.

"Yes, dear, it's covered." He adjusted the music station to his liking. I continued to remind the boys to be on their best behavior while at the bowling alley, as I refereed their premature bickering.

"We know, Mommy," they uttered in unison. A statement that was easier for them to say than do.

Our destination finally came into view; the parking lot was full of familiar cars and faces. Belle and Grandpa Matthews were standing next to their polished black *2010 Cadillac CTS-V*. I shook my hands as if to be preparing to enter the ring for a battle of survival. "You can do this. It'll be fine." He found a parking spot.

"I know, I always do, just gets exhausting after a while." I waved at Mom as she pulled up next to us.

"I got your back, baby." He turned the key, indicating our intention to stay.

I climbed out of the car with a proper smile in place. "Hey, sweetie, have you heard from Tara? I tried calling her, but I haven't been able to reach her," Mom yelled across the top of their little Saturn as she stood adjusting her wrap-style shirt. Suzy ran from the parent's car. "Did you bring the gifts?" She opened the back door. I looked to Todd, and with a simple nod, I was able to tell him to take care of the kids as I shared last night's occurrence with Mom. His returned nod showed his understanding.

I jumped into the backseat of my parent's car and told them the whole story. "How do you feel about it?" Mom crossed her arms as she jumped into therapy session mode.

"I'm happy he knows. I thought it might be awkward, but I talked to him, and I think it'll be fine. It should really help Tara and her depression," I said as my awareness caught Belle approaching the car. I nodded toward her stern advance. "I think we're done here, we better go." Mom opened her door.

"Starting your own little party?" Belle's nose pointed to the air.

"We were just going in. You ready to get your bowl on?" I joined them outside the car.

"My what?" Her forehead creased with confusion.

"Ready to do some bowling?" I swung my arm, releasing my imaginary ball down the middle of the parking lot.

"Yeah, we'll see." She turned around and walked toward the front door, leaving us to follow her lead.

"We were here last night, and Tara drank a little too much, so they'll be coming up a little later," I leaned in and whispered to Mom as we followed the stiff, snooty stance of Belle. "This could be an interesting day."

She rubbed my back. "I've been thinking the same thing." I smiled as I approached the entrance, where Belle stood firm, waiting for someone to open it for her.

"Let me get that for you, Belle." I opened the door and let her enter, controlling my itchy leg from rising to kick her in the rear.

The far end of the room had a section blocked off with black velvet ropes and a banner pinned to the wall that read
HAPPY BIRTHDAY SUZY!

Purple and white balloons were tied to chairs, and lilac-colored tablecloths decorated a half-dozen round table. "That must be where we are going." Mom pointed out my kids, who were already climbing on the chairs that faced the table with the cake.

225

Todd waved me over from across the room, and I accelerated my movement to help him with the bag of goodies. "I've got things started, but I really didn't know what you had in mind," he explained as I entered the party zone on the other side of the velvet ropes.

"You're doing great, honey. We can put the gifts on the big table with the cake or on the floor under it if we need to. The sandwich trays should be here anytime, they can go on there too." I looked over the bags to see if anything else needed to be addressed.

The kids' feet were adorned with red and blue bowling shoes, and I could see Dad and Todd had theirs on too. I looked to Mom and Belle, who were staring at each other with awkwardly forced smiles, trying to ignore the uncomfortable silence that had formed a cage around them. "All right, guys, let's go get our shoes." I stepped between them, looping my arms through theirs. Sandwiched between them, I escorted them to the counter. Belle's arm was rigid and detectably non-willing to participate in the display of affection, though her lack of struggle told me different.

I began to wonder if her behavior wasn't due to a lack of affection from her childhood. She appeared to want to be loved but didn't know how to show it. Perhaps some fun with family will help her out of her shell of destructive critique. My once bleak outlook on the day became more of a quest to reach out to someone who needed to be shown how to live happily. I smiled as I began to imagine a smile on Belle's face as she was shown how to have fun, a feature I had rarely seen associated with my grandmother. I released my hold on them as we came up to the counter.

"What size shoe would you like?" Justin, the pimply faced teen that worked the counter on weekends, asked in a squeaky voice.

"I'm a seven," Mom said, pointing to a cubby that was marked with the number she needed. He grabbed the shoes and placed them on the counter, placing a second pair for me on the counter as well. "Those are the right size, right, Clara?" I smiled and nodded as he blushed. I waited for Belle to respond, but her focus was set like a laser beam on the shoes on the counter.

"Belle? What size?" I nudged her.

She stared at the display of shoes behind Justin. "Are these shoes worn by other people?" Her hand laid on her chest below her neck, swallowing hard as if to keep from vomiting over the thought.

"Yes. But they are sprayed with disinfectant after each use, so they are clean." I pointed to a can of spray in one of the cubbies.

"Yes, ma'am, I can give them a spray before I hand them over to you too, if you like." He grabbed the can in question.

"I suppose that might work. Size nine would be fine."

She watched him closely as he sprayed the inside of the colorful pair of shoes. "Those are hideous, aren't they?" Her face cringed as she took them from Justin.

"They do match your outfit." I pointed to the blue that was the same color as her pants and jacket, which she was wearing with a white silk ruffled shirt.

"I can't remember the last time I wore something without a heel." She flipped the shoes over to examine the flat soles. I laughed as I thanked him and led them back to the family gathering back at the cake.

Grandpa Matthews was the first to line up for bowling with the guys. "Come on, Belle, get those shoes on, this should be lots of fun!" he yelled up the stairs. Her stare was intense; she looked at those shoes as if they would bite off her toes if she dared put her feet inside them.

"Belle, will you bowl with me?" Suzy's eyes were huge and hard to resist as she tried to convince her great-grandmother to take the next step and put the shoes on.

"I don't think they will fit." She set them on the floor and sat at a table looking down at the guys, who were already laughing and having a great time, no doubt at the expense of one another.

I ignored Belle's stubborn ways as I greeted everyone upon their arrival. Suzy soon gave up on her bowling partner as a few of her friends from school arrived. They put off the bowling quest and hit the pile of quarters on the table for the arcade across the hall. Grandma and Grandpa Marsh came in with their own shoes and large smiles. "So happy you made it." I hugged them and pointed

Grandpa toward the guys on the lane. "I better get my shoes on so I can show these guys how this is done." He winked as he walked away.

"Where's my little princess?" Grandma Marsh looked over my shoulder to find Suzy.

"She's playing with her friends in the arcade."

"Gammy!" Karson screamed as he ran past Belle and into Grandma Marsh's arms. I could see the vein darken across Belle's forehead but couldn't help but think *What does she expect?*

"Well there's my favorite bowling partner." His Gammy wrapped him up into a grandma cocoon of love.

"Come!" He pulled away.

"Kolton is already sitting down there waiting patiently." I pointed to the lanes over Belle's head.

"Come on. Come on. Come on!" Karson sang as he ran circles around us.

"I guess I'd better go. All right, let's go play." She took his hand. As they joined the others, I noticed Tara and Sean walking in with our sandwich trays. I rushed to help them.

"Hey, some guy just handed these to us. He called me Clara, I didn't have the heart to correct him."

"How are you feeling?" I extended my hand to assist her.

"I'm fine. I took those pills and am feeling closer to human now. How are things going here so far?" Tara slowed her walk and waited for the report.

"I'll put these on the table while you guys gossip," Sean chuckled.

"Everyone is playing nice. I got Belle to get a pair of shoes, just can't get her to put them on and bowl with us." I looked at Belle who was as still as a statue.

"Maybe you can get her to loosen up for a day." I shook my head as we got closer to her table.

"Belle, it's great you were able to make it. You wanna bowl on my team? I really suck at this stuff, so I thought maybe I'd set up with the kids." Tara sat in the chair across from Belle. "Well, it's nice that someone here has the decency to have some manners and show a little gratitude with a proper greeting." Her eyes rolled away from my direction. I restricted the urge to throw my arms into the air and scream, "I give up!"

"Your sister could learn from you. I guess it shouldn't surprise me, really." Belle talked as if I wasn't there.

"I don't know, I think she's pretty amazing. I'm proud of her and her family. I wouldn't mind having what she has." Tara struggled to defend me, as I bit my tongue in attempt to keep the peace.

"You have always been the funny and smart one, but honestly I wouldn't wish those boys on anyone. Especially that Karson, that boy needs a cage," she snickered.

I couldn't take it anymore; that one comment settled in with all the others she had aimed in my direct over the years. The collection of negativity proved to be too much as my provoked nerves exploded with anger. I lost control, and my body lunged forward. "Now wait just a minute." My tone remained steady as my hands hit the table. Our faces were now within inches of each other.

"That's what I'm talking about—complete and utter disrespect of your elders." Belle moved even closer to me without a flinch. My eyes locked onto hers, as if we were trapped in an old-fashioned staring contest.

"This is Suzy's day; let's not start anything we may regret later." Tara's hands grabbed hold of my shoulders and pulled me back.

"You're right, I'm better than that. As my grandmother, I love you dearly. As a person I find it difficult to even like you. You talk about disrespect, but you may want to look in the mirror and give yourself that same speech. I'd like to call you a coldhearted bitch right about now, but like I said, I'm better than that. Thanks for coming, it's always nice to have someone to add a little unnecessary drama to the scene. So now, if you will excuse me, I have a party to attend. There are people here who want to be here and are looking to have a good time. I refuse to allow *you* to ruin that. If you can act civilized, you may stay. But if you intend to continue to try and pull everyone else into your stewing pity pot, I will have to ask you to leave. The choice is yours."

I walked away, impressed that I was able to get my point across while still keeping my voice calm and not causing a scene. "Clara, I have a feeling you're going to regret that." Tara squeezed my hand.

"Oh, I've wanted to do that for so long, I could never resent that. It felt pretty good." I looked back to her table. She was no longer sitting in her seat. I scanned the area and found her already talking to Grandfather Matthews at the top of the steps. I could not make out any of their words, but their body language was enough to decipher the conversation.

Belle's finger was quick to point me out as the cause of her distress. Her mouth was moving rapidly, no doubt exaggerating my already harsh yet true comments. I was more concerned with the reaction that Grandfather Matthews would have to my behavior. I cringed as his attention put me in the spotlight. "I'm sorry," I said with no sound, hoping he would understand. His smile lifted the concern from my already overloaded mind. He stood stern as he looked back to Belle and pointed her back to her original seat.

My insides laughed as she lost her battle. Grandfather Matthews joined the guys on the floor for some bowling; Belle sat back down to pout, and I looked out at the crowd that had gathered to celebrate Suzy's special day.

"Good job, but you do know this isn't over. Belle will not let you win." Tara turned to face me.

"I know, but I'm not as weak as she thought either, so I think this could be a fair fight." I felt like a ball of fire, powerful and ready to take on anything.

"Down, girl. Let's just get through the day, and remember we are all family and have to see each other regularly."

I knew she was right, but enough was enough. Although I had felt like releasing all my tension out on Belle, I hoped that my initial outburst was enough to get my message across. I watched her sulk at her table; part of me felt bad and wanted to go talk to her. I didn't feel I owed her an apology, but I felt I owned her better clarification. I couldn't help but think that she didn't realize what effect she had had on me all these years and that maybe she deserved a decent explanation.

Another part of me enjoyed seeing her drowning in a puddle of humility, allowing her to get a taste of her own medicine. "I better wait before I talk to her again." I started to take a step in her direction but pulled myself back.

"That probably would be best. Wait for things to settle inside both of you a little first." Tara patted my shoulder.

Chapter 22

Milestone for Belle

Suzy's special day was undoubtedly a memorable one. I continued the day with the planned festivities, trying to act as if nothing had happened. Truth was, I was still absorbed with thoughts about Tara and her choice to spill the beans to Sean and, of course, the recent episode with Belle, which had put her in her place, at least momentarily.

"Kids want to play one more game. Why don't you go ask Belle to join us?" Tara wore a coy smile.

"Maybe I will." I adjusted my shoulders to stand tall and proud; after all, I should be the bigger person and not stoop to her level. I inhaled and marched up the steps. I approached her as if nothing had happened. "Belle, care to join us in a game with the kids?" I sat down across from her at the table.

"You really want me to?" Her voice was soft and pathetic.

"I would love for you to join us." I felt like I was talking to one of my kids.

"I'll think about it." She looked off into the other direction, indicating the conversation was over.

Feeling defeated, I shrugged my shoulders as I looked toward Tara and Grandma Marsh, who were watching the scene with Belle. "All right, well, you know where to find us if you decide to join in the fun." I turned away and walked toward the kids screaming my name to join them. I waved to my fan club and returned to the floor to take my turn at rolling the ball down the lane. "Take it easy on 'em, sis," Tara laughed as I reached for my bowling ball.

"I'll try."

I purposely sent my ball rolling toward the large bumper in the gutter. The ball hugged the edge of the lane down to the lineup of pins, where I knocked down two. "Booooo!" Suzy yelled behind me.

"Should I knock down the rest?" I barely finished asking, before my ears were ringing with the yells of "Yes!" being screamed by the kids. I retrieved the ball and released it down the lane; as the remaining pins fell on contact, I heard a familiar voice behind me. "You do make that look easy."

I spun around to see Belle standing on the stairs wearing the bright blue and red bowling shoes. "Come on down, you're next," Tara summoned her down to take her place. I grabbed Tara's ten-pound ball and walked it to Belle. "Come on, I'll show you." I grabbed her by the hand and escorted her to the end of the ball return. "Hold the ball up like this." I placed the ball on her hand and positioned it front of her. "Keep your eyes on the front pin, approach the line, and let her go." I demonstrated my approach with an imaginary ball in hand. "Now it's your turn." I stepped away and let her have her try at it.

Belle looked back at me with no expression. I couldn't tell if she was excited, nervous, or ready to run back to her table of solitude. I gave a thumbs-up and a smile of encouragement. I couldn't help but feel this was a real milestone for her and our family. She turned back to face the pins before her. She took a slow advance to the lane and quickly released her grip. She watched as the ball went toward the gutter; it bounced off the blue bumper and veered straight for the center of the collection of white pins, sending all of them down. She turned around with a wide smile—something I don't recall having seen on her face before; it was definitely a nice change to her appearance.

"Good job. That's a strike." Tara stood to cheer with the kids. Karson was jumping up and down on the chair. Grandma Marsh and the guys next to us stopped in their tracks to see the commotion. "Good job, Belle." Todd clapped. Her face lit up as everyone announced their praise.

"I'll admit, this is fun." She sat in the chair next to Karson, who was still standing and clapping for her.

"Worth wearing the used shoes?" I nudged her shoulder softly with my elbow as I stood next to her.

"Possibly." She grinned.

It wasn't until after everyone had left and we were cleaning up after the party that Belle truly answered my question. "I had a lot of fun today. It was totally worth putting on the old clown shoes." Her expression was back to its normal stern appeal, but the shine in her eyes confirmed her statement.

"I'm sorry I snapped earlier." I wrapped my arm around her and whispered in her ear.

"It's understandable. I can be a little harsh at times, I know. It's only because I love you enough to push you to strive for the best."

I knew that was the closest thing to an apology and words of affection I would ever get from her, and I took it for what they were. "I love you too, Belle." I pulled her closer to me for a brief moment then released my grip. I could see Tara and Suzy talking at a side table and smiled to see them having a close relationship. Karson and Kolton were dancing to the music playing overhead, laughing and giggling, enjoying their own personal world. I felt content; everything seemed to be perfect.

Everyone said their good-byes as they all parted to go in their own directions. "I'm happy you and Belle were able to break down parts of that wall between you guys." Tara helped buckle in the boys as Todd and Sean loaded my car with all the new toys Suzy received as gifts. "Me too." I watched the parents pull out of the parking lot with the grandparents following their lead.

"You guys going straight home?" I finished buckling Karson into his seat and closed the car door.

"Yeah, we have a lot to talk about. I'll fill you in with all the details when I call Tuesday to wish Suzy a happy birthday on her actual day," she explained as she walked around to the front of the car.

"Sounds great. I have to admit, you're doing better today than I thought you would after last night." I plopped my purse on the hood of the car and searched for my keys.

"Yeah, I don't want to talk about last night. And you may want to turn in a little earlier tonight." Her arms crossed as her lips pressed tightly together in an obvious effort to not laugh.

"What's so funny?" I dropped my arms to my side. "You gave your keys to Todd to put the presents in the back." She pointed to the back of the car.

"Smart ass." I laughed.

Once I retrieved the keys from Todd and gave my sister a farewell embrace, I started the car and waited for Todd to climb in. "Ready?" Todd took his seat on the passenger side.

"I am. The party was an eventful one, and I am exhausted." I started the drive toward the house. The ride was quiet; the kids fell asleep shortly after pulling out of the parking lot and woke instantly the moment I pulled up to the house.

The sky's hazy hue of pinks and purples grabbed my attention. I took a moment to admire nature's canvas as the sun was starting its downward voyage.

"Babe. You want to get Kolton unbuckled?" Todd's voice pulled me back to my family. I nodded as I opened the car door. I released Kolton from his seat of safety and watched him run up the walkway to catch up to Todd and his brother, who were already unlocking the door.

I gazed upon the view before me with feelings of pride and comfort. My muscles no longer held stress about what would happen if Sean found out our little secret. For the first time in six years, I was worry-free about having Suzy ripped from the happy home I had created for her. Suzy ran around the yard catching her second wind, with her brothers close behind her. "Are you coming in?" Todd watched me from the top step. I took another look at my family and surrendered to the feeling of completion they provided.

I joined Todd on the step and motioned the kids inside. "Suzy, jump in the shower and I'll bring in your stuff." Todd ruffled her hair as she ran past him. "I love you." I rubbed his hand as I walked by him to go inside.

"I love you too." He grabbed my arm and pulled me back to him. "You okay?" he asked, still holding my arm.

"I'm fine." I placed my other hand on top of his, as my heart warmed at his touch. "That you are baby. But I was just asking because you've been daydreaming, thought something might be on your mind." His voice was soft and sincere.

"That's why I love you. I'm fine really. Just feeling blessed to have you and the kids, I'm absolutely loving my life. I had words with Belle today, and I think it made things better between us. Now that Sean knows and Tara is getting back to her old self, I feel things are falling into place. I feel like I can relax."

Chapter 23

A Moment of Weakness

The feeling of relaxation stayed with me through the next couple of days. I hadn't heard from my sister and knew that was a good sign. Suzy's actual birthday had arrived, and Tara would be calling her after school to give her wishes and to fill me in on how things were going between her and Sean. I was looking forward to hearing from her. Even more, I was looking forward to my special date I had set up for Suzy and myself.

We were due to a peaceful day at Spring Park on Sunday if the weather held, but today, I had plans to surprise her after school. I was going to pick her up and take her out for a milkshake. My day was nearly done at work and I was getting excited to see the surprise on her face. "All right, Trevor, I'm out of here." I shut down my computer. "Give Suzy a birthday wish for me too."

He continued working, not once lifting his eyes from the screen.

"You got everything under control? You need me to stay?" I felt guilty as he seemed to be overwhelmed with his workload. "It's fine. Just go. I'll make sure you make up for it tomorrow." He lifted his attention from his work with a smile.

"Perfect. See ya!" I darted from the room.

Suzy was growing up so fast and becoming her own person. She wasn't just my beautiful daughter but one of my greatest friends.

Time spent with just the two of us was rare, but cherished. I clocked out, grabbed my coat, and rushed out the door. Todd would be picking up Karson and Kolton from my parents, giving me plenty of time to spend with my little princess.

The school was only a few miles away, but the traffic at this time of day always doubled the drive time. I hit all the side roads to avoid the craziness on the main highway. All the zigs and zags on the quiet rural roads didn't get me there any faster, but it did make the drive a lot less chaotic.

I pulled up behind a bus parked out in front of the school just as the bell rang. I watched as teachers escorted their students out the door in single file lines through double bright-red doors. I recognized the short blond curls of Suzy's teacher Mrs. Clark. I stepped out of the car and waited for Suzy's face to appear within the row of cheerful children. One by one the kids poured out of the building and out onto the concrete steps leading to the walkway. Soon Mrs. Clark's line-up came to an end and another teacher started leading her kids outside.

I searched the line of kids again and again. Suzy was not among the chain of kids. I refused to panic as my chest began to pound rapidly like the drummer of a rock band. I moved through the crowd positioned in front of the busses and made my way to Mrs. Clark. "Hello, Clara. Did we forget something?" She chuckled, obviously amused by my appearance. I stared at the short and bubbly figure before me, confused by her question.

"I've come for Suzy. Where is she?" I watched the smile vanish from her face. "What do you mean? You already picked her up. Are you all right?" Her eyebrows dropped with concern. Her head tilted slightly as if she thought I was losing my mind. For a brief moment I shared that same notion. Then my sister's face entered my thoughts. "Never mind. I just forgot something." I left her with a blank stare as I weaved through the swarm of students and ran into the building.

I stopped at the desk and looked at the ledger on the counter. "Mrs. Rivers, how nice to see you again." The receptionist's voice barely played in my ear as I saw my name as the one who signed Suzy out for the day. My body fought through the emotions of confusion, concern, and fear as I hurried my way back to the car.

I dumped my purse out on the seat and fumbled through the mess for my cell phone. My shaking fingers fumbled through the numbers to dial Tara's cell. "Come on, answer." I tapped my foot as I listened to the ringing but no voice on the other end. I quickly hung up and dialed her home number, again no answer. I laid my head on the steering wheel in a state of complete panic. "Think!" I yelled to myself. "Where would she take Suzy?"

I grabbed the phone, debating whether or not to call Todd or Sean. My mind was swimming with thoughts of Tara and her motive for taking Suzy without asking. Only one answer came to mind, the unspeakable, the ultimate breaking point for Tara for sure. Kidnapping. I didn't know what to do, who to call, where to go, I felt helpless. As I watched the buses and other cars pulling away, a mother and daughter walked by the car. I heard the mom mention they would be going to the park, and it dawned on me where I needed to go.

I quickly fired up the car and raced back to the highway. The conversation I had with her in the kitchen only days prior played in my head. *That would be a nice place for a mom and daughter to have some nice bonding time. She'll love it.* I could hear her voice loud and clear, as if she were sitting next to me. Fortunately for her, she wasn't in the car with me, because I wanted to choke her. I wanted to take her by the throat and smack some sense into her.

As I crept along with the traffic that was holding me back from finding my girl, I felt no feelings of worry for Suzy's well-being. I knew she was in good hands. My concern lay in the thoughts of finding them. The question of "What if?" hovered over me. What if she wasn't there? What if she was on the run with Suzy? What if I never seen either one of them again?

I rolled down my window and took in a breath of fresh air, but what if I was overexaggerating the situation? What if she picked her up with every intent of having her back by the time school was out and lost track of time? I grabbed my cell phone from the seat and tried once again to call her. My toes curled in suspense as I held my breath through each ring. I restrained myself from throwing the phone as it hit the voice mail, unanswered.

Finally able to speed around the leisurely drivers, I rushed through the curves of the road. Growing closer to my destination, I prayed they would be there. I had no other leads and was relying on this one hunch. The last mile took the longest as my gut tied itself into knots. My mind was so preoccupied that the color of the trees lining the entrance to the park never even registered. All I saw was a tunnel of gray leading me to my baby.

As I drove past the park sign, the bright-blue hue of Tara's car grabbed my attention. My eyes swelled with relief. I parked next the vacant car. My hands covered my eyes as they released their tension. My heart ached, and my blood was boiling. I got out of my car biting my lip as I tried to put myself in her shoes. I stopped in my tracks in front of the trail leading to the gazebo. I wiped my tears. Collected my composure and decided I would listen to her explanation before jumping to any conclusions.

I hurried down the trail until I spotted Tara sitting on the bench in the white pergola. Her back was to me, but I knew she felt my presence as she shifted in her seat. I quickly scanned the area for Suzy. My lungs exhaled in liberation as the view of my little girl picking flowers near the lake made its presence. I searched for words to say as I slowly walked toward Tara.

She scooted her body over on the bench to allow me room to sit beside her. We each sat in silence as we waited for the other to cut through the uncomfortable silence around us. "Sorry if I worried you." Tara stared out at the lake. I had no response as I looked to her to finish her justification of the situation. "I don't have a good excuse if that's what you're waiting for. It just seemed like the perfect plan at the time." Her eyes continued to focus on the lake.

My initial response was confirmed. Now the question was how to react, but I was too numb to respond to any of the choices that emerged in my mind. My tongue was tied, my heart was broken, and my body was frozen. "I know you're mad at me, and you should be. Hell, I'm mad at me." She finally looked at me. "I'm so confused. I want her all to myself. A part of me tells me she is mine and I deserve to take her as my own. But the reasonable side tells me she is not a doll and I can't just take her from her family and play house with her. That wouldn't be fair to her at this point. Of course I can't help but focus on what would be fair to me at this point either." A tear rolled down her cheek.

I looked out at Suzy, who was still content tossing daisies in the lake and watching them slowly float away. "It's like looking out at a beautiful painting. She's become a wonderful little person, beautiful inside and out." Tara placed her hand on mine. I considered pulling away; her hand felt cold and unfamiliar. I tussled with the feelings of anger and hate, wondering if I was confusing one feeling with the other. I felt hollow inside; she had always been a big part of me, but her actions had disconnected her spirit from me instantly. I knew I wanted to find the connection again, but I also knew that was not possible without trust. I had nothing to say to her.

"Please say something. I know what I did was wrong, and I had already decided I couldn't go through with it. We were going to start heading back when you arrived, I swear. I don't blame you for being upset. I wouldn't blame you if you wanted to hit me. Maybe that would help—go ahead, hit me." Her eyes closed tight in preparation for the strike.

I got up and joined Suzy by the lake. "Hey, sweetie." I hugged her tight. "Happy birthday." I released my grip.

"Hi, Mommy. You going with Auntie and I to the ocean?" She picked another flower and threw it in the water.

"There's been a change of plans, honey. We're going to go back home, your auntie is not well." I grabbed her hand and walked toward the trail. Suzy released my hand and ran toward Tara.

"Bye, Auntie! I hope you get feeling better. I love you." She jumped into her arms.

Tara's tears showed remorse. I wanted to understand what she was thinking and feeling. Growing up, that had never been a problem, as we had experienced everything together. This was beyond my comprehension. Had it been anyone else, I'd have killed them, or at least see to it that they got what they deserved. This was different. She wasn't just family, she was my twin—literally my other half—

and by rights, Suzy was hers. I couldn't talk to her, not until I knew what to say. "Come on, Suzy." I reached my arm out to her.

"Auntie, are you okay?" Suzy wiped a tear from Tara's face.

"Yes, honey, I'm fine now. I just had a moment of weakness."

Chapter 24

One More Time

I floated through the remainder of the week as if I had been living in a dream—or a nightmare really. I decided not to tell Todd about her so-called *moment of weakness*. I played Tara's situation over and over in my mind, wondering how I would have acted if the shoes had been on my feet. I wanted to talk to her and pick her brain, but I still wasn't sure what to say.

"Clara, phone." Todd held it out to me. I dried my hands of the dirty dishwater and grabbed the phone from him. I sat at the island on the closest stool. "Hello." My finger wrapped around one of the red spirals framing my face.

"Hey, sis." The unexpected voice answered. "Please don't hang up," she quickly added.

My first reaction was to do just that; why I didn't, I don't know. "I'm listening." I watched Todd walk outside to play with the kids.

"I just wanted to talk to you. Explain things and apologize." Tara's voice was soft and shaky.

"*I'm sorry* isn't going to cut it." I stood up.

"I know, I know. I'm not sure how I will be able to make it up to you. What I did was wrong, and I know that. I'm not sure what I was thinking. Well, actually I was thinking that since everything was out in the open, maybe I could have my baby. There was nothing I

243

wanted more. I felt lost. I thought this was my only chance to true happiness. I don't expect you to understand. I don't expect you to forgive me, I just wanted to explain myself." The phone grew quiet.

"You scared me. You broke my trust in you. That is something that can't be fixed overnight or with a simple sorry." I stared at my feet as I paced the floor.

"So what do we do now?" Tara asked, her voice still hushed.

"I don't know. I can't keep her from you. I still want you to be part of her life. But I don't know how to regain the trust. How do I know you won't have another episode and take off with her? You say I don't understand how you feel or felt, but I don't think you understand how I felt when I thought Suzy was gone. What's more is I thought I had lost *both* of you, which made it difficult for me to breathe. By taking Suzy, you took so much more from me than just my daughter. You stole from me my relationship with my sister. That's a punishment I don't feel I deserved. I'm sorry you have regrets. But what I don't understand is that we were getting along so great, why not talk to me?" I sat back down.

"I didn't know what to say. I couldn't tell you I was thinking about picking her up from school and starting a new life with her. When I got dressed in her room that day of her party; I saw her artwork taped to her walls and her dolls set up for a tea party. I realized what I had been missing all these years. I decided then that I wasn't going to miss anything else. I was going to be a bigger part of her life. I don't have regrets. I really don't. I just don't understand how I'm supposed to fill this void of parenthood, it's a struggle knowing I can't have kids when I already have one I can't call my own."

"I can't say I understand how that must feel. I can only imagine. But there has got to be a better solution to this dilemma than taking Suzy away from her family here." I could feel my left foot tapping out of control on the floor.

"I'm not taking Suzy, that would just open a whole new can of worms that I'm not prepared to deal with. I am, however, taking a little vacation. I'm attending a retreat for mothers who have given a child up for adoption. It's a weekend getaway just for me. I think it'll do me some good to get out and talk to others who understand and talk to professionals that can help me cope. I'm leaving next week-end. I'm hoping we'll be able to talk when I return."

"I think that's a great start. I would love to hear all about it when you get back." I wanted to be mad at her, but the more I heard the sorrow in her voice, the more I found myself feeling her pain. I wanted to hold and protect her like I did when we were little. I felt the urge to find a solution.

"You think we could be cool again? You think you can find it in your heart to forgive me?" Tara asked.

I found it hard to answer the question; I paused while I search for the right words. "I won't rule that out as a possibility. I will never forget, but as you rebuild your trust, I think I can learn to forgive." I choked back a tear as my heart ached at the thought of not being able to trust my best friend.

"I will make it up to you, I swear. I will earn back everything I lost with you, I promise. My moment of weakness was a real eye opener, and I have discovered my strengths and my weaknesses. You'll be proud, you'll see." Her voice rose with excitement. I knew she had a plan; I could hear it in her voice.

It was days before I calmed down enough to tell Todd what had happened between my sister and me. He responded a little calmer than I had in the beginning but shared my same concerns. "We'll give her another chance. She is family, and that's what we do." His words rang inside my head every time I thought about her. He was right, and I knew there would be a day when I would be able to drop my wall once again.

Tara attended her retreat and called me immediately upon her return. Her spirit was more upbeat; she spoke with confidence much like she had when she had delivered her graduation speech. She called me weekly after that; they were usually short conversations of basic chitchat and always ended with "I love you, sis." As the weeks stretched into months, the calls stayed regular. We never mentioned that day. The calls never contained an apology; they were short and sweet, and I found myself looking forward to hearing from her.

Todd and I were playing a family game of Go Fish with the kids when the phone rang. "Hello?" I answered.

"Hey, sis. What are you doing tomorrow night?" It was Tara.

"No plans, why?" I handed over my mermaid card to Suzy as she asked for it.

"Sean and I are coming down. I want to see you. Is that all right?" Her voice was stern as if to demand the request, more than ask.

"Sure." I hesitated in my response.

"Great. See ya tomorrow. I love you, sis." She hung up.

I wanted to see her. I was curious how I would feel once I was face-to-face with her. I hoped there would be no awkwardness. I worried I wouldn't want to be around her without wanting to rip her head off and hand it to her. This could be an interesting visit.

My brain was no longer in the game. I excused myself from family night and took a long hot bath.

I was soaking in the tub when it finally dawned on me what needed to be done. I could fix this. I jumped out of the tub and called her back. "Sis, what are you doing tonight? Can you come down right now?" I slipped into a pair of sweats, balancing the phone between my ear and shoulder.

"I suppose I can do that." Her voice was now the hesitant one.

"Great, I love you, sis." I hung up the phone and put on a shirt.

I entered the dining room with a newfound smile. "What are you up to?" Todd asked while handing over a starfish card to Karson.

"Tara is on her way over." I sat in the chair next to him.

"And you're all right?" He laid his cards on the table.

"Never better." I smiled.

"You're up to something; do I want to know what it is? No wait, don't tell me. I think that'll be best." Todd got up from the table. "All right, guys, game over. Suzy, jump in the shower before Auntie Tara gets here."

It was nearly bedtime for the kids when Tara and Sean arrived two hours later. I opened the door and watched them walk hand in hand up the walkway. "Come in," I insisted as I stepped aside for them. The kids surrounded them with yells of delight and hugs.

"All right, kids, let them in the door, come on, back up a little." Todd raised his voice over their noisy cheers then watched them withdraw from the visitors.

Tara gave Suzy a big hug and then approached me with open arms. Her eyes were impossible to deny their request, and I surrendered to their invitation. "It's good to see you. I've got something I want to talk to you about." I held her out in front of me.

"Me first." Tara walked to the couch and sat down.

Todd sent the kids to play in their rooms so the adults could talk. "I've been busy making things right with myself. I figured I needed to do that first before I could resolve my relationship with you." Tara kicked off her shoes and pulled her legs up onto the couch to get more comfortable. "I learned a lot at the retreat, and I'm feeling much better. I called Belle and talked to her and Grandfather Matthews. I told them I had gotten pregnant and put her up for adoption. I left out the part about you having her, but at least I'm no longer held up on a pedestal that's too high for me to keep my balance. The secret is no longer something that can eat away at me." She looked to me for a reaction.

My mouth dropped open, but the shake of the head was all I could do. "I've got a new job too. I'm working at a law firm, they specialize with juveniles. I'll get to help kids. I love my job. I'm loving my life, and now all I need to feel complete is to know I have a sister that can forgive me." Her gaze was glittery with moisture.

"That you can have. But I know of one more thing that would make your life complete, something else that I can help you with." I could hardly keep my plan to myself any longer.

"You forgive me?" Tara's big greens overflowed with tears.

"Yeah, I do, and I have another plan." I wiped away her tears with my thumb.

"No more plans!" Todd hollered from the recliner.

"Oh, this is a good one." I smiled.

"What kind of plan?" Tara's brows lowered with confusion.

"The greatest plan. I was thinking about the greatest gift you gave me. As a sister you have given me so many things, but the greatest of all was Suzy. True, it was not a planned gift, it was not a common gift, but it was a gift. The gift of life is a tremendous thing, not one that just anyone can provide. But you gave to me my firstborn. I, in return, would like to do the same for you." I was beaming from the inside out. I couldn't wait for her response.

"What do you mean?" Tara's forehead creased with uncertainty.

"I mean surrogacy—I will carry your child for you. This time there will be no secret sacrifices. We'll let all our family and friends know that I'm carrying my niece or nephew." I grabbed her hands and placed them in mine. "What do you think? It's perfect, huh?" My sorrow for her broken heart transformed into enthusiasm.

"Are you serious? Do you really think you could do it? It's not easy to go through the motions of pregnancy and get nothing out of it."

"I'm not getting *nothing* out of it. I'm gaining a niece or nephew that I will be able to hype up on sugar and then send home. I'd say it's the only way to go. Let me do this for you," I nearly begged.

"Okay." She nodded. I had imagined her response to be filled with more enthusiasm than she expressed, but her distant stare indicated that she was in a state of shock. The blank gaze on Todd's face told me he was also stunned. A look that told me I was sure to be hearing his opinion as soon as they left.

I was right, once the kids were in bed and our guest had left, Todd voiced his opinion. "That's a big decision. Don't you think we should have talked it out first?" His arms were crossed.

"You said you didn't want to hear it. Besides it wouldn't have changed my mind, you know me better than that." I chuckled.

"This isn't funny and shouldn't be taken lightly. This is very serious. You honestly think you'll be able to carry a child for nine months and then give it away? Because I know you as a mother, and I'm not sure it'll be as easy as you think."

"I never said it would be easy. This is something I want to do and need to do. Tara and I have always experienced everything together. Why should motherhood be any different? It's not that I'm not taking this serious—I'm taking this very serious, and I've made up my mind. If you are worried that I have not thought this though and I'm just jumping in, don't be. I've lived this scenario. Only this time the tables are turned, and we'll do it the right way. Of course, it would be easier if you'd support me on this." I placed my hands on his hips and looked attentively up into his eyes. "I love you, rebel."

"I love you too, and I do support you. I just want you to be sure before you commit." He rested his hands on my shoulders.

"I'm committed, or need to be committed. Either way, I'm sure."

Chapter 25

I Say We're Even

Six months after my proposal to carry Tara's firstborn, we attended our first doctor's appointment to set up the arrangement. The parents and Grandma Marsh were all supportive and thrilled that this go around, there were no secrets to be kept. Belle was not unsupportive, but she was Belle and showed only a trace of tolerance for our decision.

Three months after our first appointment, we held a News Year's Day party at our house and invited the entire family. I knew by the look of suspense on everyone's face as they filled my living room that they were expecting an announcement, so I didn't make them wait long before clicking my glass with a spoon to get their attention. *Clink! Clink!* The ringing of the glass filled the room, and all other sounds hushed to hear what would follow.

"I can tell you are all waiting to hear of any news we may have to share. So I'll let Tara tell you." I pointed to her as she walked across the room to join me by the dining room table.

"We're pregnant, and we just found out that we'll be having fraternal twins. I'm going to be a mommy." Her words were full of emotion, and the tears would have made you believe she was the hormonal one who was pregnant. "The babies are due mid August."

I rubbed my still-flat stomach, trying not to get used to its small stature.

The cheers of the family showed their approval. Smiles adorned my house of guests. This was, by far, one of the happiest times of my life. I felt honored to be doing this for Tara, and to have everyone else support me sent chills of pride down my spine.

"All right, now let's eat!" I hollered over all the jabber of what Tara would have to invest in for her nursery times two.

Grandma Marsh joined me in the kitchen to assist me in bringing out all the food to the table. "I'm so proud of you guys, and I'm happy to see you're doing this the legal way this time." She grabbed the bowl of green beans with bacon.

"Oh yeah, well, you know, live and learn." I followed behind her with the mashed potatoes.

"Can I help?" Belle stopped us at the entrance of the kitchen. My arms weakened with amazement at her request, and I nearly had to pick my bowl up off the ground. "Sure. Just grab anything on the island and bring it on out." I pointed to the many dishes she could assist with.

"There is a first for everything," Grandma Marsh whispered in my ear as she walked past me to retrieve something else for our feast. I laughed quietly, nodding in agreement.

Belle set out a bowl of salad and then stood in front of the sliding glass door leading to the backyard. I joined her and looked out at the rain. "Thanks for your help, I appreciate it." My expression of thanks was masking my need of approval.

"No problem. I want you to know something." Belle continued to stare out the window.

"What's that?" I looked to her firm profile.

"I'm impressed with you." She talked to the glass, avoiding making any visual contact with me.

"Thanks." I looked back to the window so I could at least talk to her reflection.

"I mean it. I could never do what you are doing. I didn't like carrying my own children, I never could have done it for someone else. Family or not, it's impressive." She finished her compliment and walked away.

I'll blame it on the hormones, but Belle's words tugged at my emotions and released a tear. I collected myself and quickly helped finish the table so everyone could enjoy the meal. At the end of the day, I was sad to see everyone leave, the kids behaved. The adults all played nice and got along great, and Tara and I were like two peas in a pod again.

As pleasant gatherings with family over holidays and events came and went, so did the view of my feet. My belly was the biggest it had ever gotten, and I was beginning to think I was carrying around full-grown children or, at the very least, a herd of elephants. I was desperate to know what we were having, but upon Tara's request, we did not find out the sex of the babies. I was stuck with purchasing greens and yellows when shopping for her baby shower.

"Wow, when are you due?" a lady standing in line behind me at the Baby Outlet asked with wide eyes.

"I've got four weeks left." I waddled closer to the counter to pay for my assortment of plain newborn jammies.

"Oh my god, you're huge." Her kind words made me want to slap her.

"I'm having twins." I handed over my card to hurry the transaction.

"Those are going to be some big healthy babies for sure," she laughed. I bit my lip as I grabbed my bag and slowly shuffled my tired feet across the store and out the door.

I knew I had to be getting close; my patience was growing thin, and my normal positive manner was hiding behind a large belly of discomfort. I hurried to the car and unlocked the trunk to throw in my gift for Tara's shower coming up in only two days. I slammed the trunk and quickly grasped the aching pain that shot across the bottom of my belly. I breathed in and out with the contraction and paused my stance until the pain let up. I glanced at my watch to note the time and rushed to find comfort in the car.

I waited patiently to see if any others would be triggered. Five minutes after the first one, I had another. The tightening in my abdomen was powerful, my toes curled, my hands grasped the steering wheel with such force my fingers shined white, and beads of sweat rolled down my spine. I tried to adjust my seating as the heat my body was creating made me think my spine was melting inside me. As I felt I couldn't handle anymore, the pain began to let up again.

I searched for my cell phone and called Todd. I started the car and began my drive to the hospital. "Hey, sweetie, it's time," I sang as I pulled out of the parking lot.

"Where are you?" Todd's voice was full of panic.

"On my way to the hospital. Call Tara and my mom and meet me there. Contractions are five minutes apart but very intense." I rushed through the traffic, trying to reach a decent pull off before the next contraction started.

"You're driving!" His voice was so loud I had to pull the phone from my ear.

"Yes! I have no choice, I'm at the strip mall. Hospital is only ten minutes away." I hung up to force him to place the needed calls.

I stopped twice on the way to the hospital and parked my car in the emergency parking lot, making sure to lock it behind me. I found support on a nearby truck, where I rested my forehead on top of my hands as I grasped onto the tailgate. The pains were getting sharper and unbearable, and I was worried I was going to have the babies in the parking lot. Tears poured down my face as I imagined delivering before Tara could arrive; I did not want her to miss the birth of her babies.

"Miss? Are you okay?" A lady's voice asked from behind me. I couldn't produce words through the pain but shook my head in response. I could hear her run off, and I prayed she was going for help. My stomach began to loosen up, and I could stand up straight again, even though my back was still experiencing some discomfort. I released my grip on the truck and started moving toward the ER doors with one hand holding my back and other holding my stomach.

My relief finally came when I saw a male nurse running toward me pushing a wheelchair. A lady about my age rushed passed him toward me. "He's gonna take good care of you now. Is there anything else I can do for you? Need me to call anyone?" Her pale face and kind words brought me comfort.

"My husband is on his way, but thanks anyway," I said as the man in scrubs helped me into the wheelchair.

"How close are the contractions?" He wheeled me across the parking lot.

"They were about five minutes apart, but they are steady across my back. They are sharp and more painful than I remember with my other twins." I held my breath and gritted my teeth as my body began to crack under the stress.

"Hee hee, whoo. Remember your breathing, it really helps." My chauffeur insisted as we reached the door. My first reaction was to turn around and ask how he would know, but I knew he was right and started my series of patterned breaths. He stopped me at the admitting counter. "Did you want me to stay here with you until your husband arrives? You can squeeze my hand if you like." The young brunette I was talking to out in the parking lot stood timidly next to me.

I waited for the pain to subside before answering, "What's your name?" I looked up at her large brown eyes and slender face.

"Lacy Donahou." Her hands were tucked inside the front pockets of her jeans. "Hi, Lacy, I'm Clara." I stuck out my hand.

"I don't mean to intrude, I just want to help." She shook my hand.

"You are very sweet. I appreciate your help. You can stay right here and keep me company until they wheel me back if you want." I smiled through the stabbing pain in my back as she nodded.

"Clara, you ready?" Cassie, one of my favorite nurses, asked from the door. "Definitely." I sighed. I waved good-bye to Lacy as they wheeled me through the doors and down the bright white halls. "Dr. Brey is off duty until next week, so you'll have Dr. Morgan delivering," Cassie informed as she walked next to me.

"That's fine, she delivered my other twins. I really like her." I stared at the lighting on the ceiling that resembled the blue sky and clouds.

In between contractions I dressed down in my fancy hospital gown with splatters of pink of blue and climbed into the cold, uncomfortable, adjustable bed. By the time I was connected to the IV of fluids, Dr. Morgan entered the room with Todd close behind.

"Shall we see what we'll be doing today?" The doctor pushed her rolling stool to the end of the bed as the nurse adjusted my legs on the stirrups. "How you feeling?" Todd grabbed my hand.

"I don't know, either I blocked out the experience I had with the boys, or these are indeed worse than anything I ever felt." I squeezed his hand as I felt a small pinch.

"All right. Well, I hope you planned on staying here a while. You are dilated to a five, I had to break your water. So don't be surprised if the contractions get more intense." She removed her gloves and tossed them into the trash.

"More intense! I can't handle them anymore intense than they already are. Call we a wuss or whatever, but you better be getting an epidural up in here quick.""How"

I nearly cancelled the order of having the babies all together. The pain was already draining all my energy; I couldn't bear the thought of having only just started.

"I'll get them up here." Dr. Morgan laughed.

"It's not funny. I think something is seriously wrong. It hurts." I grabbed my belly as a tear ran down my cheek.

Dr. Morgan approached my bedside and placed her hands on my belly "Let's see what they are doing in there." Her fingers ran over every bump of my baby dome. Her eyes closed as she went over my belly again. Then she had the nurse assist her in lifting the gown up to expose the belly and examined it closer. "Okay. So now we have some other options to explore. You have one baby head down and ready to come out the old-fashioned way. But you have another that is a little more stubborn and not ready to come out to play just yet. We are looking at a breech birth." She pulled my gown back down over my stomach.

"So what are the options?" Todd grabbed my hand with both of his. "Either we try to reposition the baby, which is more difficult with two in there. We deliver it as a breech, which is hazardous to

Mom and baby. Or we prepare Mom for surgery and do this with a caesarian section."

"I think the choice is clear," Todd answered, looking to me for a response.

"I don't care how, just get them out!" I screamed as sharp pains shot down my legs and up my spine. "And keep Tara out! I don't want her to see this." I gritted my teeth.

"She won't be here for another hour." Todd kissed my hand. I took a deep breath. The pain was mellow but still present. My initial intention of wanting to share this blessed event with Tara had been tossed out the window. The new plan was to keep Tara from having to experience anything negative with this birth. The sooner I could get into surgery, the better.

"Aw, my new best friend." I sighed as the anesthesiologist entered my room equipped to eliminate the pain.

"Your parents are on their way too with the kids. I'll go see if they are here." Todd excused himself from the room before having to see the large needle placed into my back. The pressure from the placement of the epidural was a cake walk compared to the war my body was engaged in with the process of labor.

Todd soon entered to announce the arrival of the parents. "They're about to take me down for surgery." I puckered my lips for a much-needed show of affection. "Love ya, sweets. I'll see you in there." His lips softly met mine.

"Clara, are you ready?" Cassie entered the room with a nurse's aide to assist her in transporting me down to the operating room.

"You bet I am."

The next hour went by like a blur. I recall moments of staring up at the bright hot lights while I lay helplessly on the table. I remember listening to the team of doctors and nurses all dressed in green talking in their foreign tongue as they reported every step they took, leaving me more worried and confused than ever.

With all the little things I can recall, I will never forget the sound of the first baby's cry and the doctor's announcement of it being a little boy, nor will I ever forget the sound of that second cry, the cry of my stubborn and precious little niece. Todd wasn't allowed in the room until after the babies were born; that was heartbreaking but, under the circumstances, understandable.

Tara and Sean arrived just after I was returned to my room. "I missed it? Where are they? What did we have? Are they healthy?" Tara rambled as she entered the room.

"Well, you're not at all excited, I expected more from you really." Todd threw his arm around her.

"You're a mommy to one of each. They are healthy and well, and look." I pointed to the door as Cassie arrived, pushing the clear plastic bassinet with both babies sleeping soundly. "Oh, they are beautiful, Clara." Tara reached in and pulled the blanket away from her little boy's face.

"What are their names?" Cassie looked to me for an answer.

"I don't know, these are Tara's babies, she will have to name them."

Cassie showed no expression and looked to Tara for a reply. "The boy will be Junior, Sean Tristan, and the girl will be Sadie Rae-Ann." Tara smiled as my middle name rolled off her tongue.

"I love it," I expressed as family poured into my room to see the newest members of our crazy family. Watching them be passed around, I hoped we'd be able to prepare them for the chaos that I had put them in the middle of.

"Thanks to you, I'm a mom. I could never thank you enough for all you have done. I feel I'm living a dream." Tara sat next to me on my bed.

"You are. You're living a dream come true. I don't see you as owing me a special thanks or anything. I say we're even." I yawned as the day's event started to take its toll on me. "Should we leave you to get some rest?" She stood up, no doubt ready to push everyone out the door.

"No, you guys are fine, I'll just rest as I watch everyone enjoy your new family."

"Have you held them yet?" Sean carried the little bundles over to me. I shook my head, then placed the spare pillow on my lap. "Here." He placed the pink bundle on the pillow against my right arm and the blue bundle on the pillow against my left arm. Their eyes opened and stole my heart. "You guys look like your dad." I admired the view of the newborns. Their eyes were dark and their complexions were clear. "You're perfect, try to stay that way okay? Your mommy is new at this whole motherhood thing, so take it easy on her, and remember for the future that if you ever need anything, you can just call me."

Todd was right; it was hard for them to be removed from my arms. I felt a connection to them that was undeniable, but the connection to my sister was even greater. I had been blessed to have a best friend by my side from day one. I'd never known the words *lonely* or *bored*. We had been created as two parts of a whole for a reason; we completed each other. If she was miserable, then I too was sad. If she was happy, then I too would laugh.

Helping her to achieve her goal of having her own family gave me the strength I needed to allow the babies to be taken from my grip. I could only smile as they were placed back into the arms of their rightful parents. Sean and Tara would be wonderful; those babies were in great hands and would be well cared for. I watched Tara press her lips to baby Sadie's forehead, and I regained my feeling of completion. Another plan carried through. Perhaps not a picture perfect family to most, but for us this was a job well done. A sacrifice well worth the conclusion, and if asked if I'd do it again, I wouldn't change a single thing.

About the Author

Petralia J. L. Fisk was born and raised in a small country town nestled between Mt. Rainier and Mt St. Helens in Washington State. Surrounded by the inspiration of nature, her hobbies of photography and writing came natural. Now satisfied with her first passion of raising a family, she has her focus on her next venture of sharing her stories with the world.

CPSIA information can be obtained
at www.ICGtesting.com
Printed in the USA
FSHW011253270819
61468FS